Elaine Pinkerton's latest book, *All The Wrong Places*, is the perfect way to transport yourself to the ruggedly exotic Red Mesa, New Mexico. It's an exciting read filled with stolen Indian pottery, mistaken identities set in a turbulent Native American high school.

Pinkerton, an adoptee, has a realistic and compelling subplot about searching for one's birth mother. Put more adventure in your life. Read *All the Wrong Places* for a vicarious thrill.

- Peggy van Hulsteyn, author of *YOGA and PARKINSON'S DISEASE*

Kudos to Elaine Pinkerton, who has written a first-class thriller that will keep you up long after your bedtime. Set in her home territory of the American Southwest and incorporating elements of her own adventurous life, ALL THE WRONG PLACES will stay with you long after the last page is turned!

-Jann Arrington Wolcott
Award-winning author and Lecturer

Running afoul of her latest boyfriend pulls Clara backward into a morass of murder and international crime. Who knew it would also launch her into something greater: that she herself had been the arrow sent forth from her birth mother's bow?

-Kathryn Hurn, Author of *HELL HEAVEN & IN-BETWEEN: One Woman's Journey to Finding Love*

All
the
Wrong Places

Elaine Pinkerton

Pocol Press

POCOL PRESS
Published in the United States of America
by Pocol Press
6023 Pocol Drive
Clifton, VA 20124
www.pocolpress.com

Publisher's Cataloguing-in-Publication

Names: Pinkerton, Elaine, author.
Title: All the wrong places / Elaine Pinkerton.
Description: Clifton, VA: Pocol Press, 2017.
Identifiers: ISBN 978-1-929763-72-6 | LCCN 2017939517
Subjects: LCSH Adoption--Fiction. | Schools--Fiction. | Indians of North America--New Mexico--Fiction. | Smuggling--Fiction. | Mystery and detective stories. | BISAC FICTION / Mystery & Detective / General
Classification: LCC PS3616.I573 A55 2017 | DDC 813.6--dc23

Library of Congress Control Number: 2017939517

Cover art "*Black Mist*" copyright Scott Swezy.
Courtesy **Catenary Art Gallery**.
Santa Fe, N.M.
www.catenaryartgallery.com

Table of Contents

In Memory of Peter Dechert

Prologue

No one told Corky Gonzales, but he knew. Ever since he could remember, a sixth sense warned him of murder and mayhem in the air. Here at Los Amigos Saloon, he could feel bad vibes. Evil was about to be unleashed. During his long career of bartending, Corky sensed this particular blackness one other time, and the very next day brought a report of murder. It seemed to be happening again. From behind the glossy wooden counter, he watched.

The two of them met often in the back corner booth at Tootsie's: a tall, lanky stud with oily dark shoulder-length curls and a long bony nose that looked as though it had been broken; and a medium-tall, nondescript man with the kind of bowl haircut that had gone out of style in the last century. Now and then he caught some names...Henry, Harry, Larry. He wasn't sure which guy was which. For several weeks now, through the smoke and the dim, yellow light, Corky had been sizing them up. They weren't the everyday scum that congregated between 5 p.m. and midnight. They had a topic, a project, a goal. Corky couldn't hear their words, but he knew.

When Trixie, a platinum blond who used the bar as a place to pick up men, tried to strike up a conversation with the men, Corky thought he saw bowl haircut flash a knife. The air at Tootsie's was dirtier than usual and he couldn't really see what happened. Trixie left in a hurry and didn't come around for a few days after that.

Mean, surly sons o' bitches, those two. Corky knew that whatever cursed deed they'd been plotting, IT was about to happen. Over the smoke, the stench of urine and antiseptic wafting out from the bathrooms, above the alcohol sloshed onto the floor, he smelled blood.

"Bloody Monday"

Clara Jordan's aching right foot, wrenched during a 10-kilometer race she'd run last weekend, slowed her down. She was searching all over the American Indian Academy for the VCR she'd promised to Joseph Speckled Horse for his presentation. He planned on speaking this afternoon about Native American heritage and the vital importance of preserving Indian culture. With her long jet-black hair and olive skin, Clara might easily have been mistaken for one of the students, but she was the school's new English teacher.

At last, in the far side of the Communications Building, she located the VCR. As she maneuvered the bulky video equipment down a long hallway toward her classroom, her foot throbbed. Where were students when she needed them? As she wheeled the VCR cart slowly along, she glanced down at her new Casio watch. Impossible, but it was twenty minutes later than she thought. She walked down the hallway a bit faster.

As the young English teacher neared her classroom, a strong unease settled in her stomach. She stopped pushing the cart in mid-stride. Noticing the school was unusually quiet, she looked up and down the hallway. Not another soul in sight.

Standing alone in the shadowy hallway, she glanced back in the direction of her room. Why did that brief glance make it suddenly harder to breathe? Her anxiety wasn't letting go. Clara looked again at her watch and was shocked to see how late it was. She tried forcing herself in the direction of her classroom. At first she couldn't move. It took all her willpower to push the cart toward room 221.

When she got within a few feet of her classroom, she stopped. For an instant, a feeling of panic chilled her to the core. Surely the door had been open when she left; now it was closed. She tried to open it, but the door, which had a habit of accidentally locking, wouldn't budge.

Maybe, she thought, Speckled Horse had arrived at her classroom early. He was probably in the room, setting up his presentation for the students. She knocked on the door. No answer. She waited, then knocked again. No sounds came from inside.

Forgetting her aching foot, she ran down the hall to find someone. Finally, the custodian, John Herrera, came shuffling toward her classroom with a huge set of keys. For such a huge, bearlike man, he moved quickly. "Ms. Jordan, you were making quite a racket with that door. I thought I heard you shrieking."

"I'm sorry, John. Being all alone, locked out of my classroom...I was feeling afraid. I know I'm being silly. The wind probably blew the door shut." Clara, usually assured and self-confident, looked at the tiled floor. Her cheeks burned; she fought back tears. Something felt terribly wrong.

"Could be one of your students playing a prank," Herrera said, hoping to put the teacher more at ease. "These kids can be rascals... you gotta watch them every minute, Ms. Jordan." The gigantic man shook his head as he spoke, wondering what had really scared Clara so much. One of his keys worked and Herrera shoved the door open.

"Oh my God!" Clara screamed. Beneath the blackboard, Headmaster Joseph Speckled Horse lay face down, a dark red pool of blood puddled around his upper torso. Clara felt as though she'd been kicked in the stomach. She screamed, sobbed, and moaned in pain and shock.

Clara had never witnessed death. If only this were a hideous nightmare, and she could just wake up! But the icy air blowing in from the open classroom window assured her it was all too real.

Clara stood immovable by the door, chewing on her fingernails as Herrera timidly walked to the body. The puddle of blood under the slain man's right arm made Herrera comment, "Speckled Horse was either shot or stabbed in the chest...but we really won't know until the police get here."

There was some blood on his left side, but not as much. Looking down at the sight turned Herrera's stomach. The custodian backed slowly away from the corpse and moved toward Clara. She looked sick. She had no color in her face and stared wide-eyed at him. The poor woman, he realized, was in shock.

The custodian poked his head out of the room and bellowed, "Help! Help! Someone come quick. Help, please someone help us!" From the far end of the hall came the patter of running feet. Thank God. Herrera's concerns were for Clara Jordan. She was having trouble breathing, and it seemed to be getting worse. He feared that Ms. Jordan might die too if something wasn't done quickly.

Raylene Morningbird, a recent American Indian Academy graduate who volunteered in the main office, had heard the cries and was rushing down the hall to help. Before the custodian could say anything, Raylene saw past Herrera into the room. Her hand flew to her mouth as she gasped in horror.

"Get an ambulance!" Herrera ordered. "There's a dead body, and one of our teachers might be in shock. Ms. Jordan can't breathe. Hurry!"

Raylene ran off to find a phone. As she ran, tears flooded her eyes and she began sobbing. Meanwhile, Herrera pulled Clara away from the death scene out into the hall, consoling her as if she were a small child.

Within minutes, the rescue squad arrived, followed a few seconds later by the police. The halls buzzed with paramedics and police.

Seeing Clara's shock and exhaustion, the paramedics, ignoring her weak protests, laid her on a gurney and attached her to an oxygen mask. It was obvious there was nothing else they could do for the slain headmaster, and they covered his body with a gray flannel blanket. The police cordoned off the area so they could start their investigation right away.

A crowd of students and faculty grew outside Room 221. Herrera repeated his story several times, telling how Clara rushed up to him looking distressed and how they went down to her locked classroom together. Sweeping a glance around Clara's classroom, the officer in charge wanted to ask Clara what the headmaster was doing there in the first place.

Though he basically dismissed the possibility that Clara might be the one who killed Speckled Horse, he just might question her later. From the custodian, it was clear, they would get very little information about the crime. Although he'd seen the headmaster almost every day, Herrera hardly knew Speckled Horse.

Twenty minutes after the dead body was discovered, school was closed and the students sent home. The police advised that it shouldn't be reopened until after the Thanksgiving holiday. When paramedics determined that Clara was out of any physical danger, Ms. Taggert, acting headmistress, volunteered to take Clara home and stay with her for awhile. The police remained, asking the rest of the faculty questions, but no one could tell them anything useful.

Ms. Taggert and Clara, who'd revived and talked her way out of the paramedics' surveillance, headed downhill from the main AIA academic building to Clara's cabin. Clara was drowning in a wave of depression and fatigue. The road home from school looked strangely unfamiliar. Her mentor, the man they all looked up to, was gone.

As Ms. Taggert drove her home, Clara rolled down the window for some fresh air. Fighting an odd sleepiness, she struggled to make sense of the day.

At last they arrived at her cabin. Nestled in tall, ponderosa pines at the edge of the campus, it was a welcome sight. When they entered, it was cold. Starting to feel more herself, Clara went through the routine of getting the wood stove going. This was her cabin's only source of heat.

The small rooms -- a living area, bedroom, bathroom and kitchen -- warmed up quickly. Oscar, her gray tabby cat, purred and rubbed back and forth against her ankles.

"Thanks so much, Ms. Taggert," Clara said. "You've been a godsend, but you don't need to stay any longer. I really need to be alone now."

The older woman looked surprised. "But you've been through a terrible ordeal. I can stay overnight in the living room." She gestured toward the Taos bed next to them. "I've slept on many a couch."

"No, really, I'll be fine." Eager to be free of her company, Clara ushered Ms. Taggert gently toward the door. "You must be exhausted, just like me. Please be careful not to let Oscar sneak out when you go."

Alone, she walked from room to room until the air was finally warm enough for her to shed her coat. She laid it on top of a pair of men's jeans left hanging over a chair. She thought of the jeans' owner, her sometimes lover Henry, and wondered why he hadn't answered her earlier phone calls. Sliding out of her clothes into a flannel nightgown, Clara crawled into bed.

2

Voices

*Come, let us go down, and there confound their language, that
they may not understand one another's speech.* Genesis 11:4

News of the death blazed across the campus like a prairie fire.
School authorities decided to reopen the campus after just one day.
Clara, ragged from a nearly sleepless night, knew it was going to be a
bad morning when she saw the mob gathered outside the Fine Arts
building. With the thermometer showing 15 degrees, the students would
never have been standing outside by choice. John Herrera normally
opened the classroom buildings by seven, but it was already 7:30.

Parking in the teachers' lot at the side of the building, Clara strode
briskly to the double front door of the large stuccoed building. She
threaded her way through the students clustered near the door. A few
greeted her; most were sullen and silent. She was glad to see Carnell, a
student who routinely arrived in her room as soon as she did and offered
to help with tasks.

"What's up, Carnell?" she asked the tall, slender young man. "Are
you all in training for the Winter Olympics cold endurance test?"

"No ma'am, we're locked out," Carnell explained. His flat,
seemingly calm tone of voice was betrayed by his wrinkled brow and a
worried look in his soulful, deep brown eyes.

Her students were all looking at her expectantly. Trying hard to
appear positive, Clara smiled and declared, "I'll get to the bottom of this.
Everyone just wait right here. I'll go to the Administration building, find
someone with the keys, and you'll be inside in minutes. Carnell, see that
no one leaves. Class is not dismissed."

Carnell nodded, giving Clara the distinct impression that he would
know what to do if the students did begin to scatter. With his dark eyes
flashing out from behind round, gold-rimmed spectacles, and slicked-
back, 30's-style hair, Carnell was the one comforting part of this picture.

It seemed to Clara as if the earth itself was mourning the death of
Joseph Speckled Horse. The winter campus looked dried up and
hopeless. Dead leaves trembled on the cottonwood trees, the shriveled
grass was an ugly yellow-brown, dry and wiry as steel wool. Here and
there, a patch of dirty snow remained from a late-October storm.

A brisk walk turned into a run as Clara, ignoring her hurt foot,
checked the financial office, then the admissions center. Where were the

people? Finally, Gloria Pacheco, the payroll assistant, appeared in the hall with a coffeepot full of water.

"Gloria, what's going on? All my students are locked out of the Fine Arts building. Herrera apparently didn't show up today, and I can't find anyone with the key. I told the kids to just wait and I'd be right back. Is there any chance you have the building keys?"

"You mean no one called you last night? There was a school-wide notice to all the staff and students that they were to go to homerooms at 9:00 a.m. and then proceed to the auditorium for assembly. Supposedly everyone got a call and everyone knew. Ms. Taggert set it up yesterday late afternoon."

"I wasn't informed about anything, just that we might have an assembly before Thanksgiving break. Who supposedly told everyone about this?"

"Taggert herself. She knew how upset the staff was and she personally called everyone. I don't know how she could have missed you. Were you home all evening?"

"Yeah, sure, maybe the phone wasn't working. Or maybe I didn't hear it. I don't know." She thought of Carnell and the others shivering in front of the Fine Arts Building. "Look, I've got to have a key. Can you loan me one?" She wanted to mention the "mystery car" that had been roaming around her house the night before, but felt it was more urgent to get the students inside, out of the cold. Besides, Gloria wasn't exactly the person to talk to. She needed to go directly to Taggert.

After searching through several drawers, Gloria managed to produce a key. Telling Clara she needed it returned as soon as possible, she handed it over. Key in hand, Clara raced back to the Fine Arts building. Her band of students was still there. As she got within sight of them, she held up the key. A small cheer arose, along with some sparse applause. As soon as the door opened, the ninth graders stampeded into room 224 and found their places quickly. Room 221 was closed off for inspection and Ms. Jordan's homeroom had been transferred to Room 224, just down the hall.

Clara had to say something to them, but where to begin? She would do the only thing that would really help them. She would speak from her heart. Looking directly at Carnell, she started to talk. Feeling cold and tired, she stood with her arms folded, moving her gaze to scan their faces. "This is a very sad day. As you probably know, we lost our headmaster Joseph Speckled Horse two days ago. He was on his way to give a talk to some of you after sixth period. He died right in our old classroom. That's why we're in a different space now." Fighting to keep control, Clara shuddered at her own words.

6

Raylene stared at her balefully, her eyes glazed with tears. Priscilla was biting her lips and frowning. Donald and Ronald, who always seemed too young to be in the ninth grade, were whispering and laughing as if trying to make a joke out of the situation. Others looked (but probably did not feel) impassive. An indistinct mumbling reminded Clara of cicadas in summer. Here and there, she caught a word. "A knife"... "bad spirits"... "stealing"...the elders"...an alcoholic."

She pictured these barely articulated thoughts sweeping through the class like electric currents. She needed to take control. "I know you may think that if Speckled Horse died here," she said, "his spirit still lingers. If his spirit is here with us, you can be sure he would want you to get on with your education. Yes, of course, we are grieving for the loss...to us, to the school, and to Indian people. But we must look toward the future. He would want us to do just what we're doing." The murmurs died down and everyone sat in stony silence.

"Ms. Taggert is now the acting headmistress," Clara continued, "and everything at the school will go on as usual. This afternoon you'll all go home for Thanksgiving."

Was she helping them? Clara had no idea. At a loss, she continued, "Use this time to enjoy being with your families, and don't be depressed about this. You can be sad without being depressed. It is right to be sad and to feel angry about this tragedy. I am very sad. Dr. Speckled Horse is the one who hired me to come and teach you. We met when I came out for a workshop for teachers who wanted to work with Native American kids. I was very interested in pottery and your late headmaster was an expert on ancient pottery and Indian history."

An expression of boredom appeared on some of the faces before her. Despite their blank expressions, Clara imagined that her students hid deep, heartfelt emotions: bewilderment, grief, anger. As she continued talking, she noticed that Deena, the smallest and smartest girl in her homeroom, had tears rolling down her cheeks. Clara shared her sorrow.

"OK, what can you do if you're sad?" she asked. "You can act it out in a negative way, kicking your roommate or kicking yourself, or act mean and ugly to your parents or your brothers and sisters. You can feel horrible and guilty as though it were somehow your fault. Or you can do what I try to do when I'm sad: turn your feelings into something constructive. Here's an idea. For everyone who would like to, write down your feelings about Headmaster Speckled Horse in your daily journal, the one we're keeping our oral histories in. Just put down whatever comes to mind -- maybe a time he spoke to you in the hall, maybe one of his talks in the gym, reminding you of who you are and where you came from."

Deena dried her tears and raised her hand.

Clara nodded her head in Deena's direction. "Yes, Deena, what do you think?"

"Maybe we could put them together in a little book and give it to our late Headmaster's family. It would be a comfort to them." She looked at Carnell, who was her second cousin, once removed. "Maybe we could get Carnell to do the computer stuff and make it look good. We could call it something like *Memories of Joseph Speckled Horse* by Ms. Jordan's homeroom."

"Yeah," Carnell agreed. "We could have drawings in it, too. We got a lotta talented artists. Let's put 'em to work."

"You took the thoughts right out of my head," Clara said. "I was thinking of our writing about this experience, but making it into a book is even better. Giving it to the family is a wonderful idea. It would mean so much to them. As Deena said, it would be a comfort."

She turned around and wrote the "assignment" on the board, letting the students chat excitedly among themselves. Soon the chatter threatened to turn into bedlam. It was just 8:40, and the assembly wasn't scheduled until 9:00. She could either have the students clean out their desks or have them brainstorm about their Speckled Horse memorial project. The latter would probably be better. They would begin the assignment this morning.

"OK, Deena, what do you remember about our headmaster?"

Deena waited for a moment, thinking. "Well, he was always kind. He would talk to you in the hall and ask how you were doing. He remembered everyone's name. He knew all our parents, too. One time I was running down the hall because I was late for my class and he said, 'Deena, you should slow down. The class will still be there whenever you arrive. You remind me of your mother Nadine who we used to call Nadine-waits-too-long. She always left for wherever she was going about five or ten minutes too late and so she was always rushing just like you are.'"

As Deena talked, Clara thought about the events of last week, mentally reviewing the hour when Speckled Horse had been scheduled to appear. Because of the VCR, she'd been late getting back to her classroom. If she had just arrived on time, perhaps the intruder would have gotten cold feet and vanished before he had time to commit murder. On the other hand, she could have been a victim too. The possibility sent a chill down her spine. This kind of thinking was useless and discouraging. If, if, if...

8

Homer Pacheco, a bear of a kid with a spiky haircut and a jovial smile, raised his hand.

"I have a kinda dumb memory. I was just an eighth grader, still in middle school, and I was always getting mad at everyone. Especially at the school. Well, one time me and my brother Chris were trying to get into our teacher's room so we could see ahead of time what our final grades were going to be. We were afraid the news would be bad and so we wanted to find out just how bad. That way we'd warn our Mom about the bad news, kinda break it to her gently."

"Homer, is this about Joseph Speckled Horse or about you and Chris?"

Homer waved his hand in the air. Refusing to be hurried, he spoke slowly and with a touch of humor edging his voice. "Yeah, yeah, I'm getting to that. Well, we were real mad and worried all at the same time and we didn't really think about how hard we were ramming into this door. We just wanted to get inside the building and we knew where Miss Moony kept her grade book. We even thought about changing the grades in her book, figuring she had so many grades to keep track of she might not even notice. Well, we had this big old pole and we just kept ramming the door right under the handle. It had opened that way before and we thought it would work again. Chris got carried away and started just ramming the pole without really looking where he was ramming.

"All of a sudden we hear this crash and the door's window, up at the top, is totally busted out. I mean totally. Man, we got outta there in a hurry. The next day there's an assembly in the gym and Speckled Horse talks about how sorry he is that it happened and how he wants whoever did it to come to his office and tell him. He promises that there isn't going to be punishment, just some work to do in return for the busted door which will have to be replaced and which will cost the school money."

"Homer, are you close to the end?" Clara said more sharply than she intended. "I'm glad you are sharing this, but maybe you could wind it up in a minute or so."

"This is the end. Really, Ms. Jordan. Hmmm, where was I? Oh yeah, that's right. I wasn't gonna say anything, but after a couple days, I started thinking about it. Chris and me, we go to Speckled Horse's office and tell him about what we did. He listens, nods his head, clicks his tongue and looks at us in a sad kinda way. He don't scold us or give us a big old lecture. Instead, we have to plant flowers in the beds around the Administration building, the new garden the teachers dreamed up. They were pansies. Dr. Speckled Horse said that's what we were acting like when we bashed the door, pansies. It didn't seem very funny then, but

9

now Chris and me laugh about it. I guess that's too stupid to go in the memory book, but anyway it's what I remember."

"Homer, that's not dumb. It's a wonderful memory. I want you to write it down, just the way you told me. Now, any more memories anyone would like to share?" Clara was secretly relieved that the class was talking about their memories. She could have hugged Deena for suggesting the idea of compiling a booklet.

Before the students could reply, the mood was shattered by a loud buzzer, the call to assembly. Clara hated to break up this discussion. Rarely had her students talked so freely. But Taggert needed to flaunt her new authority and let the students know that she was in charge. Almost all the teachers called her Taggert. It seemed to suit her personality better than her first name, "Wren."

In the past couple months, Clara had grown to dislike the woman intensely. Officious, autocratic, fussy, and demanding, Taggert was a micro-manager. Besides, she had a math background; what she knew about writing and communication could be put on the head of a pin. Every time Clara showed Taggert her lesson plans, the older woman found minute flaws, invisible to anyone but her. God awful.

Following a five-minute walk from Clara's classroom, they all trailed into the auditorium. The entire student body streamed through the side doors and filled the balcony. There, onstage with Taggert and William Atencio, the president of the board, was Grandma Posie (short for Cheraposie). Her cousin, the late Nathaniel Cheraposie, helped establish the American Indian Academy in the late 1980s.

As she sat with her students and waited, Clara thought back to her arrival at AIA 16 months ago. On that much happier occasion, Grandma Posie was also onstage. She was apparently loved by faculty and students alike. Today, in deep, rich tones, she talked to the assembly. After lamenting Speckled Horse's death, she attempted to inspire the students.

"We have most of the school year left. When you come back from Thanksgiving, do what he would have wanted you to. Work hard, take responsibility for yourself, make your parents proud. Set goals and work to accomplish them."

Not new advice, but Grandma Posie made it seem personal. She appeared to know the name of every student. "Doreen, I really want you to do as well as your sister Bernadette did when she went to Santa Fe Indian Academy. Paul, I knew your father when you were born and all he talked about was the dream he had of you going to college."

As soon as Grandma Posie sat down, Wren Taggert strode to the podium. A short, stocky blond, she wore a maroon wool suit that would

10

have looked great on someone taller but seemed to overpower the new acting headmistress. Clara noted that Taggert's jewel-neck blouse was gold, so that her entire color scheme matched the school colors. *Well, why shouldn't they?* she asked herself. If ever there was a time when school spirit was needed, it was now. Nonetheless, she was skeptical as she listened to Taggert addressing the students. *Power hungry witch*, she thought to herself. *She's probably glad Speckled Horse died, gives her a chance to play queen. She may have even orchestrated Speckled Horse's demise...*

Rising to her feet again with a dignified stiffness, Grandma Posie gave a prayer in Tewa. The students stood reverently, as did Clara. Even though not all of the students spoke Tewa, it was appropriate that homage be paid to Speckled Horse in a Native American tongue. Afterwards, she gave a translation of her prayer in English.

"Thank you, Grandma Posie," Taggert said crisply. "This is a dark day for our school, but it is also a day of great hope and looking toward the future. We have lost our leader, our guide through this brave endeavor: a Native American school that truly prepares young Indians for the new era we are fast approaching...

"When I first met Joseph Speckled Horse, I was a continuing education coordinator at Santa Fe Community College. Your headmaster and I were at a workshop and he told me about this wonderful new school being formed at Red Mesa. He shared his dream, a place where the youth of all Indian nations could come together and find common ground, a place where academically talented Native American youth could enjoy small college-oriented classes with highly trained instructors, individual attention, strong counseling and guidance, and a beautiful natural setting. All of this came to pass in the form of the American Indian Academy. Two years after our conversation, he hired me as his assistant director."

Clara checked her watch. Although Taggert had been talking forever, she seemed to be just gearing up. "Speckled Horse was a dreamer, a visionary. And he was a powerful man who made his dreams come true. In the years that I've worked for him, not only has he made AIA a top-notch school, with a very high percentage of you going on to college, he has made physical improvements around the campus that make us all happier to live here.

"Did we really think these things happened by magic? The new floor for the gymnasium, the new uniforms for our winning cross-country team, the Running Warriors?"

A loud victory cry, "Go Warriors," arose from the audience, followed by a long minute of foot-stomping and applause. Taggert waited for the outburst to subside, then continued.

"The landscaping that has made our campus the showcase that it is today, with flower beds, fountains, patios, and rock gardens; the new carpeting in your dorms -- it is all because of the efforts of your late headmaster. You have him to thank.

"But of course, now we can't thank him because he's gone. That saddens me more than I can say, and I know that all of you are also very, very sad. We are determined to get to the bottom of this vicious murder, to find out who is responsible and prosecute him or her to the maximum. May justice be done!"

Another cheer from the students. Clara looked over at Deena and saw that she seemed to be, if not happy, somewhat calmer. She was sitting next to her cousin Jarvis, a slender boy with a long face, smooth skin and slicked-back hair gathered into a ponytail. He had his arm draped around Deena in a brotherly way.

Jarvis was wearing a sleeveless shirt, no coat. It made Clara shiver to see his bare brown arms on these freezing cold days. Of course, he would never accept a jacket from her, so she had learned to say nothing.

Taggert rambled on. "...our beloved Headmaster's dream. The school improvements weren't the important things to our slain leader. *You* were. The new running uniforms, the new floor in the gym, the landscaping. These were secondary to you, his students...

"I remember my favorite speech by Dr. Speckled Horse," Taggert continued. "He used to tell all of you that 'We are all we have.' He meant you! If the United States ran out of Germans, they could go to Germany and get more people to become German Americans. If they ran out of Italians, all they'd have to do is go to Italy and import some more. But if you go away, that is the end of your people."

Clara stopped listening. Taggert was spouting platitudes about life and death, praising the late Joseph Speckled Horse, pretty routine stuff, but probably what the kids needed to hear. Her eyes roamed the auditorium, wondering if anyone here at the school had killed Speckled Horse. There was Phil Brennand, the science teacher, with his homeroom class of juniors. A tall, prematurely balding man who wore spectacles and walked with a slight stoop, Brennand had been known to strongly disagree with Speckled Horse on more than one occasion. Once, just outside Clara's room, #101, Brennand and Speckled Horse had been arguing in the hallway, something about the hiring of a lab assistant being too extravagant. Suddenly they had been shouting, and

12

Clara remembered Brennand saying, "Maybe we better take this outside."

But Phil Brennand, despite the fact that he was a hothead, was not a murderer. Besides, after that fracas, Clara recalled, he did get a lab assistant. No, it had to be an "outside job"...maybe someone connected to someone here, maybe another Native American, for there were those of the Pueblos who disapproved of the way Speckled Horse ran the school and felt that because of him, their youth were being "Anglicized." But that would hardly be a motive for murder. Or was it?

Murmuring arose from the rows of students. Clara broke in quietly. "Carnell, don't talk." Her favorite student was chatting with an attractive senior sitting a row ahead of him, a girl named Thelma Quick-to-See. Thelma was junior class president and had a scholarship to the University of New Mexico. Carnell decided to go to UNM, he'd told Clara. Unlike many of the kids who "just wanted to become lawyers and make tons of money," Carnell felt called to teach Pueblo children, especially those from dysfunctional families.

Thelma turned around and stared at the stage, where Taggert rambled on. Carnell scrunched down in his seat, looking embarrassed. Clara scanned the rest of her students. Several had their eyes closed, as if in meditation...or sleep. Sleep, that's what she would like right now. But of course, she had to set a good example and appear spellbound by Taggert's words.

The day after tomorrow, all of this would be temporarily behind her: AIA, the murder, her students, her cabin. A round-trip plane ticket for Virginia was tucked in her top dresser drawer, and she would, for the first time in three months, be seeing her adoptive parents.

Recently, Louise had told her that Will had never recovered from a virus he'd caught the spring before. But then, her mom tended to exaggerate and paint the worst possible scenario. It probably wasn't as bad as her mother liked to imagine. Besides, Clara told herself, she and her dad always had so much fun together. They were kindred spirits. If anyone could, Clara would cheer him up.

"Remember," Taggert hoarsely shouted, "what he was always saying to you: 'There aren't many of you left. You need to take care of yourselves.' I want you all to take care of one another. Friends don't let friends do unhealthy activities. Dr. Speckled Horse also valued your Native American heritage, and he wanted you to do the same. Value the land, value Indian pottery and artifacts, the rituals of the ancient ones, Mother Earth..."

At last the assembly ended. Clara waited to leave until the exiting mob of students and faculty were outside. Then she spotted him. His

6'5" frame propped against the wall, Henry DiMarco lounged inside the gymnasium's east doors. Surely, thought Clara, he hadn't been there before; she would have seen him. So where had he been during the last 24 hours? Even though she should have been annoyed with him for not calling, her irritation was outweighed by a flush of excitement. *Don't be a fool*, she told herself. She looked around carefully, hoping her students weren't aware of the flush she could feel in her cheeks. No danger of that. Wren Taggert had managed to lull most of them to sleep.

3
Henry Makes Excuses

Speeches over, teachers and students spilled from the overheated auditorium into the cold winter air. Clara felt a strong pair of hands on her shoulders. Henry had plowed through the mob of students to come up behind her. She felt a strange mix of annoyance, pleasure, and nervousness.

"I bet I have some explaining to do," he whispered in her ear as they continued to shuffle out toward the back doors of the gym. "You won't believe what happened to me. It's almost as unbelievable as what's happened here. If you don't have classes anymore, let's go into town for breakfast and I'll tell you about it."

By now they were outside in the freezing November air. "Tell me now," Clara said, turning around and facing him. Even though she was almost 5'10", he towered over her. "I have to pack to go home tomorrow morning. Right now is the only time I have. I might be able to go out with you tonight if I get everything done today."

Henry pushed her gently against a tree right behind the Fine Arts building, made a cage with his arms, and kissed her tenderly on her forehead, her cheeks and then her lips. "I was stuck in Los Angeles, on a business trip for the school. Trying to get a grant for the computer lab, corporate underwriting, maybe a mega donation. The Walnut Creek Consortium, that place in northern California that has an interest in the school, called me to meet with them the next morning and it was such a rush to get the tickets and get there in time for a meeting, I couldn't call. My cellular batteries were down. Hated to leave without contacting you...but, well, business." He trailed off unconvincingly.

Henry's explanation made sense, but Clara hadn't heard anything about a computer grant. Strange. She could have asked Joseph Speckled Horse about it, as he masterminded the school's improvements, but now he was gone. A dozen questions came to mind, but before she could ask them, Henry's lips were on hers and he pressed against her.

No students were in sight, but Clara felt conspicuous nonetheless. Teachers had to set a good example, and smooching in public wasn't exactly appropriate, especially during this crisis. She wrestled free of his embrace and stepped away, forcing herself to remain calm.

"Henry, I've got to go pack. I'm leaving for Virginia on the nine o'clock flight from Albuquerque tomorrow morning. Why don't we get together after I get back in a week?"

Henry stepped back, looking dejected. "I can't wait a week to see you, and I know that you don't want me to come along in your suitcase to Virginia. How about dinner tonight? I'll take you out for a pre-Thanksgiving dinner. We can go to Andiamo's in Santa Fe and try their pasta of the day." A smile played across his face. "I promise it'll be an early night. You'll be in bed by ten."

Henry was a wonderful lover, thoughtful and considerate, terribly exciting, but Clara knew she was probably using him just to get over Hugh, her abusive ex-husband. She had repeatedly vowed to cut off her affair with Henry. Before the terrible death of Speckled Horse interrupted her life, she'd been planning to tell him.

But Henry was like a powerful drug, and her addiction to him melted her resolutions. Ah well, she told herself, she would give in just this time and then swear off. Surveying Henry's tall frame, broad shoulders, dark curly hair and inviting smile, she realized that she wasn't sure she wanted to end the affair.

"I'm not making this up, Henry. I'm leaving for Virginia in the morning, and I have a zillion things to do. My father is really sick and Mom is going to need my full attention. I won't have time to go out and buy a toothbrush! I've got to have everything together, not to mention getting up before dawn to drive to Albuquerque. I should say no."

"But I made you an offer you can't refuse," Henry finished for her. "I'll make the offer even better. I'll take you to the airport in the morning and pick you up when you get back. We might have snow tomorrow, according to the weather channel, and you know how you hate La Bajada Hill when it's slick and icy. Delivery service: what more can you ask for?"

With Henry, it was always so off again, on again. The "dance-away lover" and a "woman who loves too much," that's who they were. Usually, when Clara felt herself becoming re-interested in Henry, he withdrew, became unavailable, lost interest. But now his interest in her seemed red hot. Stunned by the murder and anxious about her parents, she needed closeness. Henry, like a powerful narcotic, would help her forget. She wasn't sure Speckled Horse had been murdered, but since everyone was calling it that, so would she.

"You win," she said. "I must be crazy to say yes, but I will. Give me all afternoon to pack for Virginia and come by to pick me up for dinner, no earlier than seven. A deadline will help me get organized."

All 120 students of the American Indian Academy were spending the afternoon in their dormitories with specially-assigned grief counselors. Clara would not see her charges again until after the long

16

Thanksgiving weekend. The loss of Speckled Horse would take time to sink in, and she fully expected fallout for the rest of the semester.

When she got back to the cabin, Oscar Kitty wasn't there. Hopefully, he'd turn up by the time Annie came over, as her friend was going to keep him during the break. If it was possible, Annie liked Oscar even better than she did. She was always telling Clara that when she got tired of Oscar, he had a home at the Archuletas.

Remembering the previous night's "mystery car," Clara inspected the area around her cabin before going in. She found nothing out of the ordinary but the weather. Even though it was early, eleven a.m., the sky was darkish and somber. Heavy grey clouds were closing in, so low they seemed to touch the tall ponderosa surrounding Clara's house.

She stood at her closet door, grabbing a few skirts and sweaters to throw in a suitcase. Actually, she would need very few clothes, as her plans included nothing beyond helping Louise with mundane errands. She wasn't clear about whether or not Will could go along on outings. Her mother had been vague about exactly what was wrong with him, just commenting that he was "going downhill."

She removed two of the skirts she'd rolled up and put in her suitcase, leaving only a brown and yellow plaid cotton flannel broomstick. She might as well wear the "Santa Fe Style" that people back East liked so well. She threw her favorite cowboy boots in the suitcase, along with a pair of jeans, a soft flannel shirt, running gear, a couple of turtlenecks and a sweater. She put out a corduroy jumpsuit for the morning.

Annie's knock interrupted her musings about clothes and travel. When she opened the heavy wooden door, Oscar skittered in right by her feet. How long had he been outside trying to get in? She had been so preoccupied that she wouldn't have noticed.

"Hi, Clara, I've brought you a piece of the quiche I baked this morning and some fruit salad. You've got to eat to keep up your strength." Annie's long black hair was pulled back into a ponytail, with wisps of hair falling out around her ears. She wore trim, straight-leg jeans and a bulky turquoise sweater.

"Come on in out of the cold...what a sweetheart you are to think of my stomach! You know I don't have a thing in the house, so that's just perfect. And thanks for bringing back Oscar. I've been looking for him."

Just as Annie slipped inside, the first flakes of snow began to float through the air. "Are you sure you should go through with this trip? The predictions are for a major storm, and you know how La Bajada Hill can be before they plow it." La Bajada Hill was the worst spot on the drive between Santa Fe and Albuquerque, and even after the road crews hit it, the combination of hills and ice could be deadly. Whenever holidays were approaching, driving was even worse than usual.

"Annie, I've *got* to go! These are my parents, and Louise is counting on me. Besides, there is something seriously wrong with my father. Louise acts as though I'd better come soon if I want to see him before he dies. Henry said he'd drive me to the airport and since he's lived here all his life, he's got lots more winter driving experience than I do."

Annie was shocked. "Henry? I thought you were going to cut things off with him. You said he kept you on an emotional roller coaster. You were so determined to end things. I can't believe what I'm hearing." Her voice had grown high-pitched and slightly hysterical, the tone she used when giving Clara advice.

"Look, Annie. This is not such a big deal. You're my best friend and I love you, but I don't need you to make me feel rotten about something I already know is a bad idea. I will wean myself away from Henry, I promise, just not right now. I have enough to deal with without a broken heart. I have to at least get home and see what's happening before I'll fix the Henry situation. I just can't add one more loss."

Annie sighed and shrugged her broad, sturdy shoulders. "Sure, I see what you mean, but I don't want you to get hurt. I just think the more you put this off, the harder it's going to be. I can't say what I'd do in your situation. I know, I shouldn't act like it's easy. Changing the subject, let's eat lunch."

Annie spread a gourmet picnic out on Clara's dining alcove table: a moist, fragrant spinach and mushroom quiche, fresh fruit in a light yogurt dressing, green chile cornmeal muffins. She walked back to the kitchen and five minutes later brought out a steaming pot of herb tea. Outside, snow was falling steadily.

Clara tried not to worry about the trip to Albuquerque the next morning, focusing instead on Annie's delicious cooking. "If you ever decide to retire from your librarianship, you could make a contribution to the world by catering. Everything is wonderful! Thanks so much for pampering me."

Annie beamed. She knew she was a great cook, and she loved it when people told her so. "I almost forgot. Last night -- after Speckled Horse died -- the night watchman was checking around the school and went to the Fine Arts building to make sure everything was locked. Someone had broken into the exhibition room, smashed the locked glass display case, and taken the black pot that had been given to the school by one of the founders. It was supposed to bring good luck. Of course, with the murder, that news got kind of lost, but it's really quite a horrible theft."

"My God, what's happening to our little universe?" Clara questioned, her brow furrowed and fear in her eyes. She sat down to the table and picked at her food. "First, Speckled Horse. Then the missing pot. And now I have to fight this storm to go back to my father, who may not even recognize me and is probably dying. This school year seemed to start so well, but now it's going to hell in a hand basket, whatever that means!"

Annie laughed grimly. "I'll look it up in the library next time I think of it. I'd hardly call the murder a hand basket, and the school is going through rough times, but I don't think it will end up in hell. Oh, but here's something rather hellish: Wren Taggert has a new for us to jump through."

"Go on, I'm listening." Clara walked over to the wall thermostat. The temperature must have dropped at least ten degrees in the last hour. She turned the thermostat up from 65 to 68 degrees.

"Instead of the rough outline that we've always used at the beginning of every six-week period," Annie explained, "we have to submit the activities for every hour of the day, with methods and objectives for each section of each hour...kind of a grid. Then after the end of the six weeks, we're all going to be checked for whether or not we met the goals."

"Talk about micro-management! That sounds like a horrific plot to make our lives miserable. Surely you don't have to do that for the library!"

"Guess again. When teachers bring their students in for research papers or something like that, I have to set goals that coordinate with those set by the teacher. And I have to evaluate the time the students were working on whatever it was that they came in for."

"Oh God! Talk about Draconian measures," Clara groaned. "Joseph Speckled Horse hired me, and I've never had much to do with Taggert. You know, she's always struck me as bossy, power-mad and generally unpleasant. Now that Speckled Horse is dead, though, I'll have to deal more with her. Guess I need an attitude adjustment." She sighed. Life seemed to be piling up on her and she took a deep breath to shake off her feeling of oppression.

Clara looked at her watch. "Egad, Annie! It's three o'clock and I have to be ready to leave tomorrow morning at six a.m. If you're not in too much of a hurry, could you help me decide what to pack? I always take too much."

In half an hour, the two women had everything Clara would need packed into one medium-sized Samsonite canvas bag and an overnight tote, including running shoes, toothbrush, and extra contact lenses.

"I've got to take something to read, maybe Jann Arrington Wolcott's latest suspense thriller," Clara mused, more to herself than Annie.

"Here I am muttering. Just ignore my absentmindedness." She walked to her bookshelf and pulled down several paperbacks. "Will used to have about 3,000 books, but when they moved to Whispering Pines, everything got downsized. He lost his files, years and years of correspondence, and all but about 300 of his books. It broke his heart."

It was time for Annie to begin the half-hour drive to her apartment in Pecos. Though most of the road was moderate, there were a couple of bad hills and treacherous curves to navigate. By now they would be icy and snow-packed.

Clara gave her dearest friend a hug. "Here's the house key, and you know what to do about Oscar. If he seems too lonely, his carrier is in my bedroom and you can just take him home with you. Thanks for the wonderful lunch, and thanks for helping me pack. Drive very carefully and call me when you get home."

"Happy Thanksgiving. I'll miss you. Please promise me you'll tell Henry this is the end. If not now, as soon as you get back. And promise me that you'll see Tia Estrellita about that bad foot just as soon as you get back."

Clara opened the door and was shocked at the icy blast and the way the snow was falling harder than ever. "I'm taking my PowerBook. We can e-mail each other. I need to find out what's happening back here."

As Annie departed, Oscar seized the chance to rush outside the door. After a few minutes, his paws were completely encased in frozen snow and he meowed to get back in. Just to get it over with, she decided to feed him earlier than usual.

Oscar was a little overweight, the vet had told her on their last visit, so she carefully measured out a quarter cup of Hill's Science Diet and poured it into his bowl. Ever ready for the next meal, Oscar pounced from the table to the floor and started munching enthusiastically.

An hour later, Clara was tingling and warm from a bubble bath. She dressed in boots, a denim broomstick skirt, and a new red turtleneck chenille sweater and then curled up in her one comfortable easy chair. While waiting for Henry, she would not allow herself to do any school work.

This was "downtime," as she liked to call it, set aside for writing about the project closest to her heart: trying to find her birth mother. Taking out a half-filled blank book, she started a new page: "Search for family," she wrote, and then started a list of steps:

1. Look for Tsosie file (Ask Louise. Tell her you're writing a short story and need the information it contains).

2. Go to Santa Fe Indian Hospital and look for birth records for March, 1965.

3. Direct and record dreams.

4. Visit Annie's Aunt Estrellita to see if she has any ideas.

5. Think of a way to tell students about your origins and see if they can look on Native Net for any memories, connections, threads that will lead back to the past.

Half an hour and several cups of tea later, Clara was jolted out of her musings by a rattling of the front door. Henry, a small duffel bag in hand, was letting himself in. He wore a rust plaid lumberjack shirt that complimented his eyes. His dark brown curly hair had that wild, unkempt look that Clara loved.

"Hi, sweetheart. DiMarco catering at your service." Henry smile was its most charming, his voice soft and low. He delivered his speech with a slight bow.

Clara shoved her papers in a drawer and rose to her feet. "Come in, *andelé, andelé.* Don't let any heat out." She returned Henry's enthusiastic kiss as he lifted her in the air with a bear hug. "You look as though you're going on a trip instead of me. What do you mean, catering? What's in your bag?"

Henry flashed her a devilish smile. "We're not going out to dinner after all. I brought dinner for us from Maria's Kitchen. The roads are too bad to be driving back into Santa Fe so I thought we could go for a little hike in the snow and then just eat dinner at Casa de Clara. Tell me it's an offer you can't refuse." He leaned down to pick up Oscar, who had been attracted to the wonderful smells coming from the duffel bag.

"Well, what can I say? You know how much I love Maria's food. I really need a green chile fix before going to the land of roast chicken and pot pies. The nursing home fare at Whispering Pines will definitely have me craving enchiladas."

"Snow's let up for now. Let's go for a little hike before dinner," suggested Henry. "Just to the ridge, only about two miles round trip."

After bundling up and putting on snowshoes, they trudged through fresh powder to a path behind Clara's cabin. The snow-laden ponderosa branches glinted in the pale moonlight. Their breath made little clouds as they ascended the hill, holding hands.

"Now I know why people love this place," Clara said, "why they come here to visit and then never want to leave. If only I could move Will and Louise out here, my world would be complete. But after Louise's heart attack, she's afraid to go anywhere above sea level. And it sounds as though we might have to get some serious medical care for Will. He would hate going to an unfamiliar doctor."

They trudged briskly along, soon reaching a ridge top that went on for miles and led off the mesa on which the academy perched. As if blessing their outing, a shooting star shot across the western sky. Snowshoeing along with Henry, bringer of food and comfort, Clara wavered further on her decision to break things off with him. They hadn't talked about Speckled Horse's death, and now she couldn't bring herself to mention it. She needed to focus on something else for awhile. It was just too depressing.

As if reading her mind, Henry said, "I've heard about the murder. I know you wondered where the hell I was last night. Like I said, I should have been here to give you moral support. You know my job with the school requires occasional travel. I thought you'd remember that I was going to be away."

As Henry talked, he was kissing her arms and neck. "Wren Taggert e-mailed me the horrible news, and I sent you a message right away. I guess you didn't check your e-mail last night?"

"As a matter of fact," Clara said tersely, "I packed my PowerBook two days ago." She mulled over Henry's offhanded explanation for not calling. She didn't recall his saying that he'd be going to California, but she was having far too good a time now to ruin it. She deliberately ignored the nagging doubts about her lover's truthfulness. His kisses felt delicious. Even though heavy clouds drifted overhead, the horizon was clear. The evening star twinkled to the west as they neared Clara's cabin. By now, Clara admitted to herself that the idea of their becoming just friends was unrealistic. With Henry, it had to be all or nothing.

"Don't be deceived," Henry warned. "It may look like a beautiful evening now, but we're supposed to get another three or four inches of snow before morning. Good thing I'll be driving you to Albuquerque."

"I guess I won't argue with that."

As soon as they were back inside Clara's cabin, Henry made a fire in her small corner fireplace and spread out the indoor picnic: spicy *enchiladas*, chile *rellenos*, beans and rice. They sipped from icy bottles of Negro Modelo and she listened to Henry tell her about the pollution and craziness of Los Angeles, about how much he loved New Mexico, and how happy he was that she was part of the school.

The fire was heating things up, or maybe it was just Henry's closeness. Clara slipped off her bulky sweater and dropped it on the floor. Now her torso was covered only in a white cotton Henley-style shirt. Except when teaching or running, she didn't wear a bra. Clara was aware of Henry's eyes on her barely covered breasts. Well, what did she expect?

"And now I think I'll have you for dessert," he said, after clearing away the picnic and putting more logs on the fire. He wrapped his arms around her and began covering her face with soft kisses.

A warning voice sounded in the back of her mind. *This is the guy you told Annie you were breaking off with. You didn't really buy his flimsy excuse about the night of the murder, did you? What are you doing letting this snake-in-the-grass possess you?*

As Henry's fingers caressed her neck and gently unbuttoned her cotton shirt, the voice was drowned out by a flood of pent-up emotions. For the past several weeks, she'd kept Henry at a distance, pretending to be too busy, trying to ignore her desire for him. He was her first lover since she had separated from her ex-husband Hugh, and she was too hungry, too responsive, too eager.

Henry slipped off her denim skirt and white cotton panties. He kissed her waist and stomach. "God, I've missed you," he murmured. "I'd forgotten how much you turn me on." He pressed Clara to the quilt, kissing and fondling her, then stood in the firelight while slipping out of his clothes.

Clara gasped as Henry parted her thighs and thrust deep within her. He sent a tantalizing jolt through her, an electric current that reached from the hair on top of her head to her toes. She was melting, surrendering not only her body but her mind to his frenzied rhythms. Deeper and deeper he plunged until she crested the wave of her passion. The shudder that left her breathless and the deep moan issuing from her mouth seemed to come from outside of her. For a moment, she forgot all else.

"I love you, Clara Jordan," Henry whispered, "I want you and I need you. Please don't leave me." He carried her to the bed they often shared and covered her tenderly with a goosedown quilt.

Sleepy and weak with spent passion, Clara murmured "I love you too, Henry." Morning would be here before she knew it, and she had to get up early and catch a plane. Henry was here, and she felt safe. As she fell asleep in his arms, she told herself that everything would be fine.

4

Henry in the Driver's Seat

You are old Father William, the young man said,
And your hair is exceedingly white,
And yet you incessantly stand on your head
Do you think at your age it is right?
        Alice's Adventures in Wonderland - Lewis Carroll

The alarm clock's ring awakened Clara from a dream about running, a recurring dream set along a beautiful trail in a forest of ponderosa. In her dream she was running free of the nagging pain in her right foot. Sweeping cobwebs from her mind, she struggled to a sitting position at the edge of the bed. Henry, already dressed, was bringing her a cup of coffee.

Putting her coffee mug down on the bedside table, he kissed her on the top of her head. "It's snowing again, looks like another couple inches fell last night. This means I should drive. Listen to the voice of experience."

Clara didn't know why, but she felt uneasy. She trusted Henry, but on the other hand, she'd never driven with him in such fierce weather. She had looked forward to time away from her lover, assessing their relationship and maybe distancing herself. There were things about Henry that she didn't really trust. Nothing she could exactly name, more a feeling. Looking outside at a white world, she gave in. It was true: she really did not know how to drive in this weather. "Whatever," she murmured.

Clara needed to see her parents, to find out what was wrong with Will. Was it her mother's overactive imagination or did he really have Alzheimers Disease or that Alzheimers look-alike, "senile dementia"? Her eyes stung with tears as she thought about her father, the light of her adolescent years, her hero, becoming dependent as a baby, bitter and confused about his mental faculties.

Moving quickly, she showered, toweled off, and jumped into the olive corduroy jumpsuit and after-ski boots. These clothes would be too warm for Virginia, especially for Will and Louise's overheated apartment, but she needed them now. In less than half an hour, she was completely ready to go. There should be plenty of time. It was just six a.m., and her flight left Albuquerque at eleven.

Henry carried out Clara's duffel bag and Samsonte tote, meanwhile warming up the Bronco. Perched mournfully on the kitchen

24

table, Oscar eyed Clara. He seemed to know he was about to be left behind, and when Clara opened the front door a crack, he darted hopefully toward it. When an icy blast of wind blew through the doorway, he skittered inside with a loud "Mrrwoew."

Clara locked the cabin door and didn't look back. If she had, she would have noticed the nearly covered footprints in a snowdrift near the front windows. Someone had been outside, peering in. The snow was thicker and faster now and the evidence was nearly obliterated.

Henry put the car in four-wheel drive and revved the engine. Clara plopped into the front seat.

"I called the airport just to make sure," he said. "They reported no cancellations as of now. Don't forget, we're at a higher elevation here than Albuquerque, even than Santa Fe. It's always worse in the mountains."

A touch of impatience entered Henry's tone. Clara saw that a prominent vein in his temple was pulsing, a quirk she'd only recently noticed. He continued, "The road will be OK after we get beyond La Bajada Hill, and with my four-wheel drive in low we shouldn't have any problem. We have an extra two hours, but we'll need every minute. I have chains."

Slowly, cautiously, Henry maneuvered the Bronco down the hillock on which Clara's cabin perched. Despite the madness of starting a 70-mile trip on such a morning, Clara thought, this was a beautiful scene. The towering ponderosas on either side of the road were decked in pristine snow that weighed down the branches, as though they were wearing majestic white mantles. Regal. The dried-out terrain beyond the mesa was now a dazzling white, sparkling here and there with pinpoints where the sun caught some snow crystals. A field of stars. The dawn sky was cloudy gray tinged with pink.

Clara breathed a sigh of relief as they reached a level road that would take them through Red Mesa. Though it was little more than a tin-roofed church and a couple of humble adobe houses, a graveyard, and an old appliance yard, it was the closest town to American Indian Academy. Usually dirty and a bit sordid, like a shabby orphan, Red Mesa had been beautified by the fresh snow. It had a magical air about it now, desirable, as though the church was a place where the spirit could soar, the run-down adobes, the homes of some brilliant literati from the larger Santa Fe society, the graveyard a sober place for meditation.

The snow kept falling, huge wet flakes occasionally gusted about by a fierce, howling blast of wind. They appeared to be the only people out on the road in this frozen world. Clara contrasted the scene before them with a Virginia snowstorm. In that state, winter storms were sullen rather than wild, violent, and dangerous as they were in northern New Mexico.

"It's not safe for man nor beast," she said, "or how does that saying go...'Only mad dogs and Englishmen would be out in this kind of weather'? I don't think we fit in either category. We may be mad but we're not dogs, and you're Italian-American; I'm German-American and Native-American."

As they neared the highway to Santa Fe, the snow lightened. The sky hadn't cleared up, however, a sure sign that more was on the way. The real test would be when they reached Interstate 25, the road to Albuquerque. The narrow winding dirt roads coming out from the school were free of traffic, so it had seemed safe. Even if one slid off the road, there was a deep bolster of snow. But now, despite the weather, traffic was getting heavier.

Henry replied, "I told you my family came from Abruzzo, didn't I? I went over there to meet the relatives when I graduated from college. My father's cousin, Giovanni Cecchini, was our traveling companion, and the three of us visited San Martino Sulla Maruccina. Only 800 people in the entire town. We were treated like visiting royalty. Incredible dinners, going everywhere with family members. Not much happens in San Martino: we were the big event of that summer."

"Sounds fascinating." Clara said. Though she tried to ignore her feelings of jealousy and regret, a wave of despair swept through her. While Henry knew in detail about his roots, his people, she had only vague notions about hers. No real names or exact places. She came out to Santa Fe last summer to try to find out more about her original parents, the people who'd brought her into the world. So far her progress had been zero, and now, with Speckled Horse's death and the resulting chaos at the school, prospects of finding out anything seemed to be growing dimmer.

The highway into Santa Fe had been sprinkled with sand by early morning road equipment, and they made good time. Henry maneuvered the Bronco expertly and Clara closed her eyes to relax. She had to admit that she would have felt tense behind the steering wheel. Let Henry take care of things, at least for now. She had so much to think about with her trip to see Will and Louise, the Virginia home where she'd spent all of her years since being adopted at age five. Will was sick, however, and things would never be the same.

"Did I tell you I got a pet snake?" Henry asked her. "You know how I've been talking about it for so long. Well, a friend had some baby red-tailed boas and I decided now is the time. I named him Arnie, and he's a cute little green fellow. You'll have to come see him when you get back."

"Arrrrrg," Clara exclaimed. "I've never been able to stand any kind of reptiles, and I can't imagine what anyone could possibly see in a snake. Slithery, scaly, cold, silent. You can't pet them, you can't play with them, and -- I'm sorry Henry -- they're ugly as sin."

Henry laughed. "Don't worry. I'll keep Arnie in his aquarium when you come over. But, you know, different species for different folks. Some people are allergic to cats, hate their clawing and mewing, the messy cat boxes, their aloofness."

"Nothing could be more aloof than a snake. Well, I withhold judgment until I meet this amazing reptile. In the meantime, I'll stick with Oscar."

As they neared Santa Fe, the sky grew darker. The temporary hiatus from the storm over, snow was once again accumulating on the road. They stopped at a 7-11 to get gas and coffee to go, reached Cerrillos Road and headed south. Visibility shrank to a few yards ahead.

"I don't like this at all," Clara said, between sips of scalding coffee. "Maybe the flight has been canceled. Do you think we should go back to Santa Fe and call? Or better yet, let's call on your cellular." She looked near the dashboard, but apparently Henry had stashed the small phone somewhere and he was not about to tell her its whereabouts.

"No, let's don't waste time. We'll just keep going. Like I said, after La Bajada Hill, it will get better."

Henry kept driving, eyes glued to the road ahead. "Nah," he finally declared, "it's always worse right around Santa Fe. After La Bajada, the highway levels out and the storm will probably lighten up. I don't think the prediction was for snow all day."

Speeding away from Santa Fe on I-25 South, Henry turned up the car heater. The fan emitted a gentle whirring hum. Clara closed her eyes. She thought again about the strange, terrible death of Joseph Speckled Horse and the investigation that was sure to follow when classes resumed after Thanksgiving weekend. As long as she lived, she would never get over the shock of that dead body, the fallen leader of the school. In her classroom, no less. In a strange way, she felt tied into the murder. Further thought was impossible, as she gave in to the anxious half-sleep of nervous exhaustion.

The heater must have stopped, as the next thing Clara knew, she was shivering. The temporary respite from the storm was over. The world outside was white, snow blowing wildly outside the Bronco's windows and no sign of the sky or the horizon. Where were they?

Henry seemed to read her mind. "We're almost at Cochiti. I had to put the Bronco in four-wheel drive high, but I think we'll be OK if we can get down La Bajada Hill. You've been asleep for the last ten minutes."

The pounding in Clara's head reminded her that she hadn't eaten anything since last night. Too little sleep and no food, a bad combination. Maybe they could have breakfast at the airport, that is, if they made it that far.

She closed her eyes wearily. The brief nap only served to make her more tired, and she started to drift again. When she felt the car shimmy from side to side, however, she jumped and woke up. "What's wrong, aren't we still in four-wheel drive?"

Henry looked tense, his jaw jutting out and his neck craned forward as he strained to see where they were going. "Ice, damned ice underneath snow. Nothing helps in these conditions, and we're heading downhill." He pumped the brakes and switched to neutral.

Even so, they kept moving. Henry shifted back to first gear and kept his foot over the brake. They were descending now, the long slow hill toward the Cochiti Lake turnoff. As far as she could tell, they were almost at the bottom. As long as they didn't have to brake, Clara thought, they would be OK. After the dip at the bottom, they would be going uphill again, with less chance of skidding. Her feelings toward Henry softened ever so slightly. He was a good driver and she would have hated driving this route alone.

She reached over to rub Henry's upper back and right shoulder but stopped, horrified, when she looked at the road. A huge semi, awkwardly angled across their lane, blocked their route. Henry couldn't brake in time, and there was no shoulder on the right, just a low fence and a sheer drop-off to the canyon below.

They swerved capriciously to the left, where, if there had been oncoming traffic, they would have collided. Fortunately, the oncoming lane was clear, and Henry steered the car back in the direction they wanted to go. He over-corrected, however, and the car began to drift slowly to the right.

Drifting and sliding in a white world, moving surrealistically through what seemed to be a snowbank, they left the road. Instead of screaming, Clara closed her eyes. This couldn't be happening. She thought longingly of Will and Louise, wondering if she would ever see them again, wondering when they would ever stop falling.

Dead silence, and then a voice. Henry was shaking her, gently, by the shoulder. "Clara, Clara...are you OK?"

Where were they? How long had she been unconscious? She was shaking with a chill that seemed to go to her marrow. Managing a hollow laugh, she said, "At least we're still alive. Thank God we didn't crash into that marooned semi-truck or that we didn't go off the road at the top of the hill. I feel sore and bruised but nothing's broken. How about you? Are you OK?"

Henry put his arms protectively around her. "Yeah, same here. I feel like I've been run over, but nothing is broken. I really did a number on my shoulder but a little massage work will take care of it. I had to get out of the lane we got into after avoiding the truck, but because of the ice underneath all the snow, we lost touch with the road and started gliding.

"I did manage to bash my forehead somehow. It's bleeding like a Mother." He was dabbing over his left eye with a wad of Kleenex. "All I could do was grip the steering wheel and try to maintain some degree of control. The question is, what do we do now?"

Suddenly Clara realized they had just an hour to travel the 45 miles to the airport. While Henry called "911" on his cellular, she insisted on getting out of the car and trying to climb back up to the road to try to signal for help. Even if they got someone through phoning, chances are it would be far too late for her to make her plane.

"No, babe, you'll freeze out there. The best thing for us to do is to just stay in the car." Henry had been turning the heater off and on sporadically in order to conserve gas. Now he turned it up full blast, as if to convince Clara not to leave the relative comfort of the Bronco's front seat. "I'm still trying to get 911. We'll get someone to come help us before you can even make it to the road."

But, now the cellular wasn't working. "Damn, I knew I should have recharged this piece of crap last night. I don't have the connection along to make it work from the car. Do you want me to come with you, or should I stay here and keep trying to phone for help?"

Clara donned every extra piece of clothing she could find -- coat, hat, earmuffs, scarf, mittens over gloves. "I'm going to the road to look for help," she announced. Henry grabbed her arm, but she was already halfway out of the car.

Blood from an earlier wound started streaming into Henry's left eye. When he let go to reapply the tissue dressing, Clara escaped into knee-deep snow covering a steeply angled embankment. Surely he hadn't crashed the car on purpose, but Clara nonetheless wondered if she could have done a better job of navigating La Bajada. Too late now. She'd never know.

She struggled uphill. At first the cold was exhilarating. As she slowly clawed her way up the embankment, on hands and knees, her heart sank. This would take a long, long time under the best of conditions. Her legs felt rubbery, but at least she could see the roadside guardrail above her. It appeared to be about half the length of a football field away. If only she could make it to the road, surely someone would come along who could take her to the airport.

Blowing snow burned her eyes. Clara's hands were numb and her feet felt like stumps but she trudged slowly and painfully upward. Henry must still be fiddling with the cellular phone. While he had been tending his wound, Clara had put her wallet and her ticket in a fanny pack and fastened it around her waist under her coat. The agonizing doubts she had been having about him for the last month came rushing back. After this ordeal was over, she would cut things off.

So preoccupied was Clara that she didn't notice the stump protruding from the snowdrift and stumbled right into it. Losing her balance, she fell backwards, rolling over and over until she was just a few feet from the marooned Bronco. Pain seared through her right ankle, along her back and spine, and through her right wrist and hand, where she'd tried to cushion her fall. By now, the numbness in her hands had turned into an aching burn. She would never catch her plane back to Virginia. Maybe she would never get out of this.

Finally she reached the car, yanked open the door and stumbled inside. Henry wasn't there. For a few minutes she lay on the seat, shivering, her eyes closed. She noticed that the keys were still in the ignition, so she turned the car on to get some heat. Looking out the driver's side of the car, she saw a deep trough where Henry had apparently made his way through the snow. And there he was, 100 yards away, holding the phone at different angles and dialing.

Soon the snow, which had seemed to let up for a bit, started again in earnest. Clara could no longer see Henry. She put her frozen hands directly in front of the heat outlets and rubbed them together, trying to bring some life back to her fingers.

She must have fallen asleep because the next thing she remembered, Henry was back in the car next to her. Even though she had decided she would cut off things entirely with her soon to be ex-lover, Clara knew that now her very survival might depend on him. What happened later hardly seemed important. That is, if there would be a "later."

For now, Henry at least provided some warmth. She didn't pull away when he put his arm around her, instead letting her body go limp in his arms. They kept the heater on as much as possible but also had to watch gas consumption. Outside, the storm continued to rage. If she were still in love with Henry, Clara might almost have considered the situation romantic. But she knew now that her dealings with him had been a mistake. She couldn't quite explain why. No escaping his curious disappearance the night of Speckled Horse's death.

"I have some almonds," Henry offered. "You know how I always keep some on hand. We need to keep up our strength, especially if we're going to have to hike out of here. I finally got someone on the 911 number when I was outside dialing the cellular. It got all static toward the end, so I'm not sure anyone heard me."

"I'll have to admit, these are pretty good," Clara said between munches. "Of course after starving, any morsel would be delicious. Surely someone will be here pretty soon."

But it was another three hours before help arrived.

The snow stopped and weak sunlight filtered through the now-thinning clouds. A massive tow truck, its red and blue emergency lights blinking and rotating, drove up to the spot where Clara and Henry had managed to climb their way out of the snow pit that still held the Bronco.

"You Henry DiMarco?" asked the short, fat wrecker driver. "Ya called Triple A at 9:00 a.m.?" The man had a wide space between his teeth and hair that looked as though it had been cut while someone held a bowl over his head.

"Who else do you think would be out here?" Henry groaned. "It's not exactly picnic weather."

Clara sighed. Leave it to Henry to alienate the wrecker driver with his incessant sarcasm. "Show him your card," she suggested with a phony cheeriness. She'd smooth things over, as she always did, possibly reminding Henry that he didn't have to be so nasty.

Henry glared at her as he pulled out his wallet and flashed his AAA membership card toward Snaggletooth, who looked at it, grunted, and lowered a crane into the snowy pit that cradled the Bronco.

"I gotta warn ya. This may damage the car, throw it out of alignment."

"Look, we've got to get out of here. We'll take our chances. Do you want me to sign a waiver?" Henry had adopted a more civilized tone. It was obvious that his nerves were ragged.

"Nah, just wanted to let you know."

Surprisingly agile for one so overweight, Snaggletooth scrambled down the slope and was fastening the crane to the Bronco's front bumper. Clara guessed that wrecker drivers had to be somewhat athletic, as cars rarely got marooned in flat, convenient places.

31

"I'm going to do a little running," she told Henry, choosing not to look at the rest of the car rescue operations. Slowly at first, then faster, she jogged along the highway's edge toward the turnoff to Cochiti Lake. People at the school told her about the triathlons that used to be held there before people started dying during the swimming part of the events. When spring came, she would drive out here to run and ride her bike around the lake. Hopefully by then her bad foot would be healed. Right now it was beginning to ache again.

For the first time in hours, she wasn't cold. As she jogged, she shook her hands and wiggled her fingers. The numbness was gone, and it felt like her circulation was returning. After a mile downhill, she turned around and headed back up. Maybe the Bronco would be dredged up by the time she got back. Henry's overseeing operations might have helped or it might have hindered depending on whether or not he alienated Snaggletooth.

Just as she hoped, the Bronco was back on the road, hanging at an angle from the AAA tow truck's crane. She and Henry would ride in the cab of the tow truck, tucked in all too cozily with Snaggletooth. Clara sighed. Beggars couldn't be choosers. She tried not to think about Virginia, tried very hard to just sleep, resting against Henry, as they crept back up the same hill they had descended six hours earlier.

She must have dozed off, because the next thing she knew they were in Santa Fe.

"Where ya want me to take her?" asked Snaggletooth. "My brother-in-law has a garage that specializes in realignment jobs, probably all this baby needs." He was grinning as he said this, maybe at the prospect of getting some kind of payoff from brother-in-law. You scratch my back, and I'll scratch yours. A way of life in these parts.

"Sure, take us there," Clara said. "You didn't have any place in mind, did you, Henry? I can call Annie: I know she'll be glad to come get us." Anything to keep from having to be alone with Henry. After the La Bajada debacle, she didn't trust him. Now that she thought about it, she suspected the drive off the road had been preventable. Henry had wanted to keep her from getting to the airport. And, to her bitter disappointment, he had succeeded.

"Ah, no," Henry protested. "I'd rather have you take me to Wright Brothers Automotive. We can call a cab from there."

"Wright is closed for a week. They had a lift malfunction, had to order some new equipment," Snaggle offered. "What'll it be, folks? I gotta know before I take the wrong exit."

"Well, I guess your brother's garage is OK," said Henry. "What did you say it was called? Capital Repair?" He handed Clara the cellular phone. "You might as well call Amy to pick us up. You can use my cellular and just tell her we'll call when the Bronco's squared away."

It was obvious that Henry didn't remember meeting Annie. Also he was bad at names. "You mean Annie, Annie Archuleta?" Clara asked. "She said she'd be home today getting ready for Thanksgiving dinner tomorrow. It'll take her about half an hour to come in from Red Mesa, but knowing Annie, she won't mind."

She started to tell Henry that Annie had invited her for dinner but stopped herself before the words were out. The last thing in the world she wanted was to spend Thanksgiving with Henry. Knowing her soon to be ex-boyfriend, he might just invite himself along. Since she couldn't get to Will and Louise, a quiet Thanksgiving with Annie's family was the next best thing.

Clara felt exhaustion spread through her body as she somehow endured the next few tedious hours: the body shop, waiting for Annie, delivering Henry to the DiMarco household in Santa Fe, driving the half hour to her cabin at Red Mesa. Henry seemed oddly willing to let Annie take Clara home. He didn't mention getting together at Thanksgiving.

Once they got to Clara's cabin, Annie insisted that she would spend the night. "You don't look too good, keed," she joked. "Auntie Annabel needs to take care of you and Oscar. I've got everything ready for tomorrow and Mom doesn't need any more help." Clara was too weak to object. She called Louise with the unwelcome news that she wouldn't be with them for Thanksgiving, only to learn that Will had fallen that afternoon. Annie wrapped a wool blanket around Clara as she sat slumped in a bean bag chair talking to her mother.

"I don't think he's going to last much longer at this rate," Louise told Clara. "He doesn't want to live. I'm not sure he even remembers who I am." Her voice broke and Clara thought she heard a muffled sob.

"Mother, I'm so sorry that I couldn't get there. Please tell Dad that I love him and I'll try to get back soon. I think I better get off the phone. I'm beginning to have chills. I just need a hot bath and bed."

Annie was the perfect nurse. Less than an hour later, with a bowl of clear chicken broth in her stomach and wearing her warmest flannel pajamas, Clara was in bed. Her body ached all over, and she shook with chills despite the quilts Annie piled on her. In minutes she fell into a troubled sleep and dreamed of being buried in snow, shouting but not being heard.

33

5
Jerome Naranjo and the Third Degree

Sunlight filtered through the curtains and danced on Clara's patchwork quilt. Annie Archuleta, drinking a cup of Earl Gray tea, sat in a rocking chair beside Clara's bed. She'd been there since five a.m. It was now after nine.

Clara sat up, rubbing her eyes. She should have been waking up in Virginia, but here she was on Thanksgiving Day still at Red Mesa and 3,000 miles from her parents.

"Hi, sleepyhead," Annie said. "You were so zonked, I thought you'd sleep all day. Guess a traffic accident takes a lot out of one. I just made tea for you. Also, my Mom is more than OK with your joining us for Thanksgiving dinner. She's delighted. She'd be terribly offended if you said anything but yes."

"I feel like I've rejoined the human race," Clara announced. "And you made me an offer I can't refuse. I'd love to come and can I bring anything? Are the roads OK now? Have you been sitting by my bed all night?"

Annie laughed. "In answer to your questions, no, yes, no. I can tell you need a cup of tea. I'm glad I made caffeinated. You stay put: I'll be right back."

Annie opened the curtains as she walked to the kitchen. While she was gone, Oscar jumped up on the bed, purring loudly and presenting his head for Clara to scratch. Except for not being with her parents today, Clara felt oddly happy.

"Service with a smile." Annie brought in a tray with a steaming teapot, two mugs, a pitcher of cream, spoons, and a small basket of muffins. "While you were still asleep, a detective Jerome Naranjo called and said he needed to talk with you. He's part of the entourage that came to your classroom along with the tribal policemen."

"Oh, yeah, the tall Indian with a long braid down his back, low voice, and penetrating eyes. I vaguely remember him, even though I was going to try to forget about all of that for awhile."

"Clara, forget about forgetting. None of us are able to get away from the aftermath. This will taint the rest of the academic year. It will affect the school forever. So anyway, Jerome is coming over to interview you at eleven. Hope that's OK. I have to get just a few things for our feast. I'll be back to pick you up at two; dinner is scheduled for four."

"Everything is happening too fast, Annie, my head's spinning. What is Jerome going to ask me, anyway? I told the police everything I knew. They don't think I have any connection to the crime, do they?"

Annie, always eager to make people feel at ease, leaned over to give her friend a hug. "Don't worry your pretty head, my pet. Jerome is just doing his job. They want to find the monster who killed Speckled Horse. Don't be intimidated. Just tell him everything you know. For God's sake, it certainly wasn't your fault. Whoever killed him just happened to know that he'd be in your classroom."

Clara did not feel reassured. On the other hand, she didn't want to create a hassle for Annie, who'd been so caring and considerate, attentive and kind. The two of them had a strong bond. Annie was the sister she never had.

"Whatever you say, Ms. Self-assured. I need to take assertiveness lessons from you. Why don't I bring something this afternoon? The larder isn't completely bare and I could easily whip up a fruit salad or bake some brownies."

Annie was putting on her blanket coat, earmuffs, snow boots and mittens. "Really, Clara. You deserve a break. I have my whole family to help me out. Just have your charming self ready, but that doesn't mean dressing up. The Archuletas are pretty down home kind of people."

After Annie was out the door, Clara listened to the Oldsmobile, sputtering and choking as it was being started up. Annie needed a new car, but she insisted that her 20-year-old "green monster," sometimes called "the bomb," was reliable.

In answer to Clara's suggestions concerning a new car, she would quip, "Hey, at least I know the quirks of this buggy. Why start with something new? Knowing my bad luck with cars, I could end up buying a bright, shiny new lemon. What did Hamlet say? 'Tis easier to face known ills than those we know naught of...'? Something like that, anyway."

Annie walked out with a cheery smile, blowing a kiss in the air as she left. Her friendship was one of the best things that had happened to Clara since she'd moved to Red Mesa. Sometimes Clara thought about how lonely and frustrating life here would be without her wonderful friend and confidante. Besides, Annie loved to tease Clara, she needed someone to help her see the lighter side.

Her first task, Clara decided, was to call Louise again. Last night's conversation was a blur. Did Louise mention a fall, or did she just dream that up? Nervously she dialed the area code and number, getting two misdials before Louise finally answered.

"Oh, hi, honey, are you OK?" her mother asked. "We've been so worried about your being out in the storm. Don't worry about us. I can freeze most of the dinner things and we are probably just going to have dinner at the Club. Are you going to have Thanksgiving dinner with the new man? Is it Harold?"

"It's Henry, not Harold, and I don't think I'll be seeing him anymore. You might say we're going separate ways."

"Well, dear, we just want you to be happy. I'm sure you know best. Henry did seem to be a real gentleman, especially after Hugh." Her voice trailed off.

"That's OK, Mom, right now I just need time to myself without a relationship to worry about. I'm terribly concerned about Daddy. What do the doctors say? Does he really have Alzheimers, or is his condition just the natural process of aging?"

Louise spoke in a whisper. "I can't say too much about Will while he's listening. He's right in the next room, and lately he's been getting angry for no apparent reason. All kinds of things set him off. I never know when he's going to explode. Can you call me at noon tomorrow, that's ten your time. I'll be freer to talk then. It does not look good."

"Yes, I love you and Dad. Happy Thanksgiving, and I'll call you at ten on Friday." After she finished the conversation with her mother, Clara sat glumly in her one comfortable chair. She was losing everything. First Henry, now her father. What's more, she was further than ever from finding out about her original family.

Now that Will's mind seemed to be going, she would never be able to get any answers from him. Louise always got teary-eyed whenever Clara queried her about the adoption. Her only hope was Will's office files, and in order to probe into those, she would have to get back to Virginia.

And now she had to get ready for more questioning by this Jerome Naranjo. Should she call a lawyer? Was she a suspect? The thought was preposterous. She merely happened to teach in the classroom where the murder occurred. Her only role had been to invite Speckled Horse to speak to her students. The only Anglo person she knew who was really close to Speckled Horse was Henry, who had shared a love of pottery and petroglyphs with the slain Indian leader. But Henry had been out of town when this whole mess happened, or so he said.

Clara thought hard. Whoever had killed Speckled Horse must have known about the planned talk to her class that fateful afternoon, either that or they must have been trailing Speckled Horse. She couldn't recall any enemies that Speckled Horse had, but there were some tribal elders, she knew, that felt he didn't stress traditional values enough.

She ran a steaming tub of bath water, pouring in a generous glob of the bath gel Henry had given her for her birthday. That was at the beginning of November, back when she was still under his spell.

As she sank into the deep suds, Oscar put his paws over the side of the tub and mewed at her. The silly creature was obsessed with water. She had to cover the kitchen faucet with a dishcloth to keep him from lapping up water that occasionally dripped out. His water bowl could contain no more than an inch or so of water or he would splash the contents out, leaving water all over the floor and none to drink.

"You little goofus," she taunted him. "Just what would you do if you just fell into the tub with me?" She flicked a few drops of water his way. Oscar ran away, waited briefly, and then crept back to his water-watching perch. With Oscar, curiosity always won over caution. Clara loved his determination.

She luxuriated awhile in the hot water, then toweled off vigorously, picked out a fresh pair of jeans, a turquoise chenille sweater and her favorite cowgirl boots.

Why, she asked herself, am I'm acting like this is a date? She rubbed her body with moisturizer, put on lacy underwear and struggled into the tight jeans, stiff from laundering. Well, why not? Maybe it would help soften the end of her relationship with Henry. She smoothed on foundation, eyeshadow, mascara, blusher, and just a touch of lipstick and gloss, and fastened her best gold hoop earrings into her earlobes. This same outfit would be fine for dinner at Annie's.

A gentle rapping brought Clara back to the present. She opened the front door to Jerome Naranjo, taller and more handsome than she remembered. He was wearing a red flannel shirt, Levis, and a serious expression.

"Sorry to disturb you, Ms. Jordan, but there are still a lot of questions about Joseph Speckled Horse that we can't resolve, and I need your help. Mind if I come in...this shouldn't take more than an hour. Lots of times people remember more about a crime after the fact rather than right when it happened."

Clara let Oscar dart out the door even though he would want back in moments later. "Of course, Annie told me you'd be stopping by, and besides, I remember you from Monday night. Come in. Drop the 'Ms. Jordan.' Even my students call me 'Clara'."

Jerome sidled in the door as though he were trying to keep cold air from rushing in alongside his tall body. He gently pulled the door shut behind him. "Thank you ma'am, I mean Clara." His coal black eyes looked friendly even though his words were spoken in a matter-of-fact tone.

"Here, have a seat and ask away. I'll try to be helpful."

She waved him toward her one good chair and dragged her rickety garage sale special from the kitchen. "I still can't believe this happened. Why anyone would want to murder Joseph Speckled Horse? Why did it happen in my classroom? Very few people even knew about his after-school talk. It was part of a series of...I guess I should call them ... motivational talks that I'd planned for my homeroom class. He had to arrange everything carefully to have time to come for the visit. In fact, we'd been trying to plan this since Columbus Day, a holiday that of course AIA doesn't honor."

Jerome looked as though he were about to comment on Columbus Day but instead of saying anything, he just frowned. "Ah yes. Well, Clara, we think that whoever arranged Speckled Horse's death may have been a mutual acquaintance of both yours and Speckled Horse's. It seems to have been an inside job."

"My God, really? Do you have any likely suspects?"

"You know a student named Johnnie Tsosie?" asked Jerome. His voice had a sharp edge. "Apparently he was seen leaving the school in a hurry right after the body was found. He's the only obvious suspect so far."

Clara thought for a minute. "Well, I have two Tsosie sisters, Treena and Deena. And I think they told me they have an older brother, probably Johnnie. The two sisters are some of my best students. A very good family. I can't remember their ever mentioning any problems with Johnnie. But they wouldn't talk about that anyway. All I knew is that Johnnie dropped out of school for awhile to go on a kind of vision quest. The kids told me he was gone for nearly three weeks last year but that he wasn't suspended because what he was doing was his own personal education project."

"Well, Johnnie hasn't been seen or heard from since Monday night," said Jerome. "Seems like an odd time to start a vision quest, right as the headmaster of the school is being murdered. A little too coincidental. I talked with Daryll Reid, his science teacher, and he said that Johnnie has an attitude, been moody and uncooperative lately, something eating him. He didn't know why, guessed that it could have been something against the way the school was being run...or something against who was running it. Not much to go on, but it's all we have so far."

"Have you talked to the Tsosies?" Clara asked.

"Yeah, complete dead end. They told me that Johnnie is 18 and on his own, that they thought he learned more from his quests than he could in the classroom. The father has a drinking problem. The mother seems weak and easily intimidated. I felt like I was really unwelcome. No sign of Treena or Deena when I was at their house talking to their parents."

"So what do you want me to do?" Clara asked. I can quiz the girls about Johnnie, why he left Monday night. But anything they've ever mentioned about their big brother made him sound wonderful. Not your rebellious type, sort of a family guy."

Jerome scribbled notes in a small green tablet. "What was Speckled Horse's attitude toward coming to spend time with your class?" he asked. "You say he first started planning this after the school talk in October, but he was just getting around to it in the end of November?"

"Speckled Horse was really fired up about the talk. He sounded as though the talk was something he really looked forward to. He was concerned about nature conservation and preserving Native American culture. He was very big on pottery, relics, petroglyphs, that kind of thing. He was so proud of the school's endowment collection, some rare pieces of pottery that he'd managed to come by from various benefactors of the school."

"Did he ever mention a black Tewa pot with an ancient motif, something like an arrow or snake, a pot with mystical healing powers? One disappeared the night that he was murdered. There may be a connection between the theft and Speckled Horse's death."

"Hmmm, it does seem too strange to be mere coincidence. Do you think there's a connection between Johnnie Tsosie and the pot? Or a connection of all three -- the murder, the stolen pot, and the flight of Tsosie?"

Jerome didn't answer right away. "Some of the elders are saying that with the disappearance of the pot, the future of the school is endangered. Apparently the pot had been in Joseph Speckled Horse's family for many years. Speckled Horse's mother had received it as a wedding gift from a Suina family known for their fine pottery. That was long ago. When she died, she gave it to the Indian school for their endowment collection. Only Speckled Horse and a few of the older people knew about the mystical qualities of the pot. Of course, just from the standpoint of beauty, it was highly desirable."

At the name "Suina," Clara jolted to attention. As well as she could recall, that was the name on the file that, years ago, she'd found in Will Jordan's home office, the name that she was born with. Of course,

39

there were probably lots of Suinas. How would she ever find out which family was hers?

There was something else about what Jerome said. One of her students commented that Speckled Horse was involved in some unethical dealings. She couldn't quite remember who'd said that, and when she questioned the accuser, he had backed away, saying that she wouldn't understand.

"A student who didn't like Speckled Horse said that he would sell the roof out from over his mother's head. The conversation ended when I arrived. The students must think I'm a direct spy for the administration. Whenever I'm in the area and anyone on the staff is mentioned, there's a dead silence."

Jerome scribbled more notes. He folded the green note pad back together and slipped it into the chest pocket of his lumberjack shirt. "I understand. A lot of these kids are shy around Anglos, even those they like and trust. But without being too obvious, maybe you could try to get the gist of these rumors. Could be important."

"Well, of course. I do want to help, and everyone will feel better when we can get to the bottom of this horrible crime. I'll keep my ears open for clues. Oh, and by the way...Am I in any danger because it happened in my room?"

Until now, she hadn't really thought about this, but suddenly she realized that whoever killed Speckled Horse might want to eliminate anyone who might be a witness or even close to the crime. After all, she did live alone. Now that her romance (or whatever it was) with Henry was dead, Annie was the only person who knew her whereabouts on a day-to-day basis.

"Yes," Jerome said, "I'm glad you mentioned that. We don't feel there is any real danger, but there is the possibility that someone might feel you know too much. You may be trailed by the assassin or his henchmen. Just be aware of any strange calls or any unexplained footprints around your cabin. Maybe you should have a dog."

As if in response, Oscar jumped up on Clara's lap and nuzzled his head next to her hand to be scratched. "I'm afraid my friend here would run away at the first sight of a canine," Clara said. "I can't give up Oscar, but I will tell you if I see anything suspicious."

Jerome tore a sheet out of his green note pad, wrote his phone number on it and handed it to Clara. "Really, just call me if anything seems to be out of order. I'm going to be at an all-day meeting at the Corn Dance Cafe in Santa Fe tomorrow, but I have my pager number written down with my regular number. Just be careful."

Clara, scooping Oscar from her lap to her arms, got up and walked Jerome to the door. "Thanks again, Jerome. I'd shake hands but Oscar doesn't like to be put down and if I do it before he's ready, he digs in his claws. Happy Thanksgiving."

Jerome stepped up into his tan Ford pickup. He rolled down the window and called out as he was driving away, "I'll be in touch."

She stood watching until the pickup was a tiny dot at the end of the hill. Oscar squirmed in her arms, the feline signal that it was time to be put down. The cloudless sky dazzled turquoise, contrasting with the gloom of yesterday.

Clara breathed in the cold, fresh air. She walked the quarter mile downhill to her mailbox. From the midpoint in her long, curving driveway, she could see across a ravine all the way to the main campus buildings. She could just barely make out the Fine Arts Center, the large adobe structure that housed her classroom, the dorm and the gymnasium.

She was removing two days' collection of bills and ads from the mailbox when Annie's green bomber came chugging up the hill. "I'll give you a lift," she called out as she pulled up alongside Clara.

The two women called Oscar out of a tree and coaxed him indoors. Even though it was warm and sunny now, by the time Clara returned, the temperature would once again drop below freezing. After filling the cat's dishes with kibble and fresh water and getting a fruit salad from the refrigerator, Clara grabbed a coat. She climbed in the bomber, and they headed to the Archuleta residence on the outskirts of Espanola.

The Collectors

Retired heart surgeon Dan Eastgate and his wife Carol walked through their hilltop mansion in La Mesa, California, feeling smug. This was their first Thanksgiving after Dan's retirement. He'd had an extremely lucrative practice, his retirement made more appealing by the city of San Diego's two-million dollar compensation when they decided to build the interstate right through his office.

Eastgate was a handsome, dapper man, short but powerfully built. His sparkling blue eyes and smooth, tanned skin contrasted interestingly with his snow white hair. Dan looked at his slim, attractive brown-haired wife, a woman of 55 who looked 35, and felt a surge of pride. She was a retired English professor, had been assistant head of the department at the University of California, and was the author of several popular nonfiction books.

As always on special occasions, Carol wore black. She looked elegant in her velvet broomstick skirt, a Navajo style blouse, black granny boots, and silver Indian jewelry. And Carol was the only woman Dan knew who looked sexy in spectacles. She was an intellectual, he mused, better read and more articulate than anyone he'd ever met, and her round gold-rimmed glasses -- rather than looking school-marmish -- were part of her charisma.

He had arrived. It wasn't just Carol, whom he loved deeply, that made him proud. It was his home, the pinnacle of his success and the manifestation of good fortune that he had not been given but earned. They'd invited the Boyntons, a young doctor and his wife, to Thanksgiving dinner. The Boyntons were bringing their infant son, but Lana promised that little Jimmy would be sleeping. He was a "perfect" baby and would not disturb them during their meal. If he awakened, Lana said during a phone conversation the day before, she would just nurse him or Clarence would carry him in the back pack. And the back pack, Clarence added, always calmed him down and put him right to sleep.

"Darling," Carol sang out, "it's going to be warm enough to have the patio doors open, and we'll be able to hear the fountain and watch the butterflies. Lately I've seen so many. It reminds me of when we were at the Royal Lahaina in Maui and the terrace room was filled with tiny brown and red birds. They were perched on everything, twittering and looking for crumbs. Remember how the hotel didn't like them but all the guests thought they were charming?"

The tantalizing aroma of roast turkey wafted through the marble-floored rooms, traveling gently over polished surfaces and overstuffed chairs and sofas. Since her retirement, Carol had become quite the homemaker, taking gourmet cooking classes and haunting antique shops for just the right pen holder or sconce for certain niches in their "hilltop hideaway."

Not that she needed to settle for domestic treasures, for Dan was an inveterate traveler, taking trips with or without Carol to exotic spots all over the globe. Every time he left, he would come back with treasures: ivory from India, silks from China, weavings from Guatemala.

A gentle ringing interrupted the Eastgates' self-congratulatory tour. Carol strolled by the gurgling fountain in the entrance atrium to open the carved double doors, which together weighed several hundred pounds.

"Hi, you two!" she called out cheerily. "We knew you were coming so I baked a cake! Actually, I baked three, along with pie and whole wheat poppy seed rolls."

Standing outside the double doors, lightly flushed from the trek up a long, steep flight up to the top of Eastgate hill, stood the dinner guests. "Your new place is fabulous," gushed Lana. "We saw the elevator when we first drove up, but knowing the feast you've prepared, we thought we needed all the exercise we could get." Lana, dressed in white silk wide-legged pants and matching mandarin-style top, looked as though she could use less exercise, not more. Looking even younger than her 38 years, she was absolutely tiny, wearing only the smallest size fours and often finding clothes in the children's department.

Clarence Boynton followed his wife into the Eastgate palace, his arms cradling their pudgy nine-month-old, Jimmy. The new father wore an ivory suit of expensive lightweight fine-woven wool highlighted with a mahogany satin vest. Even little Jimmy was in on the family color scheme, wearing off-white overalls, a tan turtleneck, chestnut colored baby Reeboks and a baby-sized white golfing hat.

Carol groaned inwardly at their "togetherness" and cutsie outfits. As she often did, however, she said the opposite of what she felt.

"Oh, you beautiful Boyntons! I just love your color-coordinated outfits. You're simply the height of fashion." She tickled little Jimmy under his double chins. "And look at the young Mr. Boynton. Isn't he decked out? Say, if you get tired of that hat, Mr. Jimbo, would you pass it on to me!"

Little Jimmy burst into a huge smile, cooed, burbled and kicked his short legs.

"Good God," said Dan, "what is this...a fashion show or a dinner party? Let's sit in the living room and wait for the bird to finish roasting. What can I offer anyone to drink?"

Lana suppressed a gasp when they entered what appeared to be a medieval guild hall. The walls and ceiling were covered with a dark, silky wood. Placed about a foot apart, carved columns topped with delicately carved heads decorated the wooden walls. Each head was distinguished with the marks of a different trade: a butcher's hat, a tailor's beret, a cook's carving knife and fork.

"This is incredible," muttered Clarence, "the butcher, the baker and the candlestick maker, all etched in wood. Where did you find this blast from the past or whatever the hell it is?"

"Hoping you would ask," Dan said. "You know how Carol and I love to browse for antiques. Well, the last time we were in L.A. for a medical convention, right before I retired from my practice, we found this secondhand shop in the heart of one of the forgotten streets off the strip. When I saw all this dark wood, I asked the owner what it was, where it was from, and how old it was." He paused. "Can you believe...a medieval guild hall!"

"I think Carol and I both knew we wanted it, no matter what. We'd been planning to remodel the living room when we were both officially enrolled in the 'leisure class'. I had already decided to retire after convention and Carol was tired of teaching according to the political correctness ultimatums that were controlling the English Department at UCSD. The idea of a medieval guild hall appealed to us both. It represents a kind of going back in time, our own chance to return to the way we were before we both got wrapped up in our careers."

Dan interrupted his account of the acquisition, "But, I haven't gotten your drink orders. I'd like to recommend a French Mont Chapelle chardonnay, fresh from my wine cellar, very crisp and delicate. Or we could have my best bottle of champagne, vintage 1998, Napa Valley."

Instead of getting drinks, however, Dan put on his newest CD, startling with its sound of crickets against symphonic strains, the crickets starting out softly and becoming loud, urgent, strident. The music seemed oddly out of place with the deep, dark wood and the somber medieval tradesmen visages.

Carol was rocking little Jimmy in her arms, crooning, making him laugh. "Anytime you get tired of this little one," she told Lana, "just bring him to Auntie Carol. We seem to have a real rapport." One of her deepest sorrows in life was that after they lost their infant son Jordan years ago, she wasn't able to get pregnant again.

Sometimes Carol thought the loss of Jordan was why they had flung themselves so wholly into their separate careers, why they now seemed to have trouble finding ways to spend their considerable wealth. While other people struggled with orthodontist and college bills, they took exotic trips and collected treasures from all over the world. She sighed, not loudly enough for anyone to hear.

"I don't want to bore you," Dan was saying to the Boyntons, "but you've got to see the incredible photos I took last summer of our African safari. We still have time before the bird is done, don't we dear?" He passed around drinks.

Carol handed Jimmy back to his mother. "Well, yes, but maybe Lana and Clarence would just like to sit and visit for a bit. After all, they've been driving for at least an hour." She hated to say too much, for she knew how important to Dan it was to impress their guests. It was as though the safari photos would convince him that they were spending their retirement in a productive way. The Boyntons had Jimmy. They had collections.

Clarence picked up on Dan's eagerness. "Hey, we'd love to see photos of Africa. Lana and I plan to go there someday, right sweetie?" He looked down at his wife, who was gently bouncing Jimmy in her arms. Gradually the whimpers stopped and Jimmy nodded off to sleep.

"Well, I guess it would be fun to go on a safari, Clarence. I've always wanted to see animals running free. Of course, we'd have to take Jimmy. I couldn't stand leaving him with anyone. Carol, is there a bed where I could leave the baby? He's finally asleep and since he didn't get his nap this morning, I need to put him down. He's such a good boy, he never cries. That is, unless he doesn't get his naps."

The two women walked down a long hall to the master bedroom suite and the king-size waterbed that dominated a garage-size bedroom. After placing little Jimmy in the center of pillow bolsters and under a baby-sized flannel sheet and a hand-knit Afghan, Lana followed Carol around on a tour of the eight-rack walk-in closet.

"These are just my clothes," Carol explained. "Dan's are on the other side of the bedroom in another walk-in." Row after row of shoes filled one shelved section, dozens of chenille, silk, and cashmere sweaters were stacked in another, and an entire hook-covered wall displayed Carol's purse collection. Except for the blouses and shoes, black, deep teals and grays seemed to predominate. The same plushy white carpeting that covered the living room and hall floor muffled their footsteps in the enormous closet, a room that looked as though no one ever walked in it.

While the two women walked through the master bedroom, pausing at every family picture or piece of collected art for Carol's explanatory footnotes, Dan and Clarence were downstairs in the basement looking at 8 1/2" by 11" glossy color photos of the Eastgates' African vacation.

There seemed no end to the stacks of albums and photos piled on tables and bookcases. Photos of rhinoceri, fields of tall grasses with grazing antelope, giraffes, and zebras; and Dan and Carol standing in scenic desert locations covered every inch of available wall space.

After admiring the African photos for what he hoped was a sufficient length of time, Clarence asked, "What are these rows of file cases, more African memories captured on film?" He gestured toward a bank of 12 wooden files lining one side of the room.

Dan laughed. "Those contain thirty years of medical practice. I have every record of every patient I ever treated, from the earliest days right after Carol and I were married in Seattle through when I put up my shingle in Los Angeles, right up until I retired last year. That's a lifetime, man. At least it's one lifetime. I'm starting another one now."

Carol and Lana, who'd finished the upstairs tour, walked into the safari/medical records room. Lana wore a bored expression. She did not want to listen to safari stories. With bogus delight, she chirped, "Oh Dan, I'm so sorry I missed hearing about your fabulous vacation, but with babies, you just never know how long it will take to get them to fall asleep. Can I take a rain check for the Africa tour? I'm just dying to see your legendary wine cellar. Carol's been telling me all about it."

She didn't add that what she'd really like was another drink. She was irritated by the Eastgates' ceaseless bragging. Lana, as always, had tried to look very special for this occasion, and with all the possessions, memories, trip stories and collections, she felt that no one even noticed how good she looked. Least of all, Clarence. If she drank enough, it wouldn't matter that she was being slighted.

"Oh my God, our drinks. I totally forgot them," Dan apologized. Anyway, we're switching to champagne. "You see, you're our first guests since the remodel and I was just so eager to give you the grand tour." He left for the kitchen.

Carol led the Boyntons into the wine cellar, assuring Lana she could have a look at the photo collection after dinner. Dan returned with four tall goblets of crisp, dry champagne, and the four clicked their glasses in a toast.

"Here's to Thanksgiving," said Carol, "and may the turkey be moist."

"To Carol," added Dan, "the best thing that ever happened to me, and to our beautiful friends, Lana and Clarence."

"To all of you," said Lana, "and to little Jimmy."

"To our hosts, Dan and Carol," said Clarence, "adventurers and collectors. May our paths cross often in this adventure called life."

"Here, here," proclaimed Dan. "Now for a crash course in vintage wines. He pulled out a bottle from the wall rack. "Here's a 1996 Merlot from Sonoma, the Milagro Verde vineyards. Wine buffs are still talking about '96 -- a real vintage year. The sun and rain were just right, and the grapes had a crisp, sweet edge. This wine has personality, so much personality that by 2010 one bottle will be worth $100. I've got three cases and if no one else has any, the value will be double that."

As Dan talked his way through several more vintage merlots, some rare ports and an extensive selection of Rieslings, he kept pouring champagne. By the time he finished talking, they'd finished three bottles. Lana felt just fine. She suggested they have a look at the "African safari collection."

After his elaborate wine cellar lecture, Dan was mildly drunk, festive, and slightly rowdy. Everyone else seemed equally festive. He might as well show off his latest treasure, a sleek, black Indian pot. Even though he'd promised the seller to reveal nothing about its background or how he'd obtained the exquisite piece of pottery, he couldn't help mentioning that he'd acquired it through an Internet transaction. Dan's face was flushed and he was talking fast.

"Some computer hack in New Mexico has an obscure home page. It took me forever to get there. The guy put me through the Spanish Inquisition before he would deal, almost as though he wanted to make sure I was a legitimate collector and not one of the feds making sure that this wasn't a stolen artifact of some kind. Really kind of weird, but don't you think it was worth it?"

They stood in front of the glass fronted case as Dan talked. Atop a red velvet pedestal shone the gleaming black pottery, a perfect pear shape with the top slender and fluted. Around the sides were stylized snakes, some aimed up, some down.

"Oouuu, that's gorgeous," cooed Lana. "It just looks so cool and silky, I want to touch it. If you could take it out of the case, Dan, I promise not to drop it. And I love those snakes on the sides."

Clarence got interested. He usually hated anything even remotely artistic, especially if Lana showed enthusiasm. More often than not, if she liked something, she wanted to buy it or have something just like it.

But the beauty of the Eastgates' black pot was irresistible. "You bought *that* through the Internet? Man, that's not like anything I ever saw online. I better find this guy's web page. I know Lana, she'll be asking for one before we get back to San Diego."

"Aw, Clarence," Lana protested. "You make it sound as though I have to buy everything I see. I'm not like that, ya'll. Clarence likes to see me dressed up, so it's true I buy a lot of clothes. But pottery is something we don't have. Our house needs some decorating."

When Clarence frowned, Lana changed her tune. "But really, I just want to hold it. If you want to give me the e-mail address of your supplier, I can check him before Christmas. I never know what to buy."

Dan went to a small chest of drawers, took out a key, and unlocked the sliding glass door. "Of all the artifacts and folk art we've collected from all over this world, this has got to be my favorite," he said.

Lana stretched out her hands. "Let me hold that elegant treasure," she crooned. "Come to me, my baby."

"Calm down," said Clarence. "It's just a damn pot, for Christ's sake."

Slowly, carefully, Dan removed the pot from its pedestal and placed it in Lana's outstretched hands. Just as she took it and hugged it to her breast, a high pitched scream pierced the air.

"Oh no," she gasped. "It's Jimmy. He must have rolled off the bed." Dan rescued the pot just as Lana seemed about to drop it.

7
Clara Meets the Archuleta Family

"Hey, this is a residential area and you're doing sixty," Clara said. "We don't want to get a speeding ticket on Thanksgiving. Of course, when would there ever be anyone in Red Mesa to issue a ticket? But, then, you never know." Clara did not want to criticize Annie, so she tried not to look at the speedometer, instead closing her eyes and leaning back against the headrest.

Clara sighed. She wished so much that she could see her parents, the only family she really knew. Of course, there were those other parents, from long ago, but they were only a vague memory. She'd been adopted when she was five.

"A peso for your thoughts," said Annie, as she turned out onto the highway to Santa Fe. "I know it must be sad to be away from your folks at Thanksgiving. You should have asked me to drive you to the airport. I know I would have gotten you there, snow or no snow. Damn Henry, anyway."

Because of Annie's breakneck driving, they were already at the dip in the road that signaled Canoncito. The only sign of the tiny settlement was the red-roofed church next to the highway. "Yes, Annie," Clara said, "I'm really sad about that. Louise and Will and I have spent every holiday together since they adopted me when I was five years old. When I was living with Hugh in Seattle, they came out for a couple Christmases when I couldn't get away even though Louise is deathly afraid of flying. They were the most wonderful parents. They always made holidays so festive. But my father is going downhill fast, and Louise was really counting on me to come out and help her decide what to do about him."

Annie reached over with one hand and patted Clara on the back. "I'm really sorry, but I can understand how you must feel. My mother's sister, Aunt Loretta, had Alzheimers, and it was terribly hard on the entire family."

"But we don't really know if it is Alzheimers," Clara said. "It may be senile dementia. I guess as far as the effects, it doesn't really make a lot of difference. All I know is that Louise took care of me when I was little and helpless, and now that she needs me in the same kind of way, I'm not there for her."

"I think what you need to do is get Will into some kind of facility, or if he wouldn't go along with that, have some help come in for your Mom."

"I agree," Clara said. "That would be a good idea. But I know right now that Louise couldn't afford it. Well, actually, she could. I told her I'd send money for a caretaker for Daddy. She will still worry about running out of money though. Will had a small retirement from his career, but it won't keep up with inflation."

"I see what you mean," Annie said. "When our parents get older, we have to help them make decisions. It's the opposite of when they were taking care of us and they knew best."

Huge puffy clouds, snow white and clustered like sheep, filled the sky as they neared Santa Fe. The sun came out. Remains of yesterday's fast-melting snow sparkled in patches here and there.

Clara took a deep breath and thought about Annie's suggestion. Hiring a caretaker for Will, or at least partially paying for one, would be a way she could help, seriously help, without having to move back to Virginia. And if she didn't have to move back, eventually maybe she could even get to the search that brought her out here in the first place. She knew that her original family might have come from here, but how could she find them?

Reaching Santa Fe, they stopped on St. Francis Drive for gas. Annie wouldn't let Clara charge it on her credit card. "You've given me rides often enough, all the times when the green bomber has been out of commission. This is the least I can do. Besides, today is my treat: Thanksgiving dinner and transportation to and from. Like the commercial says, 'You deserve a break today.'"

"I'd rather have an Archuleta break than a MacDonald's break any day," Clara said. "Did I remember the fruit salad?" She had a vision of it sitting on the kitchen counter in its Tupperware container.

"Remember, I carried it out to the car. If you'll turn around and look in the back seat, it's on the floor. You can be so silly, Clara. I think I should be hired as your official memory. Or maybe a mindguard, you know...kind of like a bodyguard."

Clara laughed. "I can't tell you how good it is to be worried about something as innocuous as fruit salad. I keep having flashbacks to Joseph's dead body. That, and the blizzard that kept me from getting home. Oops, I'm sorry, Annie. You know how much I've been wanting to meet your family and how much I appreciate the dinner invitation."

Try as she might, Clara no longer felt hopeful about finding out about her original family, her roots. When she first came to New Mexico to live, she saw her mission clearly. She would do everything possible to find a trail leading to the Indian half of her family. And at first, talking with her students, hiking to petroglyphs, getting to know families in the pueblos surrounding Red Mesa and the American Indian Academy, it seemed possible.

On the other hand, if she lived here long enough and people grew to know and like her, the missing information might surface, or so she hoped. Coupled with that dream was her plan to go through her father's files to look for information about her past. The latter, of course, would be possible only when she went back to Virginia for vacations or holidays. She thought about the "Tsosie file" she'd located in the basement of the split level ranch-style house where she spent most of her childhood.

Twelve years old at the time, she'd felt sneaky going through her father's papers. The file label read, "Suina or Tsosie, baby Clara." Inside were a lot of official looking papers and the tiny photo of an infant. She was that infant! She recalled the hot flush of excited curiosity that led her to remove the file and start reading, her fear when Louise had popped into Will's office and asked her what she was doing.

Just as she'd always done, Louise became tearful and her voice sad and faint whenever they got anywhere near the subject of Clara's adoption.

"Oh no, sweetheart, please don't meddle in your father's papers. We plan to go over everything with you someday when you're older. It would upset Will very much if he knew you were so unhappy with the home we've provided that you wanted to go digging in the past. You're our daughter now, and we couldn't love you any more if you'd been born to us. In fact, I think we love you more than parents whose children just *happen* to them."

Across the decades, Clara could still hear that hurt, tender, sorrowful voice. Still feel the emptiness when Louise gently removed the file from her hands. Still recall the feeling that she would never again be as close to finding her origins.

But of course, she did love Louise and Will. She was grateful to be one of the "real children," no longer shuffled about to uncaring and often horrific foster homes. She would do anything to keep from making Louise unhappy, and she idolized Will.

She had begged Louise not to tell her father about the file episode, apologized for meddling, and agreed to go shopping after school the next day with Louise for some new slipcovers. When she next managed to sneak a look in Will's files, there was nothing where the Baby Clara file had been. She looked for an hour through the rest of the file cases, until she heard a car rumbling up the driveway. Heart beating, she'd raced upstairs two steps at a time, ready to pretend that she had been doing nothing other than waiting to go shopping with Louise.

If only she had saved that file, Xeroxed the contents, really talked with Louise about her burning desire to know about her biological parents. But a month or so after the file episode, Louise had a heart attack and everything changed.

The memory of that time remained starkly in her subconscious, a kind of Loch Ness monster, ready to rise to the surface at any time. She remembered feeling responsible, as though her burning curiosity about those original parents had caused Louise's heart attack, as though if she were a better daughter, it would not have happened.

The two women were north of Espanola now, headed toward the Archuleta homestead. Like Clara, Annie had been silent for the last ten or so miles. Uncharacteristic. But the two were such good friends that they did not need to fill up the gaps with words.

Finally, however, Annie asked, "Did I tell you about Tia Estrellita?"

"Oh, you mean the dinner guest I'm going to be meeting? Yeah, you mentioned her, but you didn't really elaborate. All I know is that she's a *curandera* of some type, a natural healer. I love her name, 'Estrellita.' It's so light and airy, like some delicate, gauzy scarf wafting through the air, lacy and fanciful. Tell me more."

"Well, first of all, *estrella* actually means 'star,' as in celebrity. The 'ita' is just a suffix that her friends and family add, kind of like a term of endearment. She's really the opposite of 'lacy' or 'gauzy.' She's more a pillar of strength. If you ever have a bad back or muscle aches, she can massage the sore parts and give you herbs to help cure them. The herbs can be used in many ways. Sometimes she has you brew a tea from them, sometimes boil them in water and soak your sore *whatever* in them."

"Do you think Estrellita could help me with the ache in my foot?" Clara asked. She longed to be able to run again the way she used to. Before the ache in the bottom of her right foot, around the toes, she could run for ten miles without getting tired. Now, after just five miles, she couldn't bear the pain.

It wasn't just running that was affected. It hurt when she walked. If it hadn't been for the soreness, she probably would have returned to her classroom with the VCR before Speckled Horse's death. Her sore foot might have cost his life. Alas, nothing could be done about it now. Or could it? If her life depended on it, would her foot let her down? She'd been injured before and gotten over it, but this seemed to be a permanent condition.

"Your foot?" Annie asked. "I think Estrellita can cure anything, but she has to get to know you first. She is not a healer for money. She does this for people she loves and for the people who are dear to them. I think Estrellita will like you because you are my friend and therefore want to help you. But her ways are not like those of Western medicine. They take time and patience. She will have you learn the herbs, and she may even have you seek them out where they grow. It is all part of the process."

"Yeah, that could be pretty neat. I could run to find the plants that will help me perform better in races. The stronger I get, the further I'll be able to run for them."

As they passed the new Black Eagle Gaming Center, the sun burst through. The only reminders of yesterday's snow were fast melting. The sky was a brilliant turquoise, now nearly cloudless. The fierceness of yesterday's weather seemed like a bad dream.

"You know, this is what I love about northern New Mexico," Clara said. "One day you have winter, and the next day it's spring. I've gotten so I don't even miss green grass and big trees. This place grows on you."

"I feel the same way," Annie said, "and I've lived here all my life. I'm really sorry you can't go visit your parents because I know how much you were looking forward to seeing them. On the other hand, I'm so glad you're spending Thanksgiving with us. Like I keep saying, my whole family can't wait to meet you."

Clara described yesterday's episode with Henry once more to Annie. "It was the only place where there wasn't a guard rail at the edge," she mused. "If we'd had to slide over anywhere else, we'd have been stopped. It's almost as if Henry knew where he could get us grounded, almost as though it were deliberate."

"Hmmm, I know the spot you're thinking of. It hasn't been that way very long. There was a huge accident about a month ago, a big semi went over the edge. The driver died of a concussion, and a family of four in a Geo, right in the path of the semi, were blind-sided. They all ended up in critical condition. I think the little girl is going to be paralyzed for life. The father can't walk. They'll all be permanently disabled. I'm surprised you didn't read about it."

"God, how awful. I've been recycling the papers mostly unread, just too busy with school. It's terrible that nothing has been done about it. Maybe after our mishap yesterday, they'll make repairs."

"Don't count on it. This is the land of *manana*, and we have the holidays coming up. Yeah, eventually something will be done, maybe next spring."

A disturbing thought flashed through Clara's mind. With almost all of the guard railing in place, how had they happened to slide off in the one area where there was a gap? In retrospect, it almost seemed deliberate. No, that was crazy. There had been a big rig across the road they'd had to swerve left to avoid. That's what caused the fishtailing, and that's why they swerved. The big rig couldn't have been planted, and besides, Henry's goal had been to get her to the airport on time, not to spend the morning frozen and floundering in a snow bank. Or had it? Her imagination was running away with her. She needed to get a grip.

They passed through the busy main street of Espanola and headed north toward Taos. Just before they reached Velarde, Annie turned left on a side road.

"On our way to Casa de Archuleta," she called out gaily. "I can smell the turkey from here! Carmen's *posole* is probably bubbling away as I speak. And just wait until you taste Estrellita's enchiladas. They're *muy rico*. You see, we have both *gringo* and Mexican food at our holiday feasts. Something for everybody, the best of both worlds. It will give Shelby Melton something to write about."

"Shelby who?" Clara shot her friend a puzzled look.

"She's a friend of our family's and a freelance journalist doing a series on how northern New Mexico families celebrate the holidays. She was interested in us because we have not only our own extended family but people who would otherwise be alone for the holiday, so -- we agreed to be the Thanksgiving family. I hope you don't mind being part of an article."

"No, I don't have a problem with that," said Clara. "I think it sounds like a great story. I won't mind if she wants to interview me. It'll give me a chance to promote the school, which we're all supposed to do...ambassadors for the AIA, you know."

They traveled about a mile on a road paralleling the main highway, and then Annie drove up a craggy bluff overlooking the frontage road on one side and the Rio Grande River on the other. A rambling adobe *hacienda,* surrounded by towering cottonwood trees—Annie's family home—dominated the bluff. Several dogs, barking and wagging their tails, trotted out to meet them.

"Well, this is it, *mi casa.* And, as we like to say, *mi casa es su casa."* The rambling adobe looked warm and inviting, nestled as it was amongst towering cottonwood trees. The front portal was whitewashed and the wooden door as well as the posts holding up the roof over the portal were painted turquoise. "To ward off the evil spirits," Annie explained.

Dried out hollyhocks splayed out by the front door, which was festooned with a wreath of corn cobs, dried flowers and ribbons. Clara thought of her parents' lonely apartment and felt a wave of disloyalty for not being with them. But after all, she'd tried and it just wasn't possible. She would call them tomorrow morning, maybe send flowers to Louise.

As soon as she walked in the door, Clara quit worrying about what she should have done and where she should have been. The Archuletas welcomed her with sangria and salsa, served with a huge basket of tortilla chips. She met Annie's siblings. Judith was a staff development specialist for the state, twins Sharon and Karen were college students. Shelby Melton, a tall, thin woman with a crew cut, was interviewing cousin Raul about his music. She freelanced for several newspapers in the area, she explained.

The only Archuleta son, Tom, was off on Naval Reserve duty, but the whole family had talked to him just before Clara and Annie arrived. Estrellita Gonzales, *curandera* and close friend of the family, had recently sprained her ankle and was seated in an easy chair, cane by her side. When not answering Shelby's questions, Raul was singing Spanish folk songs and accompanying himself on the guitar. Last, Clara met Mama Maria, a widow, a matriarch obviously well loved by her large family of mostly daughters. "Mamacita," they all called her.

"You can call me 'Mama, too, *mijita,*'" Maria told Clara. "The friends of my children are my friends. You've come on a good day. We have two feasts in one, all our native foods and the turkey and trimmings. I hope you brought an appetite." She glanced at Clara's slender waistline. "You could use some good home-cooked food to put meat on your bones."

"Mamacita, you know how we are." Annie laughed and put her arm around the short, rotund woman. "We are always on a diet. We don't want meat on *our* bones. Clara is fashionably thin, the way I want to be."

"You are beautiful the way God made you. Always fussing and worrying about your weight. What's important is what's inside." Maria tapped her fingers against her heart. "Ah, it's no use. You just diet on some other day, not when Momma has baked the best turkey she's ever cooked." She smiled warmly at Clara. "Annie's told us much about you, all good."

Clara smelled wonderful aromas wafting from the back part of the rambling house...turkey, spicy chile, some sweet baking fragrances, probably rolls or pies. Suddenly she felt ravenous. It was comforting to be in a household, away from the death and weirdness at school, not focusing on Will and Louise, just soaking up the Archuletas' warmth.

The sangria went straight to Clara's head. Otherwise, she might never have told everyone about her injured foot and gotten involved in a discussion about herbal remedies with Estrellita. This wasn't like her usual reaction in large groups. More often she would just listen.

But the pain in her foot was important. It had, after all, kept her from running for the past several days, and it was responsible for her not getting back to the classroom in time to save the headmaster. She recalled the throbbing of her right foot as she scurried from room to room in search of the VCR. It had slowed her down, possibly kept her from either saving Speckled Horse or perhaps even from becoming a murder victim herself.

"Estrellita knows all about how to cure muscle pains," Annie told her. "She's helped people walk and even regain use of their arms. She does it all with her healing touch and with herbs that she finds in the mountains. You should go see Estrellita. She'll tell you how to treat your foot without drugs or prescriptions. I bet you'll soon be learning about and gathering the plants for yourself."

Estrellita just smiled and nodded during Annie's speech. "Ah, little one, you make me sound too big and important. All the gifts I have are directly from God, the healer of us all. True, some of my friends have recovered after they've been to see me. But it is God's will that they recover, and it has very little to do with me. I am just His instrument. He works through me."

Annie looked at Clara to see what her reaction was. "Estrellita has been an honorary family member ever since I can remember," she told her friend. "When Uncle Jake was sick with a virus that looked like it was going to take his life, Estrellita went out every day to collect herbs for healing teas. It took weeks, but against everyone's predictions, he regained his strength and his will to live. Six weeks later, better than new, he got out of bed and danced. That was ten years ago. Since then, he's never been sick a day in his life."

When she saw Clara's expression, she hastened to add, "I am not making this up. It really happened!"

Everyone went through the lines in the kitchen to heap white china plates with food, mountains of food -- *posole*, rice, *enchiladas*, *frijoles*, turkey, stuffing, gravy, sweet potatoes, mashed potatoes, peas and onions, two kinds of salad, sauteed mushrooms, broccoli. Dessert plates were provided at a side table of cakes, pies, cookies, and a huge Pyrex dish of bread pudding. Soon they were all seated in upholstered high backed chairs around the wooden dining room table or at satellite dining areas composed of card tables and folding chairs.

The tables were decorated with burgundy tablecloths and candles. In the center of each was an arrangement of gourds, dried grasses and flowers, corn cobs and pine cone turkeys that had been crafted by various family members.

Clara felt honored to be seated at the main table. Unlike her sparse family of just three people, the Archuletas spread out like branches of the cottonwood trees that towered outside the picture window.

As afternoon faded and everyone ate themselves silly, she talked with Mamacita and Annie's brothers and sisters. Judith was a teacher at Santa Fe Indian School. Fred managed a new health spa, Planet Health. Sharon and Karen, the twins, both worked for the state. Sharon was a caseworker for Children, Youth and Families and Karen worked in telecommunications. Cousin Raul, who wasn't getting along with his immediate family, had dropped out of college to follow his musical interests. His group, *Los Compadres*, had just made a CD and hoped to get some national bookings. His parents, he said, were very upset that he wasn't choosing a career with more stability.

"Mamacita likes people for themselves," he added. "My parents just care about what people do for a living, how much money they earn, what kind of house they live in. Frankly, their values are all off. They've never understood why I choose to follow my heart. I finally just couldn't take it, so I moved out. *Casa Archuleta* is my home away from home."

"Yeah, I kind of feel the same way, I guess," Clara said. "My parents are in Virginia. I was supposed to fly home yesterday but because of the snow storm, I missed the plane. My Dad is sick, and I was really looking forward to being there for them. But being here, it's impossible to be sad. Especially with the wonderful ballads you keep playing for us."

"Ah, a lady after my own heart." Raul smiled. "Don't worry. I'll be playing more ballads after dinner."

Karen and Sharon were coming around with coffee and tea, much needed, Clara thought, after the hours of feasting. While he was talking with the twins, she quickly appraised Raul. Like all of the family, he was good-looking. A tall, slim man with broad shoulders, sharp, chiseled features, a warm smile, and sparkling dark eyes. They weren't just sparkling, Clara told herself, they were sexy.

No one could eat another bite of pie or another *empanadita*, so they walked outside, their feet noiseless on a cushiony carpet of leaves. The graceful cottonwood was lovelier up close than through the window. The Archuleta land went all the way down to the Rio Grande.

Clara breathed in the cool air, tinged with the smell of damp leaves. A wan sun filtered through the overgrowth. Cookie, one of the Archuleta's five dogs, trotted around and between them. He was a shaggy, black beast with ragged ears and huge paws.

"He needs to grow into his paws," Annie said. "I think he may get as huge as Ralph, the biggest dog we ever had. I remember that we had a cat named Bill who sort of grew up with Ralph and they were great friends. It was a riot, this big, shaggy black beast and a little orange kitty. They both got old and died at the same time, sort of like an elderly married couple."

Clara thought of Oscar at home, probably yowling for food. Not much of a Thanksgiving for her little fur person. At least he'd been inside with his special catnip mouse and an extra bowl of food in the bathroom. She'd make it up to him by letting him sleep in her bed tonight.

After the walk, they all ambled back into the house for more coffee and tea. When Henry's name came up (Clara had been hoping it wouldn't), Judith said, "Oh, the DiMarcos...They're the family who gave such a big endowment to the school. There was a joke going around that they were going to name the new gym the Carlos DiMarco Sports Arena. I think they lost their enthusiasm for the DiMarco family name when their delinquent came back from New York with his tail between his legs. What was his career? Investment banking, computer consulting...something like that."

An awkward silence followed.

"Clara is dating Henry," Annie said.

"Used to date," Clara corrected.

She hoped that more would be revealed, but Judith changed the subject. On the way back to Red Mesa, she would remind herself to ask Annie exactly what Judith meant by 'delinquent.' Henry never said much about his New York past, except that he got tired of the hectic pace and he missed the mountains and weather of New Mexico.

Later, after music supplied by Raul, more steaming cups of coffee and Mexican chocolate, and more conversation in the big, family-filled living room, Annie and Clara said their goodbyes and headed back to Red Mesa.

A spectacular sunset exploded in the western sky as they drove through Santa Fe and out the Las Vegas Highway. With Clara driving, the pace was slower. She felt better than she had for several days. The ordeal at the school seemed far behind her, replaced by a mellow Thanksgiving at the Achuleta's.

"I can't thank you enough," she told Annie, whose eyes were closed, her head back. "Except for missing my parents, I can't remember a better Thanksgiving."

Annie wasn't asleep after all. "Hey, what are friends for?" she said in a drowsy voice. "My parents and brothers and sisters want you to

58

visit again. And Estrellita told me to tell you to come visit her at the Indian Hospital, where she works part time. She really can help you with her herbal remedies, and she'll show you what to look for when you gather your own."

Clara had a vision of herself running over grassy fields, up hills, along sylvan paths, running the way she used to run. Without pain or worrying about distance. Along the way, she would stop and pick sprigs growing near rocks, select leaves and roots from trees or shrubs, finding the herbs that would cure her foot. It was a delightful fantasy, and somehow it didn't matter that she had to be healed in order to do the running she imagined. In her fantasy, the running itself made her stronger.

Clara went to sleep that night thinking of the outing she planned to take at dawn, and in her dreams she raced lightly through a field of green, leafy plants.

8
Running into trouble

The murder was over a week old now, Thanksgiving break was over, and students were back in the classroom. Clara felt refreshed after the gathering at Annie's house, several long runs over the break -- one a ten-miler -- and a good conversation with Louise last night. She tentatively planned to go back to Virginia sometime in the spring.

For the past two days, her students had been hearing from grief specialists and talking about their feelings at Speckled Horse's death. The first counselor was a large, jolly man from the Governor's Children, Youth and Families Task Force. He had them crying one minute, laughing the next. Clara noticed that they seemed to be less tense than when classes first resumed.

Today's speaker, a petite woman with short light brown hair -- from the Attitudinal Transformation Society -- was less relaxed. She reviewed the stages of loss and asked the kids how their bodies reacted to sadness. Clara suspected that they were tired of talking about their feelings and just wanted to get on with life.

When she asked Clara at lunch time if she needed to come back in the afternoon, Clara said thanks but no. It was time for them to focus on something else. She also needed a break from the Speckled Horse affair.

"Let's try to get back to what we were doing before the break," Clara told her class. "Who remembers the 11-sentence paragraph? But first, does anyone want to talk about what the grief counselors said?"

"Nah," Deena said. "Our dorm counselors have been talking with us about it every night. I think we're grieved out."

"Anyone else?" Clara asked. "The police are investigating the murder and hope to find more clues before too much longer. I'll let you know as soon as I know anything. But let's get back to our work. As Ednay St. Vincent Millay said, 'Life goes on. We forget just why.'"

"OK, remember the elements of the 11-sentence paragraph?"

"Yeah," said Carnell. "You start with a thesis statement, something like, 'I like the Internet because...'" and then you write down as many reasons as you can all around the thesis statement. Then you group together all the reasons and turn them into sentences."

Clara sat at her desk while the students, chewing pencils and jotting notes, worked on their assignment. She knew this kind of writing assignment could help ...it worked well with her ninth graders back in Virginia, and this bunch was taking it seriously.

Carnell's essay pleased her. This gifted young man wrote about the time he spent with his grandfather and how much he missed him. "I would go to his house every day after school and ask him to tell me about the old days, when he was young and we didn't have gambling casinos. There were fish in the lake and instead of new roads through the Pueblo we had lots and lots of space. If Anglos came to see the dances, they were special guests, friends of somebody's, not just tourists with cameras dangling from their necks."

Carnell added that they honored the land, studying the birds and vegetation in their hunting grounds. His grandfather said they didn't call it environmental concern, it was just a way of life. "They knew every kind of bird and where they nested. They even knew how many eggs were in each nest and which birds didn't nest the next season."

Before he died, his grandfather had given Carnell a sacred medicine pouch, telling him to wear it around his neck for protection. He came to his grandson in dreams, and he was there for guidance. "When I am undecided about something," wrote Carnell, "I close my eyes and imagine what the wise one would say."

"This is wonderful. Can I use his in a class anthology?" Clara asked. "I haven't announced it officially, but I'm thinking we might compile our work by the end of the year."

Carnell's dark eyes glowed and a smile played around his lips. He was usually solemn, and the smile transformed him. Instead of answering, he shrugged and slowly nodded.

But not all the essays were good. Some were disturbing. Christine Littlebird wrote about why she liked concerts.

"The best thing about the music and being with lots of other people all having fun is that I wake up in the morning and can't remember anything. When I am there, I have a blast, but things go to my head and I black out."

Alarmed, Clara asked, "But what is so good about blacking out? Why would you not want to remember? And what makes you lose consciousness?"

Christine looked down, silent. That was answer enough. The kids had told Clara about Christine's drinking problem. The girl would drink four or five beers and some brandy or whiskey and then pass out. Her parents both drank too much and she had a brother who was always ending up in fights, brawls that usually landed him in jail.

"I like not remembering what happened," Christine replied. "I get too bored with everything. This way I don't have to wait until things get finished. It's kind of like I can be there but not be there. Then I don't have to remember because there's nothing to forget."

The essay was grammatically correct and well-written despite the disturbing nature of the contents. Clara didn't ask more questions. She made a mental note to try to get Christine to talk to Steve Duran, the school counselor.

"You've got the form down well," she told Christine. "Your writing is fine, but I think you can do better with the topic. Do you have any favorite relatives you'd like to write about for the next assignment? Remember how I said we'd be doing family histories. If you chose that, you'd have a head start on the next assignment."

Christine looked down at her desk quietly. Finally, she murmured, "I guess my grandma."

"I'd really love to read about her," Clara said. "Do you want to go ahead and write about her now? You can turn that in instead of this paper about parties you don't remember."

Without saying anything, Christine tore up the party essay, took out her notebook and started writing on a fresh page. Her face looked serene and unperturbed, Clara thought. She so much wanted to help these students. If only she weren't such an outsider; if only she could win their trust.

Later in the day, Christine came to the classroom with a brand new essay. The title read "My Grandma is my Best Friend." Clara glanced over it and saw that while Christine compared her mother unfavorably to the grandma, it was far more positive that the party essay.

An hour after classes ended, Clara was in the girls' deserted locker room changing into her running clothes. She remembered what Christine's friend Loretta had told her at the beginning of the school year. Christine lost both her grandparents in a fire. She realized that the entire essay was probably a fabrication. Christine had made it all up just to please her. Irritating, but hardly surprising. She felt her face flush with embarrassment at her gullibility.

Would she ever be able to really help these kids, to get through to them? She wanted so much to reach them, and sometimes --as with Carnell -- she felt that she really did. Others were reassuring as well, and she could see big improvements in their writing. But then something would come along to deflate her sense of progress.

Besides, she reasoned to herself, maybe Christine was writing about her other grandparents. Everyone has at least two sets of grandparents, right? Or maybe she just didn't want to write about her grandmother in the past tense. Sighing as she pulled her long black hair back into a ponytail and slipped into running tights and an oversized sweat shirt, Clara decided that she would simply put the entire episode

62

out of her mind. She couldn't solve everything. At least Christine cared enough to hand in a second paper.

She carefully put her clothes in a locker, slipped her key into a wrist wallet, and went through her five-minute stretching routine. Hands to floor, leaning over. Pulling her knees, one by one, to her chest, and rotating her feet in small circles. Hands over her head above and then to either side. She'd just had time for before-classes runs for as long as she could remember, and it was going to be wonderful to cut loose and go for six, eight, or even ten miles. As an afterthought, she returned to her locker to get earmuffs and gloves from her running bag.

When she walked back into the locker room, she was surprised to see the locker door ajar. She was certain she'd locked it before starting out. A vague uneasiness possessed her as she finished bundling up, locked once again and double checked to make sure that everything was secure. She was probably just tired and inattentive from a long teaching day, Clara told herself.

The minute she stepped outside, cool, crisp air greeted her. She leaned against the gymnasium wall, palms flat, legs stretched out behind her, and tensed all her muscles. After ten seconds, she relaxed, then repeated the process three more times.

Setting her stopwatch, Clara jogged slowly at first, then faster, toward the track behind the gym. Her left foot throbbed insistently, reminding her that she was going to visit Estrellita as soon as possible for some herbal remedies. The asphalt parking lot was unforgiving, and she was grateful to reach the clay track at last.

As she almost always did, Clara warmed up for a mile on the track before starting out wherever her feet led her. The first time around, she felt slow, fat, sluggish. The second was better, and during the third and fourth circuits, she felt light and speedy.

Beyond the track was a field nearly bare of vegetation. The kids called it Prarie Dog Heaven because of the dozens of holes in the ground created by the burrowing critters who lived there. There must have been a thousand, thought Clara, as she picked her way across to the rising land beyond the pitted field. She'd heard about a trail through the foothills that led to the top of Bentano Peak, so named for an earlier Native American educator who had tried to start a school in the early 1900s and failed. Of course the Pueblo still called it by its Indian name, *Multonomah*.

Running at a smooth, even pace despite the prarie dog holes, she checked her stopwatch. Fifteen minutes. She'd go for at least an hour, then see how she felt about continuing. It wouldn't be dark for another two hours...

Twenty minutes later, Clara headed up a narrow, rocky trail in the middle of ponderosa pines. The steep angle meant slower, harder running, but by now her heart rate was up and the extra exertion didn't strain her. Up and around, the trail undulated for another mile or so.

She was fit, Clara realized, strong despite the temporary running cutback she'd suffered because of her bad foot. She took deep breaths of the cool forest air and ran faster as the trail dipped downhill for a few yards before heading relentlessly back up.

To her left, the hill dropped into a deep ravine. One false step and she would have gone hurtling down. Occasionally, some low shrubs separated her from the precipice, and at times she was running on a narrow ledge. It was necessary to pay more attention here than at the beginning of the trail.

Then, just when she thought of turning around to avoid a fall, the terrain was more moderate. No steep dropoff to the left, a gentle up and down with few boulders in the path. She was coming to the crest of the hill, only to find another rise beyond that one.

Her wrist chronometer showed 40 minutes. She felt like running at least 20 more. Here was a split in the trail. One branch turned sharply left and followed a steep downhill slope; the other forged ahead to the right and up the next rise.

Clara slowed her running briefly to drink from her lightweight canteen and admire the hint of a sunset. The sky was rose tinged with peach, big white puffy golden white clouds billowing above the extravaganza of color.

She was energized, adventurous, free to follow a whim. Using her arms to stabilize and propel, Clara charged up the steep path on the right. After running for five minutes, she settled into a pace that was fast enough to move her forward but slow enough to keep her from slipping. After nearly a mile of uphill, the trail flattened out.

Even though she was running the same trail, it was as though she had entered a different world. Suddenly Clara found herself surrounded by rock bluffs and fantastic turrets. Many of the rocks looked like loaves of bread or haystacks.

Instead of the dark, slightly damp earth of the earlier part of the trail, her feet now pounded sandy terrain. The rock formations on either side grew narrower, steeper. For a moment, Clara panicked. What if she couldn't find her way back to the school? But that was ridiculous. The path hadn't branched out and if she just retraced her steps, surely she would end up back where she started...

The rocks around her grew closer to the path until she could touch them on either side. They were gray and rough, sandy in texture, layered as though they had once been part of an ocean floor.

When the walls opened up and Clara scanned the horizons, for miles around there stretched more of this strange gray rock, sometimes in gargantuan spires, capped with knobby tops; sometimes forming huge stone loaves of bread, the tops of which lopped over the sides.

The stone walls on either side grew narrower and a large rock incline blocked the path. Or could it be that this was the end? She could turn around and go back, or she could climb the obstructive boulder and discover what lay beyond. Clara decided on the latter.

Crawling on hands and knees up the four foot incline, she reached a higher level of this fantastic rockscape. Here was the path once again, snaking across a sandy desert. At the same time, it resembled the ocean. Incongruous in this land-locked terrain, the ocean-ness made it all the more exotic.

From the east, toward Red Mesa, thunder shattered through Clara's musings, followed by a bolt of lightning that traveled from the middle of the sky overhead to the ground. Still more rumbling was accompanied by the first drops, and soon the rain fell in hard-driven sheets.

Clara searched in vain for shelter, but the only trees were short and scrubby, no more than bushes. Already she was beginning to shake with cold, and she knew if she didn't find refuge soon, she might not survive.

The roar of pelting rain filled her ears. She could barely see for all the water in her eyes. Her shoes seemed to weigh 30 pounds each, and she could feel them growing soggier with each step. She tripped on a boulder, twisting her ankle and gashing her shin on a sharp branch that had blown across the trail.

Just when she felt like giving up, simply lying down and letting the rain beat her to death, Clara came to a rock shelf that jutted out over the trail, forming a partial shelter. The ground underneath the overhanging ledge was dry, and she gratefully went to the furthest reaches. By now her shin was streaming blood, her ankle throbbing, her vision blurred.

Outside her ledge shelter, wind howled. Torrents of rain continued to rage. It was impossible to see more than a foot beyond the roof of her stone haven.

Even though she was injured, cold, and disoriented, Clara felt encouraged. At least for now, she could quit fighting the elements. She lay down and curled up in the innermost reaches of the sand shelter, closing her eyes in exhaustion, Clara fell asleep.

She dreamed of being at home with Louise and Will. They were sitting at Christmas dinner, and she was reciting. "You are old, Father William, the young man said, and your hair is exceedingly white. And yet you incessantly stand on your head. Do you think at your age that is right?" In the dream, Will wasn't addled. He was a jokester. She and her mother were laughing, humoring him. He didn't rage or throw things. Instead, he smiled and performed magic tricks. In the dream, Clara felt safe. She was interested in his eccentricities, not alarmed by his looniness.

But the real world crept back into her consciousness. After half an hour, she awakened. At first, she couldn't remember where she was or how she'd gotten there. It was still drizzling but enough daylight remained to get back to the school. She'd been gone for an hour and a half. This meant it had taken an hour to get to the ledge hideaway, about six miles of running.

It was now five p.m., and she just barely had time to get back to the school before dark. Her shin had stopped bleeding, and her ankle, while sore, felt capable of at least holding her weight. At first staggering, then settling into a slow, lumbering jog, Clara started back on the now slippery path. It was even harder than running in the rain had been, as now, water sloshed about and visibility was dimmer.

She had to make it back to the school, as it could start raining again, or even snowing. She was so hungry and tired. She could feel her strength ebbing away. She fell on a small boulder, wrenching her already painful ankle, gouging the palm of her hand on some sharp rocks.

This was impossible. In spite of her resolve, Clara feared the dark, the uncertainty of the path, the pain in her ankle. Despite the wetness...it was still drizzling...her mouth was parched and dry. Breathing was difficult. She couldn't seem to get enough air into her lungs.

Sheer terror, that's what it was. She'd felt like this once before, when she'd scuba dived on her honeymoon with Hugh. Her first husband had insisted she go with him into deep waters off Maui, where after just one lesson, they would suit up and plunge into 60 feet of water. Clara wasn't able to breathe deeply enough and she kept floating back up to the surface. The instructor explained it afterwards, a fairly technical, anatomical explanation. The main point being that fear kept Clara from breathing properly. Even though she didn't THINK she was terrified, the body didn't lie.

The difference, however, was that now she knew how worried she was. Dread permeated her every pore. Her run slowed to a jog, then finally to a walk. She turned around and headed toward the only shelter she knew of in this dark wilderness, the place she'd just left. Better to get back tomorrow than not at all. Oscar had plenty of water to last, and he was so fat that he wouldn't suffer too much without fresh food for one night.

The light was failing, a silvery, gray cast giving everything an eerie glow. What she would do back at the ledge, she wasn't sure. One certainty, however, was her desperate need to rest. Barely able to put one foot in front of the other, she slogged on through the moist air, over the slippery, damp path. Occasionally, she shut her eyes and swayed, nearly falling over.

Just when she couldn't move another foot, she spotted a rock outcropping. She ducked down under the rough canopy and sank to the ground.

Sometime later, she opened her eyes, looked overhead and saw stars. How long had she been asleep? The drizzle had stopped, and maybe she could make her way back to the school. It might be light enough to make out the path. But then she remembered how she'd had to crawl up the steep section of her trail on hands and knees. Going the opposite direction in the dark would be risky. Her ankle was none too strong. One slip and she could end up breaking a leg.

No, she was stuck here for the night. Clara stretched out on the bumpy ground, closed her eyes and tried to go back to sleep.

Impossible. Her mind was racing, as she remembered how breathless she'd felt earlier on the trail and back still further to the time when Hugh forced her to slip into the unknown ocean. But now there was no one else to blame. She'd gotten herself into this mess and she would get herself out.

Breathing was easier than before, but her mouth was dry and parched. Rather than lying on the ground, sleepless and worrying, she would explore her immediate surroundings, as much as the dark would allow.

She groped her way along the wall of rock, using her hands to keep track of where she was. Suddenly she felt a gap. Her hand reached into a hole in the rock wall. She stopped to explore, moving her hand carefully along the side of what turned out to be not just a hole but the entrance to a cave. As her eyes adjusted to the dim light, she walked inside. Cautiously, fearfully, taking small steps with her feet barely lifting off the ground.

While she couldn't go too far, as she didn't know what the cave held, this provided some shelter from the elements. It might start raining again, and a cold wind was beginning to sweep across the mesa.

Compared to more wandering in the dark, the shelter of a dark cave seemed absolutely inviting.

Finding a ledge at what seemed to be the cave's entrance, Clara slept fitfully, shifting her position often to get more comfortable. Somehow the night passed.

A dim light announced the soggy dawn. It was raining lightly outside the cave, with occasional gusts of heavy downpour. Just 5:00 a.m., so she could wait until it grew lighter and hopefully less rainy. Clara longed for something warm and dry.

Partly to keep warm, partly from curiosity, she walked briskly around the parameters of her rock haven. Rain and wind, renewing themselves after a hiatus, raged beyond the sheltering cave. No point in venturing out now, so Clara walked along the borders of her prison.

Her mind wandered as she went from boulder to ledge. Rock of ages, ancient rock...If only these stone walls could talk, what tales might they tell? Rain was falling, harder than ever now. Despite downpour, dawn's light was illuminating the stone walls. There was far more to the cave than she'd thought originally. Forgetting the time, Clara ventured deeper. Stepping cautiously, she trailed her hand along the wall, feeling the rough grainy texture with her fingertips.

Suddenly she felt a groove in the stone. She ran her fingertip along its length, feeling a deeper groove at the end of a long line. This seemed like more than an accidental formation, maybe some kind of message written in stone. Leaning over, peering intently, she tried to tell what she was feeling.

A snake or lightning bolt? She knelt down lower so her eyes were even with the carving. Finally her eyes adjusted to the partial light and she was able to make out a stylized arrow. It was about a foot long and aimed toward the back of the cave.

Astonished, Clara looked for more carvings in the same area. There was something about an arrow, a distant memory, a repeated motif...As she searched for more petroglyphs, Clara tried to remember where she'd seen a stylized arrow like this. Was it on the pot that had been stolen from the school on the night Speckled Horse died?

Yes, there had been arrows carved around the sides of that lustrous vessel. Clara recalled when Speckled Horse, just a few days before his death, had taken the pot out of the school's locked case and shown her a close-up view. The arrows were a trademark of the potter, Sophia Running Woman Suina. Clara remembered holding the pot up to the light and admiring its symmetry.

As she continued her walk around the interior of the cave, she remembered arrows from longer ago. Before she was adopted by Will and Louise, she used to spend long hours with crayons and paper. Her topics were the usual childhood representations...houses, spindly stick people, trees, flowers. But there were also arrows. In fact, she had some pictures from her early childhood that Louise had given her in a box. She was almost sure that some of them were arrow drawings.

Maybe she was somehow connected to the arrows on the pot and the arrow on the cave wall. It was too impossible, too far-fetched, and yet...

She reached the other side of the cave entrance, her circling complete. Nothing else of interest within, and it was time to go back to school for a day of teaching. As she started to run along the path back toward the school, she vowed to explore the cave further. That wouldn't be until the next time she could escape for a long run. For now, she had to beat the clock to reach her classroom before the students did.

9

His Master's Bidding

Dan and Carol Eastgate had finally arrived, at least in the eyes of their neighbors on Altavista Lane, La Mesa, California. Debbie Shubert, who used to talk over the fence with Carol as they were taking a break from transplanting petunias and marigolds, never saw Carol with a trowel in her hand anymore. Instead she had hired a fulltime gardener to tend her manicured green carpet of a lawn, lush flowerbeds, fake waterfall and brimming fishpond.

Carol busied herself with society luncheons, the symphony board (of which she was the secretary/treasurer), and the Arbutus Club. She had actually founded the Arbutus Club, whose primary purpose was to review the latest books, mostly mysteries.

Gone forever were the days of faculty luncheons and having the neighbors in for afternoon tea. Carol was too busy making appearances in her expensive garden dresses and elegant broad-brimmed straw hats. She was on more boards than she could keep straight track of and her endorsement was solicited by a dozen worthy causes in town.

The Boyntons were the last of the former friends that she and Dan kept in touch with, and she was certain that the Thanksgiving dinner was the last time they would socialize with them. It wasn't that they weren't nice people, attractive, enjoyable. The Eastgates had moved up, however, and the Boyntons hadn't.

Carol was busy on this sunny November Wednesday with beauty treatments. Ordinarily she would be playing tennis, a long-standing doubles match at Encantado Estates, the health-spa/sports complex she and Dan had added to their list of clubs when they learned that their country club had less competent aerobics instructors than Encantado Estates. Besides, they liked contacts in high places, and Encantado included half a dozen top CEOs in its ranks, men that Dan wanted to rub shoulders with. He'd confided to Carol that he might decide in a year to run for a county political office. Everyone influential would be grist for his campaign mill.

At 8:30 a.m., she drove her red Lexus out the double garage door and down the hilly, asphalted driveway. She was about to click the electronic gate controller as she left, but then she remembered that the gardeners were coming. She had asked Louie, her regular guy, to bring several helpers, in order to have everything ready for some big events coming up at the Eastgate residence in the next few weeks.

Dan was hosting a meeting of the neighborhood association next Wednesday, to discuss water usage and the threat of drought. But more important to Carol, the Arbutans, as they called themselves, were coming to her house, and everything had to look perfect.

She and Dan decided to remodel the kitchen after the Boyntons' Thanksgiving visit. Lana had inspected every nook of the old-fashioned Eastgate kitchen, telling Carol about her own, superior Corian counters, glass topped range, the glass doored refrigerator and designer fixtures. The next morning, even before the good china was completely put away after Thanksgiving dinner, Carol was on the phone with contractors to see who could do a kitchen makeover in the shortest timeframe.

Now the kitchen was only half-done. Even though the Creative Kitchen people promised it would be complete well before the Arbutus Club was scheduled to meet at her house the first weekend in December, Carol couldn't take a chance on having things in disarray.

She'd decided that the meeting could be in the family room, part of an addition she and Dan had added last summer. There was a half kitchen off the family room and that would suffice for the luncheon preparations. Besides, she was having things catered so she wouldn't even really need the big kitchen.

The only problem with meeting in the family room was that it looked out on the worst part of the yard. Thus, all the last minute landscaping and the need for some extra gardening help. In addition to tending all the plants and installing new ones, Enrique was supposed to build a pool and waterfall and make three xeroscape boulder gardens. He said he could do it, no problem, but he'd need some helpers.

Carol told him to hire up to three extra people to work with him for the week. She would pay him and he could dole out the money to the others. As she drove down the drive out to Foster Boulevard, Carol smiled to herself. She was lucky to have such reliable help, lucky to be able to afford to beautify her house and grounds. She and Dan had worked hard to be where they were, but still, she felt blessed.

As Carol headed the red Lexus out Foster and onto Route 5 for her appointment in San Diego, a dirty brown Ford Tempo slowly cruised up in front of her house. If she had looked in the rear view mirror, she would have noticed it, but she was totally preoccupied with her beauty appointments that day and the exciting prospect of at last having her favorite club over for a luncheon.

As she was reviewing the menu for the tenth time -- tuna melt squares, vegetarian minestrone, a fruit compote, meringue shells with hot fudge sauce -- a compact man of medium height got out of the

Tempo, which was parked in front of the house across from the Eastgates'. A Mr. Nobody type.

He had light brown hair, badly cut in a bowl style. His features were regular and unremarkable, and he had an impassive face -- the type of man who could easily get lost in a crowd. Mr. Nobody strolled briskly up the brick walkway and rang the doorbell. In his left hand, he carried a soft leather attache case -- looking much like dozens of salesmen that visited thousands of front porches every day.

But unlike the briefcases of most salesmen, this case was nearly empty. It contained only a .38 revolver and a piece of paper with the Eastgate's address, #10 Altavista Lane. He knocked, and receiving no answer, walked around to the back yard, where several gardeners, who must have entered from a back entrance, were just starting to work.

"Can I help you?" asked Enrique Rodriguez, a longtime employee of the Eastgates. He took a proprietary interest in not only their garden but also their security. He was leaning on a hoe, his brow furrowed and his dark eyes narrowed into slits.

"Um, well, I was hoping to talk with the Eastgates, the owners of this house, just a little business with the insurance company. Routine but fairly urgent." He tapped his briefcase and gave Enrique a knowing look.

"They will talk with you when they get back from work," Enrique said. "Do you have a card? I will see that they get it."

He had no idea about the Eastgates' private affairs, but this nondescript little man seemed to be just going about his business. Normally, Enrique would check with Guadalupe, the Eastgates' housekeeper, but Lupe was taking care of her daughter and new grandson today.

"Uh, well, I just ran out of cards," said Mr. Nobody. "I can check back this evening, no problem. This is just a routine matter, nothing urgent." As he spoke, he backed away from Enrique, toward the side gate from which he'd entered.

"*Jefe*, we don't know where these boulders are supposed to go," interrupted Louie. Enrique's 16-year-old nephew, who was working with him to try to save up money for a used car, was more energetic and diligent than the other two men that Enrique had rounded up to do this job. If he continued through life with this kind of energy, he would go far.

Mr. Nobody scurried through the gate, rushed down the front lawn to his car, and was driving away fast as Enrique was directing placement of three moss-covered "character rocks" that Carol had ordered for the small garden area on the east side of her rambling back yard.

72

As the day wore on, Enrique and his crew dug, pruned, mowed and planted Carol's back acre into shape. Sweat poured from their brows until noon, when they sat under the shade of the Eastgate's back awnings, opening sacks and lunch pails and chattering away about their children, sports, women. Enrique, who had a lot on his mind, forgot all about the businessman who came to call on the Eastgates. When Carol returned from her facial, manicure, pedicure and leg waxing, they talked only about the garden.

Since leaving the Eastgate's house at ten that morning, Larry Butt had been killing time. He drove all around La Mesa, thinking about nothing much, having a burger at the Dairy Queen, buying the local paper, The *Courier*, and reading every page. He was just finishing the Classified Section when he noticed the clerk staring at him. A cheap looking blond, his favorite type, but today he was in no mood for flirtation. It was almost as though she wanted to ask him for a date. Damn. No one in this miserable burg could know that he'd even been here. He threw the paper down, left a ten dollar bill on the table and stormed out of the Dairy Queen and into his car.

Only three o-clock, so more hours to kill. His plan was to wait until the Eastgates got home, knock on the door, force his way in, grab the pot and then leave. That Boynton character, the one who'd contacted Henry to see if he could get a pot like the one he'd seen at the Eastgates, had told exactly how to find it. Go in the front foyer, through the living room to the display cases by the stairwell. The key to the case would be under the picture hanging to the right of the stairwell.

Damn that clerk. He was sure she'd seen him clearly, probably well enough to give a complete description. And damn Henry, for not getting it right the first time. When he got orders to get the pottery, Henry said that his bosses (dudes in town leading a sort of double life) had a buyer for it. What were their names? Corlett, Ramirez, Johnson...something like that.

Later he found out that Henry hadn't talked to the bosses at all. He, Henry, was the one who had a buyer and he hadn't consulted with the bosses before he sold it to Dan and Carol Eastgate. Then, weeks later, when Ramirez and the gang really did have a buyer, Henry had to get it back in a hurry.

This was crazy, this waiting. Damn those Eastgates. Maybe the Mrs. would get home before Mr. He'd drive by just one more time and look for a car. If he could get the pot while no one was home, that would be best, but Henry had made it clear that if he had to hurt someone, it better be final. No leaks could get out, and that's why Larry had a .38 revolver in his briefcase.

As he eased the Tempo from the Dairy Queen parking lot, Larry Butt's face settled into an angry mask. If anyone had been there to look, they would have seen his eyes tightened into slits, the blue irises angry and glinting. His jaws were clenched, teeth gritted, and the veins in his temples were throbbing. His breathing was shallow and choppy. He was perspiring heavily. Butt held the steering wheel tightly in both hands, handling the car in a smooth manner that contrasted dramatically with the way he felt.

He hated the rich. Spoiled bastards like those Eastgates deserved to be blown away. Because his mother, poor Thelma, couldn't keep a husband, they'd been poor almost all of his life. Not destitute, but on the edge enough so that until Thelma married his hateful stepfather, Larry had to wear Goodwill clothes or hand-me-downs sent to them from his cousins in Virginia. Poor white trash, that's what his cousins called them.

Larry Butt's face was now under control, his jaw no longer clenched, his eyes returned to their original size. The rage did not escape him but had gone within. By the time he drove into the Eastgates' posh suburb, he was breathing normally. He could have been one of thousands of commuters coming home from work.

As he drove through the well-manicured lawns near the Eastgate estate, Larry slowed his car to a crawl. The last thing in the world he wanted was to be noticed -- by the Eastgates or any of their neighbors -- until he made the actual housecall.

Ah, he was in luck. There was Carol's red Lexus, pulled right up into the driveway, next to the front walkway. He had a story all ready about the insurance company he represented, even a business card reading, "Aden Wardwell, Agent/Capitol Family Insurance. For all your needs, from cradle to the hereafter" followed by a phone number, fax, and a bogus e-mail address. He had played Aden before. In fact, he was so good at it that he'd only had a door slammed in his face once. Most people ended up being quite friendly and extremely interested in the bogus insurance. Fortunately, his business was such that he seldom had to actually sell anything. The potential "customers" were usually silenced before he had to pop the question.

But with the Eastgates, he would not get to the end of the orientation, the history of Capitol, the litany of satisfied customers' accolades, the incredibly low premiums.

He would begin by complimenting the Eastgates on their lovely home and gardens. They would offer him coffee, maybe a glass of wine.

They would soon be chatting like old friends. Then he would demand the black pot. There shouldn't be any trouble, especially after they saw the .38 revolver.

If just the wife were at home, it would be a pushover, probably no nasty work. If the husband arrived during the process, he would use the wife as a shield.

It was close to 5 p.m. and as Larry neared Altavista Lane, the traffic grew heavier... He checked the rearview mirror to make sure no one was trailing him, scanned the lanes alongside, and looked ahead for his turn onto the Eastgates posh road.

The lawns grew greener, lusher and more manicured as Altavista climbed a gentle hill. The deepening shadows of afternoon made the neighborhood even more elegant. The place reeked money, fumed Larry as he crept along in the dirty Tempo. He noticed lattice work fences, climbing vines, gazebos and old-fashioned bulb-style streetlamps. And an abundance of flowers: luscious roses, tall yarrow, tiger lilies, daisies, geraniums, pansies and petunias, pink and purple cosmos.

Funny that he should know so many flowers' names, but when Thelma was desperately trying to make a home for them -- back when they were so poor he had to wear clothes from Goodwill -- she tried to have a flower garden in their rock-hard New Mexico back yard. He remembered the endless trips to find rocks for her flower beds, and the extreme disappointment when all the flowers withered and died and only the rocks remained. They would water, fertilize, and nurture the plants but no matter what, nothing lasted for more than a few weeks. The perennials never returned and the petunias were blasted by July heat and barely lasted the summer.

So, Larry knew about plants, more than he wanted to know, and it only served to remind him of how miserably unhappy they had all been back years ago. It filled him with a well of unfocused rage, so the Eastgates would be enjoyable. Something he knew he could do and do well. He would bring back the sacred pot to Henry, and if he had to waste those spoiled bastards in the process, so much the better.

He felt cool, calm, efficient. As his mother used to say of herself when she was working in the garden, he was "in his element." Unlike Thelma, however, his efforts were going to be successful. As he drove closer to the Eastgates, he smiled. He imagined how satisfying it would be to demand the gleaming black pottery and watch as they groveled. They would fumble around looking for the key, lean over and open the glass case, and reluctantly hand him the pot. With his .38 aimed at them, they would be very quiet as he left.

75

Henry, who had all kinds of connections in La Mesa and everywhere else, had arranged to have the phone lines cut off sometime that afternoon. The Eastgates would have to run to a neighbor's to telephone, and by the time they contacted anyone, he would be at the outskirts of La Mesa, headed toward the airport.

At the airport, he would dump the car (which he'd stolen in the first place, one of the skills he'd developed over his years of gainful unemployment).

That was one scenario. Another was going in to an empty house, unlocking the display case, slipping the pot into his Aden Wardwell, Insurance Agent briefcase, and just driving away. Somehow, he liked the first scenario better. He needed to see their faces.

Ah yes, this was the Eastgates' block. Up ahead loomed their house, neat and tidy now but, Larry mused, soon to be the scene of terror. He pulled the Tempo off on a side street, Primrose Lane -- stupid, the names these yuppies came up with -- and parked in front of a house with a "For Sale" sign in front. Because he wouldn't be seeing this awful piece of junk car again, he checked the back seat, the floors, and the glove compartment for anything he might have left behind. Pulling a handkerchief out of his pants pocket, he wiped off the steering wheel.

Larry Butt stepped out of the Tempo, walked across the street and up half a block until he was standing directly across from the Eastgate house. There was a red Lexus in the driveway. Good. Somebody was home.

Nonchalantly strolling, Larry crossed the street and walked up to the door. Briefcase in hand and a bland smile across his face, he knocked. Once, twice, a third time. He stood and listened. Not a sound from within. Pushing against the front door, with his shoulder, Larry entered the foyer. Still not a sound.

They must have stepped out. Just as well. He would be fast and by the time they came back from wherever it was, he would have the pot and be out of here. As he stood in the shadows of the foyer, Larry caught his reflection in the long mirrors that lined both walls of the entrance.

Flashing black eyes, expressive eyebrows, slicked back brown hair. When he wasn't frowning, Larry realized that some people might consider him handsome. If the Mrs. was home alone, she might be so taken with him, he could help himself before taking care of business.

He walked softly down the foyer hall, pupils dilating to adjust to the semi-dark. The place was bigger than he'd imagined and suddenly he couldn't remember if the display case was supposed to be on the right or left. Groping his way along, one hand on the wall next to him, he had almost reached the end of the long entrance hall when he heard a door slam and then voices.

Larry Butt caught his foot on a table leg, slipped on the Oriental hall runner, and barely escaped crashing to the floor. He'd banged his shin on something and it hurt like hell. He'd also hit his head. Now wasn't the time to meet the Eastgates. Scuttling on the floor like a crab, he straightened out the Oriental rug, pushed the table back into its original position, and slipped into the closet just as the voices got closer.

It smelled of dust and shoes in the Eastgates' front closet. Larry scrunched down into a corner and tried to make himself stay perfectly still. He'd done this before, long ago. When Thelma first started going out, after the divorce, he and Bobby had to put up with all kinds of rotten boyfriends that their Mom dragged home. Together, they stole airhead Michael's shoes from under the bed and put them in the garbage. Michael started yelling as soon as he awakened and couldn't find them. Larry could still hear him, as though it were yesterday... "Where are those two little bastards? I'll tan their filthy hides and I'll step on their shoes. We'll see how those shit eaters like that." He swore and raged, throwing things and pushing Thelma around.

That was before Larry lost all respect for his mother. Back then, he was worried for her, and he started to cry. But Michael was stoned, his permanent condition, and he was vicious when he got mad. Larry hid in the closet, while Bobby, who'd been caught before he could hide, convinced Michael that it was all Larry's fault.

That was when Larry first ran away from home. He would wait until Michael left, anything to avoid the beating he imagined from Michael, with his nasty temper and bleary mind. Larry was angry with his Mother for choosing Michael over him. But because Thelma was his mom, he couldn't be too angry. Maybe he was really a rotten person; maybe he deserved to be locked outside overnight.

Larry willed himself back to the present. The voices outside the closet had gone away. He cautiously opened the closet door and peered out from the darkness. He would steal out, try to get the black pot before anyone discovered him, and leave as quickly as possible. Just as he was about to step out, however, the doorbell rang.

It turned out that the Eastgates were having a dinner party. He would just have to stay in the closet until they finished, everyone went home, and the Eastgates were asleep. That was OK, he could outwait the scumbags. If only no one opened the closet. Fortunately, it was very hot for November and it was unlikely that anyone would have brought a coat. Larry's legs were beginning to cramp up, so he squirmed back into a corner of the closet so he could stretch out.

Larry detached himself from the present as he waited silently in the closet. He drifted into a half-sleeping trance, during which he imagined that Bobby was still alive. They had been buddies, soulmates, the two Musketeers...until Bobby squealed on him. That was when he realized that he could never trust Bobby again. He would have found it out sooner or later, so what the hell...Michael, the scumbag, really should have been thanked. He just speeded up the process. Larry knew from the time of Michael that he would always be alone and that he had to guard his back every waking hour.

Finally, all the noises in the Eastgate household had died down. It was time to make his move... He slowly opened the sliding wooden door and peered into a dark foyer. The smells of cigarette smoke and liquor filled his nostrils as he stretched his arms and legs out. No lamps on, the only illumination came from the light-sensitive night-sensors permanently in the wall sockets.

After nearly slipping on the Oriental carpet that ran the length of the foyer, Larry fell to his hands and knees and crept toward what he hoped was the direction of the display case. His eyes were adjusting to the dim glow of the night lights.

Glints of light exploding in a starburst right ahead...that had to be the display case. Larry's heart began to pound and sweat poured from his brow. He had a cotton mouth; his stomach growled loudly; a throbbing ache pounded through his head. None of this mattered, though. He was almost there and he remembered clearly where the key was. Creeping, creeping, he neared the glass case.

Maybe it was because he was looking so intently at the glass, maybe it was because he hadn't slept or eaten in three days. Whatever the reason, Larry Butt -- just when he was so near the prize, fell face down a flight of stairs right in front of the display case. He landed in a heap at the bottom. His ankle was viciously sprained and he'd torn the right side of his face on a flower pot that had broken and snagged his cheek. Blood streamed down his face, making it hard to see. Before he could scuttle away to another hiding place, he heard a male voice roar, "What the hell?"

Lights were on everywhere. Larry reached for the .38 revolver in his right front pocket. Just in time, for at the top of the stairs loomed Dan Eastgate, the ultimate yuppie in his navy blue silk robe.

"Carol, did you give that fucking gardener the key? I told you to be more careful!"

Larry realized that Dan couldn't yet see him in the shadows of the downstairs den. He'd make Dan open the case for him at gunpoint, like a good little rich bastard yuppie, then he would be able to get away without having anything else to do with these scumbags...

"No, Dan, of course I didn't give our key out. Do you think I'm a fool?" The sound of weeping followed... "If you don't mind, I'm going to call 911."

Suddenly a bullet whizzed within inches of Larry's head. Good God, that fool was trigger happy. He must have seen him, or maybe he was just shooting at the dark, shooting at nothing, shooting at the Boogie Man. Well, he'd give Dan Eastgate a real enemy, but there was only one problem. Dan wouldn't be alive to talk back.

Another bullet nearly shaved Larry's right ear. Moving, snake-like, on his stomach, he sidled to a more protected position, under a table. In the process, he knocked over a glass vase full of flowers, getting doused with rotten smelling, slimy flower water and hit on the cheeks with shards of shattering glass.

Dan Eastgate switched on the lights. His face an angry mask, he stomped loudly down the steps to the den. He was aiming his Magnum in the general direction of Larry's hiding place. "OK, wherever you are, you cocksucker, come out with your hands up or I'll blow your brains out. Come on out, you goddamn coward."

From upstairs came the sound of forlorn screams interspersed with sobbing. The Mrs. had apparently tried 911 and realized the lines had been cut. From the sound of her, she wasn't about to come out of the bedroom. If only she would cut out that God-awful caterwauling. He wanted to go strangle her right now.

In the meantime, here was the wailer's troglodyte husband, nearly on top of him. Taking careful aim from under the table, Larry blasted Dan Eastgate through the heart. The vermin's body crumpled to the white carpeted floor and blood began to seep out from around the edges of the dungheap. Larry couldn't resist a kick of the body as he headed upstairs to the display cabinet.

Now the screaming upstairs reached another level, from hysteria to dementia. If Larry could have been two places at once, he would have put a bullet through her vocal chords. But he was a professional; he could not let himself be distracted. Work to do, deadlines to meet.

So here was the cabinet, barely visible in shadows, and there on a red velvet pedestal was the sacred pot. Never mind using the key. His vision was blurred from the fall, and the only person who would have stopped him was dead. The screamer wasn't going anywhere, and besides, he would take care of her soon enough.

Larry smashed the display case with the butt of his gun, stepping back to avoid the spray of shattered glass. He unzipped his briefcase,

79

formed a pouch with the soft sides and gently lifted the gleaming black pot from its stand. After wrapping the velvet cloth around the bottom and sides, he lowered it into the briefcase and rezipped. He thought about just leaving. After all, he did have a plane to catch, and Henry was expecting a call from him by midnight. It would not pay to make Henry mad. When Henry was mad, he did nasty things. The last time Larry angered his boss, he'd been locked in a closet without food or water for a week.

On the other hand, the screamer had to be silenced. She might attract neighbors. The last thing in the world Larry needed was a commotion. His head was pounding from the bitch's shrieks: it would be satisfying to put her out of her misery.

Slinking up the steps, Larry followed what was now a muffled sob to a closed door at the end of a carpeted hall. It was locked, but one good karate kick punched a hole right under the doorknob. A few more kicks and there was an opening big enough to get his hand through to unlock the door on the other side. Crappy door, simple lock.

The whimpering had stopped and the bedroom appeared to be empty. An open window looking out to the stars was flanked by white curtains. A night breeze lifted and billowed the curtains. It was almost as though they were dancing.

"OK bitch, come out, wherever you are. If you cooperate, you might escape with your life. Come on, dammit, I know you're in here."

Larry closed what was left of the door behind him, pushing in the lock. This way, he'd hear if she tried to bolt. He had to hurry. Henry didn't like to wait. He would go through everything methodically, until he routed her out.

If nothing turned up soon, he knew just what to do. He'd spotted a gasoline can in the tool bin next to the front door. He'd lock the bitch in, get the gas can and douse everything on the first floor, toss a few matches and bolt out the front door. Larry had used fires a lot in his work, and they were very effective in masking other evidence.

But first, he would finish his search. He had a strong desire to see the bitch's face when he told her about blasting away that fucker of a husband. He wanted to make her grovel and beg for her pitiful life. He would see her face and then waste her, neat and tidy. Damn her for screaming and giving him the Excedrin headache number 2000.

The bed was a mess, covers all twisted, sheets pulled out, half a dozen pillows all over. Next to the bed lay a phone off the hook. Larry imagined her trying frantically to call out and crying in frustration when the line was dead.

He looked briefly out the window to see if there was any chance she might have jumped. It was at least 20 feet to the ground and a brick patio lay beneath. If she'd jumped, chances are she'd be splattered there on the ground.

No, she had to be somewhere in the bedroom suite. He lay down on the floor and looked under the bed. Nothing but a lot of slippers and a vibrator. Next, the monster closet...shelf after shelf of shoes, purses, sweaters. His and her sides, ever so tidy. Larry kicked his foot into every corner. She could be in a crumpled mass somewhere, just like she would be after he finished.

Meanwhile, a massive pounding began in Larry's temples. His eyes felt like they would pop out of his head and his mouth was on fire. It was that screaming...it had made his blood pressure rise. Boy, would she ever get it.

Then Larry thought about Henry and imagined being locked in the rat room. When he sinned before and was locked in the room for a week, Henry threatened him. "If you ever let me down again, you miserable cur, this will seem like paradise. I'll put the live snake food in here with you."

Henry raised rats to feed his collection of pet snakes. Larry had seen them...filthy, disgusting vermin. And if he didn't take care of everything, they would be locked in with him when Henry next doled out punishment. He wouldn't be able to ward them off: they would eat him alive. Larry broke out into a cold sweat.

Enraged and panting, he stalked into the bathroom that adjoined the walk-in closet. God, it was huge. His anger flared up once again at rich bastards who could have bathrooms this big. On the left was a sliding glass door. Larry pushed it open roughly, causing a high-pitched squeal from the metal casing. Once more his temples started throbbing. He felt like his head was being squeezed in a vice. His arms and legs tingled, and he nearly pulled the trigger of his gun out of sheer impatience.

Nothing in the shower and sunken top except for fresh drops of water. He looked under the sink, a cabinet large enough for a scrunched up person to lurk. Nothing there, either.

Around the corner was the toilet and beyond that, a tall wooden wardrobe. This bathroom was bigger than some of the houses he'd grown up in. For the hundredth time that night, Larry checked his watch. It was 9 p.m. and he had to be on the plane back to Albuquerque by 10. Henry was expecting him to come by his house before midnight with the pot. He couldn't be late, but on the other hand, he couldn't leave anyone in the Eastgate house. Especially since he'd talked to the gardener.

After pulling open the double doors to the wardrobe, Larry stepped back and waited. A tumbled mass of clothes and shoes revealed nothing. But she had to be in there, the miserable bitch.

He stood for a few seconds, his loaded pistol aimed at the center of the wardrobe, then he shot at the bottom of the wardrobe. Just as he suspected, she was there. The filthy trollop fell to the floor, bleeding at the ankles.

Looking ridiculous in her dishevelled pink robe, the creature was grovelling, crying and pleading. She was on her knees, tears streaming down a face contorted by raw terror.

"No, no please don't kill me. I'll give you money. I'll give you the car. Anything...please, please..." Her long blond hair hung limply in stringy tendrils, her eyes red from crying.

God, that voice again. He'd toyed with the idea of raping and then killing, but the thought of Henry's rats drove the possibility from his mind.

No time, no time, get it over with, just do it...

More screaming, more pleading. That horrific edge of terror was making his temples pound. If only she would shut up for even a second. Larry couldn't stand it much longer.

"Help, help...please don't shoot, please, please." Sobbing. Hysterical. Desperate.

Unbidden, he saw an image of Bobby in the pool under the boulder. So long ago, but he could hear Bobby's screams clearly, blending with this Eastgate woman. Larry could swim. He could have saved Bobby. But Bobby was in the water, and eventually the water took him. This thing in front of him, on its knees, was actually creeping closer.

Aiming the .38 toward the creature's vile, gaping mouth, he squeezed the trigger and it fell in a heap, blood immediately seeping into the white carpeting.

Larry slipped his gun back inside his coat pocket, secured the brief case on his right arm and raced downstairs. As he left, he remembered the gasoline. There was time for his little mission, and surely Henry would be pleased to have everything so clean and neat. That was one thing he could be proud of. When he had to do the dirty work, he did a clean job of it. He smiled to himself.

Carefully putting the brief case under a rhododendron bush ten feet away from the front entrance, Larry took the gasoline can from the woodbox, went inside and poured it out over the wooden kitchen furniture and magazine rack in the kitchen, which lay just beyond the display case and fatal stairwell.

He lit a match and threw it on the table with its crumpled up morning paper. Racing out of the house, he could hear the satisfying whoosh. Resisting the desire to look back and admire his handiwork, he locked the front door, grabbed the briefcase, jumped into the waiting Tempo, and sped toward the airport.

Henry would be pleased.

10
A Meeting with Estrellita

The day started with bright, promising sunshine, but by 8:30 a.m., the weather gave over to icy splats of rain, some of them laced with snow. The last leaves of autumn rustled and gave up their hold, drifting to the ground in mournful gusts of wind. The KVSF weatherman predicted a 10 percent chance of snow.

The gray sky outside matched Clara's mood. As she took attendance in her big green book, she stifled a yawn. What had she gotten last night? One hour of sleep? Three? Four? It was hard to say. Her students seemed glum as the weather. Though she had planned to tell them about last night's misadventure, after seeing what kind of a day it was going to be, she decided against it. Even though she wanted to see if any of them knew about the cave and could tell her anything useful, she just didn't have the energy to explain her ordeal. It was too fresh, and still a little painful.

Oh, somehow she'd get through the day. They had just finished reading *The Running Man*, an early Stephen King novel, written under the Richard Bachman *nom de plume*. Fortunately, that day just about everyone had a copy of the novel. For those who'd left them in the dorms, she passed out a few extras.

"OK, class, thinking about the world of *The Running Man*, I want you to write what you would have done if you'd been Ben or Sheila? How would you have protected yourself from Free-Vee? Remember, Big Brother is watching you, and you have to be very clever. Remember the setting: It's an environmental disaster. The air is so bad everyone has to wear nose guards. People, even very young children, are dying of cancer."

The first period students were paying attention. As much as grammar basics bored them, they absolutely loved the apocalyptic Stephen King vision they'd all just read together. Notebooks were out and open, pencils and pens were jotting notes. The assignment captured their imaginations. Clara smiled to herself.

"Picture the world of *The Running Man*, It's around 2050, and things have deteriorated. Ben and Sheila are victims of a totally corrupted government and inhuman living conditions. It's a sinister, dog-eat-dog kind of life. Imagine that you live in the same ratty tenement complex as Ben and Sheila. Pretend that you've just watched the contestant on *Treadmill to Bucks* who missed a Bonus Point and had a heart attack at the same time. You don't like what's happening, but you're determined to figure out what to do about it."

Assigning *The Running Man* was one of the best things she'd ever done with her students. They could all picture the world portrayed in the novel, and it inspired even the inarticulate among them to at least draw the sadistic game shows or scenes of the wrecked neighborhoods and struggling everyday people. Nature devastated amid the tyranny of "free vee" were all too conceivable to them. In their discussions, Clara had used the world of *The Running Man* as a metaphor for the dire consequences of ignoring humanistic values in life. The students who didn't like writing, had a field day with illustrating scenes from the novel.

They were all busy, writing or drawing, even fidgety Donald and moody Christina. Carnell looked deeply engrossed, as though he were writing his life story. For one of the first times this year, Clara was able to just sit at her desk as the students worked. Unheard of. She might as well enjoy it -- before the next hand went up or somebody asked to be excused.

"Ok, class, work on this until nine o'clock, and then we'll compare notes." After one last walk around the classroom perimeter, Clara sat down at her desk once more. She sighed softly, as the exhaustion of last night sank in. She was deeply tired, but the intent expressions and total immersion of her students in the assigned project energized her.

She reached into her briefcase for the mail she'd retrieved from her slot in the faculty mailboxes. Mostly routine...something from the Teachers' Association; a schedule of home basketball games for both the girls' and boys' teams; a plea from Mike Sutton, the running coach, for an assistant (she was tempted by this one) and finally; a sealed envelope from the office of Wren Taggert, interim headmaster.

Just then, hands started waving. Clara had trained her class to raise their hands when they'd finished a writing assignment. That way, they didn't disturb people who were still working, and she had some idea of how to pace the class.

"If I were Ben," Carnell read from his essay, "I would hold secret underground classes so people could learn how to read again. I would also teach them how to disconnect free vee and then connect it back up when the inspectors came around. That way, people could think more clearly and figure out a way to escape from the evil watchers who controlled them..."

It was lunchtime before Clara had time to open the letter from Wren. Surely it would be a contract renewal. Some of her colleagues

85

were getting renewal letters, and she needed to know where next year's salary was going to be coming from. The nursing care for Will had turned out to be a big success, but unless her contract were renewed, she didn't know where she'd find the money to help Louise.

She closed her classroom door and sat down. Even though she'd brought her usual sack lunch, she was far too nervous to eat anything. She tore open the envelope.

"Dear Clara," began the letter, "I regret to inform you that funding for the enriched ninth grade English class has been drastically reduced. One of the school's benefactors died, and until the estate is settled, this resource will be in limbo. While we do not know anything with certainty, it seems likely your ninth grade advanced communications class might have be curtailed. You have done a good job with your students, and this situation in no way reflects upon your teaching ability. As you know, you were hired as a language arts teacher for one year. We had hoped to make it a permanent position, and until last week, it seemed a real possibility. Furthermore there are not enough advance enrollments in the other classes that you teach to justify continuing your position on that basis. While it is true that our situation may change between now and the end of the current academic year, I would advise you to look for another position. Yours truly, Wren Taggert, Interim Headmaster."

Clara was stunned. This letter expressed the opposite of what she'd been told when she was hired at the end of last summer. Back then her interviewer was Speckled Horse, not Wren. Until Wren became assistant headmaster and then interim, Clara was barely aware of her existence. There had been a team observation last September, and Wren had been one of six assessors who checked Clara's teaching style during a day of classes. All her marks had been high, and she never gave the assessors much thought. Why, if her teaching had been fine, would they be getting rid of her? Frankly, she didn't really believe that her position was being eliminated because of financial reasons. From what Annie told her, the school currently had plenty of financial backing. They could do whatever they liked with hiring and firing.

Suddenly she remembered what she'd heard about Wren Taggert: "Watch out, or she'll stab you in the back." So, this was it. But why would she pick on her? Maybe because she'd been such a favorite of Speckled Horse, and everyone knew that Wren and Speckled Horse never saw eye to eye. It was rumored that he and Wren had an affair years ago and that Wren hated him after it was over.

Weary and discouraged, Clara put her head down on the desk, hot tears stinging her closed eyelids. She *had* to keep this job or else find another that paid as much. She could just barely afford the money she sent home each month; otherwise, there was no way Louise could keep the daily nursing care for Will. The reports Clara received each week were most discouraging.

Though she tried valiantly to stay positive, Louise's phone calls and letters brought her down. Will didn't recognize Louise much of the time; he didn't know where he was; he often lashed out angrily, once even pushing Louise against the wall and bruising her arm. Against her will, Clara wept.

Clara had decided against going home for Christmas. She couldn't afford the plane fare, and Louise was so burdened with extra medical care bills, she didn't really have it either. Just as well, she thought bitterly. If Will didn't know Louise, he wouldn't recognize his daughter either. It would be more than she could bear, seeing her wonderful father a mere shadow of himself, a parody. He was going, leaving her, and there was nothing she could do about it.

A knock on the door interrupted her dreary thoughts. They had only thirty minutes for lunch, so brief a break that Clara nearly always ran out of time.

"Just a minute," she called out, throwing her uneaten sack lunch in the trash, sticking the miserable letter back in her brief case, taking out a compact and powdering her face. Her eyes were red and swollen, but what could she do?

Thank God, it was Carnell. He was sweet, sensitive, concerned about her. The little brother she never had. She'd told him about her Alzheimer's Dad and also her secret determination to find her biological mother. He was so thoughtful, always trying to help her and always way ahead of the rest of the class.

"Ms. Jordan, you look upset. I'm sorry for just coming in but I've got some good news."

Clara smiled at him and smoothed back her hair. She hoped her eyes didn't look too puffy. "Oh, that's OK, Carnell. It's almost time for the fifth period. What news?"

Carnell beamed. "Well, you know how I always hang out in the computer lab and how I like to surf the net. I've been spending nights there, lunchtimes, after school...mega hours...and you'll never guess what I found! There's a web site called "Lost Deer" and it's all about birthparents looking for their children, who were adopted by white people, and adopted Indian or part Indian children looking for their real parents. I know we'll be able to find out about your original family if we just hang out there. Man, there's all kind of links, all kinds of e-mail addresses. Can you come see it today? I think we can find your real family. They're probably looking for you too."

"Wow, Carnell, that IS exciting news." Clara could hardly believe it. With all the things she'd tried in her quest for roots, it never occurred to her to search the Internet. "But it's got to be tomorrow or the next day. I have only after school to go running, and I have to prepare midterms tonight."

"Sure, tomorrow's fine. Hey, please give us all easy questions." He grinned, a rarity for Carnell. His deep brown eyes sparkled. "Just kidding. I know we're your genius class."

"Don't worry. It'll be fair. Besides, you've been here, you've paid attention, and you've kept up with assignments. You'll do real well."

Students were streaming in from the cafeteria, so Carnell, still smiling, went to his seat in the middle of the back row. While other students sat in the back as a place to goof off or escape the teacher's close attention, Carnell seemed to use the backfield position to look over the classroom, and his attentiveness set the tone for other students. He was a good influence on the class, Clara realized gratefully. If only this Internet search would work!

All afternoon, she reviewed her students for the upcoming midterms, not allowing herself to think of either the disturbing letter from Wren or the exciting prospect of starting an Internet search for her origins. For so long, that goal receded ever into the distant future. Now it seemed imminent.

The final bell shattered her musing. Before going for a run, she would have to talk to Wren to see what the letter really meant. Was she being quietly fired? Was there a possible recourse? She dreaded the encounter with her supervisor, but on the other hand, she knew from experience that it was better not to put off this kind of talk.

By 4 p.m., it was raining, a slow, steady downpour. Clara looked out her window as students, holding newspapers or books over their heads, scurried to the dorms. Just a few degrees colder and the rain would turn to snow.

It seemed especially odd, Clara mused, to be getting rain rather than snow. Usually in November there would be snow. Global warming, some were saying. Because the last few summers in northern New Mexico had been dry and winters snowless, everyone was hoping for a wet winter. Rain or snow, it didn't matter. Moisture in any form was welcome.

Clara felt overwhelmed. All these worries about the climate's future, and she was not even able to find her parents. She couldn't do anything about what was going to happen with the temperature and rainfall. But as far as finding her parents, maybe, just maybe, there was hope.

The last period of the classroom day was over. Sitting at the old-fashioned wooden desk at the head of her classroom, Clara listened to the radiators sizzling. She finished writing the answer sheet for her set of exams. How wonderful to be ahead of the game! It would be a first in her teaching career, not having to take home a mountain of books and papers the night before tests.

By 5:15, she finished everything she needed to do for the next day. She put tests in the right-hand lower desk drawer, locked it, and put the key to the drawer under some paperclips in the top middle desk drawer. A primitive system, perhaps, but it seemed to work. She slipped the answer sheets into her brief case, which she would take home. This way, even if someone found the tests, they wouldn't have the answers. However, Clara really didn't expect snooping. Her students had kept up pretty well this fall, and the questions weren't hard, just thorough.

When she went to Wren Taggert's office to discuss the letter of dismissal, the interim headmaster had already left for the day. There was barely time, if she hurried, to go by the Public Health Service hospital in Santa Fe to see Estrellita if she hurried. Just as important as her job problems was the ache in her right foot, that nagging pain that kept her from enjoying any run. And running was central to her sense of well-being, the thread that kept her going.

At the Archuleta Thanksgiving dinner, the *curandera* had assured her that natural remedies could cure her foot. Clara remembered how she said she would be happy to share her knowledge.

As she maneuvered her red Cherokee Chief out toward the interstate, Clara thought about Carnell's discovery. He might really be on to something. What would it be like to have her real parents back in her life? Would they even like her? Would she like them? And what would her reunion do to Will and Louise?

As Clara drove toward Santa Fe, the huge, puffy clouds loomed over the *Sangre de Cristos*, turned from white to pink, tinged with a peachy gold. Around the gilded clouds, the sky was rose. The pinon studded foothills glowed in reflected sunset, and the snow-covered top peaks of the *Sangres* looked pink. Clara remembered that this natural phenomenon was the reason they were named "blood of Christ" in the first place.

As she neared the city, traffic grew heavy, and she had to devote full attention to driving. Annie was always telling her how light the traffic used to be in "the old days," how you could get from Red Mesa to

Santa Fe in half the time it now took. Clara liked to remind her friend that everywhere, not just Santa Fe, was changing. She liked to tell Annie, "The pace of life will just keep accelerating, and time has become the most important commodity."

Time. She needed time to find her parents before time ran out, while they were still alive. It had taken years for her to realize that it was not disloyal to Will and Louise to find out about the other parents. There was enough love to go around. Just because she wanted to know about her roots did not make her any less loyal to the people who had raised her. In today's world, one needed all the parents one could get.

Old Pecos Trail was jammed with traffic, and Clara's progress was abruptly interrupted. After sailing along with her innermost thoughts, the lovely cloudscape and the prospect of seeing Estrellita again, it was irritating to be stuck behind the big semi ahead. It made a lot of sense to live in Red Mesa, where it was unusual even to see another vehicle, much less get stuck behind it.

The Indian hospital was just beyond AIA on Cerrillos Road, one of the main business arteries in Santa Fe. Clara stayed in the far right lane so she wouldn't miss the turnoff. A sign announced "Lady Braves versus Prep tonight. 7 p.m." The Indian School was known for having winning baseball, track, and basketball teams. What they lacked in height, they more than made up for in strength and agility. At least that's what AIA coach Sutton told Clara.

The driveway to the Indian hospital popped up right after the sign, and Clara had to turn rather abruptly not to miss it. After she cut out of the stream of traffic, she looked at her watch. It was 5:35, and she'd probably missed Estrellita. Oh well, she'd at least go inside the hospital and leave another message. There was a teacher's retreat day next week, and if she was too late to see the *curandera* this time, she could always come back.

But as it turned out, Estrellita was still at work. The receptionist, a beautiful young Indian woman with two braids wrapped around her head, directed Clara.

"Just up the hall, third door on the right. You're lucky she's still here. Usually everyone is gone by this time of day. And especially with the weather so threatening and all." The woman gestured up the hall and then turned her attention back to the paperback romance she was devouring.

Clara caught the title - *Ecstacy Reclaimed* by Brandy LaRue. This was somehow incongruous. She would have expected the woman to be reading *Sacajawea* or a Tony Hillerman novel. But then Clara noticed that underneath her white clinician's coat, the woman was wearing black suede high heels and leopard skin lycra tights. She had long talon-like, manicured, scarlet fingernails and lipstick so dark it appeared almost black. Still, she was so pretty that even the weird attire couldn't hide her natural beauty.

"Estrellita Rodriguez" announced a name placard above the glass-plated office door. Clara stopped for a moment before knocking. Just what was she going to say, and what could she offer Estrellita in return for advice? Not that the *curandera* would expect anything. Estrellita would do anything for Annie, and just as she said at Thanksgiving, any friend of Annie's was a friend of hers.

Still, Clara felt a little presumptuous. She stood for a moment in front of the beveled glass door, hesitating. The sound of a chair being moved across a marble floor inspired her to knock.

"Coming, coming." Estrellita opened the office door and stepped back to let Clara in. She looked elegant in a crushed velvet broomstick skirt and a starched white tunic style blouse gathered at the waist with a silver concha belt. Strands of liquid silver hung around her neck and matching earrings hung from each ear lobe. Her long salt and pepper hair was pulled back in a bun at the nape of her neck.

"Oh, hello, *hola, mi querida*...come in, come in. I know you're thinking this is what she wears to work every day. No, no, usually I wear slacks. But tonight is the baby shower for one of my nieces." She pulled out a chair on small wheels for Clara, sat down at her cluttered desk, and looked expectantly at her guest.

"Well, I guess you know why I'm here." Clara lifted her right foot, shod in a black leather boot. "But, Tia, you're all ready to go to a party. I don't want to hold you up. I should have called first. Just tell me if this isn't a convenient time, and I'll come back later."

"No, *mi hita,* the shower isn't until eight. I had to bring my party clothes to work today rather than driving all the way back home. Don't forget, I live next door to the Archuletas. And since they put up all the casinos, traffic has become a nightmare. Don't worry, I will tell you when I have to go. Besides, I'd much rather talk with you than tend this paperwork." She waved her hand over the unruly stacks on her desk, as if by magic they would just disappear.

Following Estrellita's orders, Clara removed her boot and sock, and described the pain in her foot. Estrellita held the sore foot in her lap and gently probed.

Pressing the area above the big toe, she asked, "And what about this spot? Is this sore?"

Clara nodded. "Yes, a little."

Then pressing the space right above the little toe, she asked again. And so she went around Clara's entire foot, probing and testing. Estrellita's strong hands reviewed her entire foot, and after each new location, she asked how it felt. Some places were excruciating to the touch; others felt normal.

Clara tried to report with complete accuracy. No one had ever touched her feet, at least not that she could recall. It was comforting to have Estrellita cradling her foot in her ample velvet-covered lap. She became aware of foot parts she didn't even know she had.

Finally Estrellita was done.

"Well, you don't have a neuroma, at least it doesn't feel like it. And I don't think it's tendonitis. It may be a bone spur or a stress fracture. If you want to, you could go to a western doctor, have x-rays, maybe an operation. But if I were you, I would let time and Mother Nature cure you."

"Does this mean I can't run?" Clara asked. "I think I'd be worried about my sanity if I couldn't run. I'm an addict, in case you didn't know."

Estrellita chuckled, a deep, throaty rumble that seemed to travel up from her stomach. "Oh, I know about your running. Annie's told me all about how you get up before the light of day, how you ran nine marathons and took an hour and a half off your time to complete 26 miles. Most people would be half dead if they ran 26 miles without stopping. Maybe your foot is trying to tell you something."

"Well, yes, I used to be a fanatic, I guess. When I did all that running, it was the one thing in my life I could count on, the one thing that was going well. Everything else was falling apart, but I kept making better and better times, getting stronger and thinking clearly. It was during a run that I decided that I would move out here and teach at AIA. I still run but it's just for enjoyment. Surely I don't have to lay off completely. Isn't there anything I can do to make my foot less painful as I heal?"

Estrellita had let go of her foot, so Clara leaned over, slipped her sock back on and shoved her foot in the black boot. She felt a little foolish, coming here to ask Estrellita's advice when the only solution was probably one she couldn't even consider.

To her relief, Estrellita did not say "Quit running." Instead, she recommended a bath of eucalyptus leaves combined with an herb that grew in a *bosque* near her house

"I'm not sure what the scientific name is, so we just call it *yerba buena*. I've never seen it anywhere else except in this one spot, either.

So here is a big supply." She opened a file drawer and pulled out a large, clear plastic bag full of dried brownish leaves.

"I don't have any eucalyptus leaves, but you can buy them at Herbs, Etc., right up Cerrillos Road from here. And my herbs, I'll be able to supply you with whatever you need." Estrellita stood up, as if to end their meeting.

"Remember that everything must be dried well before you use it. Just brew a very strong tea and pour it in a tub with warm water. Make it as hot, not boiling, but as hot as you can stand. Do this every night for 20 minutes and let me know in one or two weeks how it's going."

"You didn't tell me to stop running. Does that mean that anything is OK?" Clara hated for the time to be up so soon, but she could see that Estrellita was eager to get to her next engagement.

"Listen to your body and your heart. If you feel worse, let up and just do two or three miles. When you're feeling better, you could run for an hour. You need to maybe take more rest days. Give your foot a chance to heal. I wouldn't run any races for a while, at least not on a hard surface. Lay off the competition. I'm serious about letting me know how you're doing. You can come by any day after work."

On the off chance that Herbs, Etc. might be open late, Clara drove by after leaving the Indian Hospital. The place was locked, but there was a light on inside. She rapped a few times and was about to give up when a young Hispanic man opened the door a crack.

"I'm sorry, but we're closed. We'll open tomorrow morning at nine."

Speaking fast, Clara explained that she needed only one thing, eucalyptus leaves, and she needed it for medicinal purposes. "It's an emergency," she added.

Supplied now with Estrellita's magical herb and a sack of dried eucalyptus leaves, Clara headed back to Red Mesa. Just thinking about the healing foot bath lifted her spirits. Her foot would be better and she could return to the kind of running that made her feel alive.

Traffic was light, and the threatened snow never came. It was a brilliantly clear, starry night. She would be home in time to curl up with a pot of tea, Oscar on her lap, and do a final review of tomorrow's lesson plans.

At peace, Clara smiled as she traveled back to Red Mesa. She felt, as she often liked to say, "cautiously optimistic." Despite the difficulties of this year, maybe everything was going to settle down.

11

Larry's World

The red eye flight back to Albuquerque was rotten. Irritating, crowded, no food. Larry Butt was wedged in between a blond woman dressed in a sweat suit, a screaming baby in her lap, and an enormously fat man who oozed over into his seat.

Larry felt like he'd been mugged. Bone tired and weak with hunger, he ached all over. Ever since leaving the hot flames from the Eastgates' house, that satisfying inferno, he'd been racked with chills. The noise in his ears might have been the subliminal whine of the plane's engines, but it reminded him of when he'd offed the Eastgate bitch. Damn, it was messy, but she asked for it. If she had just shut up, he might have spared her. Oh well, Henry said to do whatever was necessary. And he was coming back with the pot, wasn't he?

Despite conditions on the plane, he must have dozed off, because the next thing he knew, they were landing in Albuquerque. He reached anxiously under the seat to make sure the brief case was still there. The baby was dozing in its mother's arms, but the fat man was halfway over in his seat space. Larry had to press against the man's arm as he reached over to get his brief case. Fortunately, no one paid attention to the jostling.

The seatbelt sign went off. En masse, the red eye passengers stood up. It was 5 a.m., plenty of time to make it to Henry's place by eight. Larry fingered the keys to the Jetta that he'd left in Airport Fast Park and clutched the brief case, with its precious contents.

Shuffling along with the other weary passengers, he looked like just another business man. His brown suit was inexpensive but not the cheapest, his shoes just the same color and newish. There was nothing at all distinctive about him, unless it might be the bowl haircut, a style left over from the 70s, a style that met its demise before he was born. Just like Thelma to be lagging behind, Larry often thought to himself. But for some reason, the bowl cut remained. It hid the ugly cleft in his forehead, a reminder of when he'd fallen off his tricycle under Thelma's haphazard mothering.

With nothing to claim, Larry strode purposefully past the baggage area out into the raw morning air. Even without looking at the card on which he'd recorded it, he remembered his parking space: F5.

He badly needed coffee, so despite the deadline looming ahead of him -- 8 a.m. at Henry's or else -- he drove up Gibson Avenue until he found an Allsups. He bought a large travel mug and filled it with black coffee, picked out five candy bars, and a medium bag of Cheetos, then got on I-25 north to Santa Fe.

Once on the highway, Larry pressed the accelerator until the Jetta was doing 80. Sipping the scalding coffee and munching on Snickers, Milky Ways, and Heath Bars, he began to feel better. The sacred pot, safe in the brief case next to him, would be delivered to Henry in plenty of time. Since they were both dead, the Eastgates wouldn't be talking.

Larry started laughing to himself. It began as a low rumble in his throat, then developed into a huge bray that nearly engulfed him. No, no, they wouldn't be talking. They wouldn't be doing anything. They couldn't bear witness against him, and they'd never expose Henry's cybersmuggling. Yes, he'd shut them up all right. Dead ducks, dead dopes, dead silent.

Right in the middle of a gut-wrenching guffaw and his third candy bar, Larry remembered the fire. God, what if Henry was angry about that little addition to the execution of his plans? Logically, Henry should be pleased. There would be less for the police to find, less evidence to go on with everything reduced to ashes. Surely Henry would see the logic of this.

"Whatever you do, don't make a mess." Remembering Henry's parting words, Larry choked on the candy. A fire wasn't really a mess, was it? How would they ever know who had set it? Fingerprints, evidence of struggles, everything would be obliterated. Except, of course, bullets didn't burn.

He'd throw his gun in a sewer grating when he came to Rio Rancho, where it would be time to buy more coffee and candy bars anyway. Surely Henry wouldn't ask if he still had his pistol. He could make up something. Maybe he just wouldn't tell him about the fire. It wasn't so important in the big picture. Smoldering ashes, that's all that would be left, and that wasn't really a mess as much as a really effective cover-up.

Suppose someone had discovered the fire right away and had it doused? Suppose the evidence hadn't gone up in smoke...his bloody footsteps on the white carpet in the Eastgates' bedroom, the broken display case where he'd claimed Henry's black pot, evidence of the struggle on the staircase when Dan Eastgate cornered him. Just thinking about what might be left behind, Larry started to sweat.

No, it wouldn't do to mention the fire to Henry. Even if it was the best thing he could have done, Henry might not agree. Besides, the master would be furious at the insubordination. If there was one thing Henry demanded, it was absolute obedience. March to his orders or die.

The fields along I-25 were growing more visible as dawn approached. Just as he passed the turnoff to Rio Rancho, a meteorite shot across the sky directly ahead of him. In his exhausted, half-crazed condition, Larry suddenly realized that if Henry decided he'd botched the job, he would be just like that, blazing brightly, then snuffed out.

Thinking about it made him drive wildly. The Jetta was doing 85, then 90, 95, 100. Now, instead of sweating, Larry was wracked with chills. He turned up the heater full blast. The roar sounded just like the fire he'd left behind, and in his mind, Larry traveled ahead to the pending interview with Henry.

Abruptly, a stomach cramp nearly doubled him over the steering wheel and a wave of nausea engulfed him. Yes, of course Henry would know. He would see right through his facade. Larry steered the Jetta to the right of the highway, put on the emergency brake, opened the door, and retched. He lost the five candy bars, the coffee, the miserable conglomeration of junk food he'd been downing for half an hour - everything. The vomiting went on until there was nothing left in his gut, leaving him so weak that he passed out briefly on the car seat.

The motor was running, and so was the time left before he had to report. He promised Henry the pot would be in his hands by eight a.m. It was now five minutes after seven, and traffic was getting intense. There were several wrecks on I-25 so he could easily get caught on the highway and held up for hours.

No, despite his weakened condition, Larry realized, he had to keep moving. Nothing could be worse than the possibility of Henry's wrath, Henry's scorn, Henry's punishment. And if Larry was sure of anything, it was his master's sense of justice. Total submission or a life not worth living.

Larry forced himself to sit up just as a police car approached, its lights on. He had been speeding, but then so were a lot of other people. Surely the pigs weren't after him. Nonetheless, he ducked back down on the seat until he was sure the police car had passed. It was half a mile ahead, its whirling light now accompanied by a siren. Probably pursuing a DWI.

But that was not Larry's problem. He was sick from worry, lack of sleep, and rotten junk food, but he was definitely not drunk.

The eastern sky was growing lighter, with delicate pinks and blues spreading across the horizon, a beauty wasted on Larry. As he sped north toward Santa Fe on Interstate 25, he imagined his imminent meeting with Henry. Everything had gone according to plan except for the fire.

Over and over, he told himself, "The fire never happened." He wanted to forget about it so totally that Henry would never suspect, never ask. He knew that Henry could read his mind, so the only way he could hide anything was to erase it from memory. In fact, he'd gotten pretty good at what he thought of as "creative remembering." If only there were enough time to reprogram his visual pictures.

The clock was racing. He passed the Pepto-Bismol colored San Felipe gambling casino on the right. Despite the hour, the parking lot was jammed with cars. Fools recklessly throwing away their money, Larry thought to himself, which reminded him of the money Henry owed him. It was a cool 20K, enough for him to leave the mainland and go hang out in Maui for a while -- with cash to spare.

That is, unless Henry was displeased, in which case there would be hell to pay.

By the time he passed the Cochiti Lake turnoff Larry realized that he no longer remembered the fire. It might have been something he dreamed. Just as, so long ago when Bobby sank into the water and never came back, he was not part of the disappearance. Years later, when someone mentioned Bobby's drowning, it never seemed odd that he remembered everything about it even though he wasn't there.

As he roared down the highway, constantly checking the rearview mirror for police cars, Larry allowed himself to picture that afternoon so long ago. Thelma and that sleazebag Abe were busy with the police. They completely swallowed his story about being at the camp while Bobby had wandered off. At the time, Larry distinctly remembered Bobby's telling him he'd be right back, in time for the birthday party.

Abe and Thelma were the searchers. In their panic about Bobby, they forgot all about him and his birthday. They were having a search party rather than a birthday party. Larry crawled into the back of their van and found the ice cream and cake. The cake was fudgy chocolate, the ice cream -- which had grown soft -- was butter pecan.

He took the bag with the cake box, ice cream and plasticware, and ran into the tall trees down a ravine away from the camp. He wrinkled his nose at a burning smell. The bacon, in its skillet on the rocks, was up in flames, but of course no one noticed. They only cared about Bobby.

Well hidden, as if anyone would notice or be looking for him, Larry sat down with his cake and ice cream. The cake was very chocolatey. Larry forced himself to eat the whole thing. He had to be both host and guest of honor. No one to sing Happy Birthday, no presents, just this stinking food. He took a bite of now soupy butter pecan ice cream, then another and another, until he had polished it off as well. Then he was sick.

Not a pleasant memory, but at least it took his mind off the meeting. Henry the all-powerful, his *bete noire* and worst nightmare. But, if he had the black pot in time to do with it whatever he was planning, he would be Henry the beneficent. Why he needed it at any cost was not information that Larry was privy to, for Henry did not tell his underlings more than they needed to know.

Just as the sun was fully up and traffic was approaching gridlock, Larry was at the top of the last hill before descending to Santa Fe. Feeling protected by the presence of other speeders on the road, he pressed on the accelerator. He was traveling so fast, he nearly passed the off-ramp at the Pecos Trail Exit.

12

On the road again

The herbs were doing their work. Clara was amazed at the difference in her foot since she'd started using Estrellita's remedies. The soothing eucalyptus plus foot bath before bed, a castor oil pack in the afternoon, as well as the mental boost of knowing she was doing something to help. All of that gave her hope that she might someday run the long distances she loved. Maybe she would work her way back up to marathon strength in a few months.

But for now, six a.m. on a school morning, Clara was going to try running just five miles, about twice the distance she'd been logging since Speckled Horse's death. After several yoga stretches, she slipped into a lyrca running suit, black stirrup pants with a florescent pink stripe running down the outside of each leg, a matching pullover top, a big baggy t-shirt from her last 10-kilometer race over that, padded socks, and her favorite pair of New Balance running shoes. She pinned her front door key to the waist of her pants, grabbed earmuffs and wool mittens, checked to make sure Oscar wasn't about to dart out, and stepped into the cold, dark pre-dawn.

When Annie scolded her for running, she would tell her friend not to worry. "It's safer than driving your car. People have a one in three chance in their lifetimes of being involved in a collision, much worse odds than those for runners. Besides, I always carry my pepper spray and it would at least distract an attacker so I could run away. I change my route every day, so even if someone were waiting for me, he wouldn't know where to wait." And so on. But it didn't do any good. Her best friend insisted that she quit running at dawn or dusk.

As Clara headed down her drive to the dirt road that ran to the village of La Mesa, she realized that she'd forgotten her pepper spray and that she was running the same route she'd run for the last month. Because Annie just didn't understand why Clara was so devoted to running, she focused on all the negative aspects of "addiction." Clara would respond, "If you've got to be addicted, then run."

It was a gloriously crisp, clear morning. After descending from her house, which topped a small hillock, Clara turned left on the dirt road that ran perpendicular to her driveway. After just half a mile Clara had warmed up enough to increase her speed. She swung her arms and raised her feet higher, soon leaving her cabin far behind. At a mile, she turned left and climbed a path up into a forest of Ponderosa pine.

She had to look at the ground frequently to keep from stumbling on embedded boulders and protruding tree roots. The path zigzagged up the side of a hill before leveling out to a ridge. When she first moved to her cabin, Clara ran here frequently, but since Speckled Horse died, she hadn't been back.

The ridge went on for about a mile, commanding a panoramic vista of the school before a gradual downhill that paralleled the road in front of Clara's cabin. In late summer and early autumn, it was covered with a fantastic display of wildflowers. Sunflowers, purple astors, brilliant red paintbrush and Elephant's ear. But now the hills were sere. Dried, dead grasses and the skeletal remains of flowers gone to seed were all that remained.

Running-wise she felt in gear, as she liked to think of it. Heart pumping, arms and legs propelling her forward, lungs at work. She covered two, then three miles. At mile four, she stopped at a mossy boulder to tie her right running shoe. When she did, she remembered the note, a piece of paper from an appointment book that she had found right about at this spot. She had forgotten about it until now.

The note mentioned a meeting between Ramirez and someone with the ridiculous name of Butt, an event that was to have taken place sometime in November at 3 p.m. There was another name, mud-stained, that she couldn't read. Because the note meant nothing, she'd picked it up and stuffed it in her windbreaker. The death of Speckled Horse was right afterwards. Did she still have it? Could it possibly provide answers in the still unsolved mystery?

People were saying that a student who disappeared the same night of the murder was the most likely suspect, but they were grasping at straws. The school was under a cloud that would dissipate only when the crime was solved. Even though she had tried to stay as far from the investigation as possible, the stray note troubled Clara.

She ran further until the path started to descend. She felt strong, as though she could run forever. It was wonderful to go all out and not feel the sharp ache in her foot. But now that she could breathe more easily about her foot, she started to worry about the note. Probably it was nothing, but what if it could help? As soon as she had time, she would search all her pockets and junk drawers. Her habit was to hoard objects that might be important at some later date, especially items found along the road during her runs. She would find them months or even years later, ferreted away in drawers or pockets.

But for now, she had to concentrate on her footing, for the trail grew very steep, and the ground was so dry that the loose dirt acted like ball bearings. Moving her arms away from her body to balance, Clara ran sideways, in small steps, and made it down the last descent with only one or two slides.

Then, another mile on the lower jeep trail and across to her road, and she was headed back to her cabin. Amazingly, it was only seven a.m. She would have no trouble making it to class by eight.

Her feet, legs, in fact, everything, felt better after the five-miler than it had for a very long time. She would write an entry in her mileage log, a custom that she'd followed for most of her 20 years of running. It was only when she started the teaching year at AIA that she'd gotten out of the habit.

As soon as she got home, she opened a blank page in the latest of twenty spiral notebooks and wrote:

November 30, 2000: Left the house a little after 6 a.m. and ran the ridge. Foot much better, almost well. About 45 minutes for five miles. Could've done better but path was rocky. Note: look for paper found here last month (May shed light on Speckled Horse case).

Showered and wearing her favorite denim dress, Clara gathered up her briefcase and looked for Oscar. He was always disappearing just when she needed to leave the house for school. These cool fall days enticed him outdoors. But this was coyote mating season, and the hungry critters were out in full force. Oscar would make a convenient meal.

"Here kitty, kitty, kitty. Here, kitty, kitty, kitty," she screeched out the front door. "Time for breakfast. Mommy has to go to work. Here Oscar."

Finally a small gray head peeked from behind a tree and Clara coaxed Oscar into the house. "It's about time," she scolded.

Oscar's left ear was bleeding, as though he'd gotten into a fight. She looked more closely and saw that the ear was cut, as though with a knife or scissors. Fresh blood dripped from the half-inch wound.

Clara scooped up the drooping cat in her arms and carried him to the bathroom sink. She tried to comfort him. "Oh, Oskie, what happened, fella? Poor Oscar, let's get you fixed up."

She put her cat in the sink while she rummaged through the bathroom cabinet for hydrogen peroxide. Oscar limply complied, letting out an occasional pitiful *Meow*.

"If only you could talk, kitty...Who did this awful thing to you?"

She was going to be late for school, but she couldn't leave without taking care of Oscar. She found gauze and hydrogen peroxide, made a compress, and pressed it gently against either side of the injured ear.

After putting out cat kibble and fresh water and giving Oscar a new catnip toy she'd been saving for Christmas, Clara locked the front door behind her a few minutes before eight. If she hurried, she could make it to her classroom just before the first bell.

In her haste, she didn't notice the drops of blood on the front porch, and by the time she returned home that night, they would be dried, even easier to overlook. Instead she revved up the Cherokee and sped to the Communications Building.

With five minutes to spare, she walked into her classroom. As usual, Carnell was already there. Seated in his overseer's position at the back of the room, he was engrossed in *The Stand* by Stephen King.

"How are you enjoying the book?" Clara asked. She remembered staying awake just to get to the end of a chapter. Since they'd finished *The Running Man,* several of her students were on a Stephen King reading binge. It made Clara happy. Despite the school board and the higher-ups insistence that Native American students wanted more material about their own culture and history, she found that kids liked the same things other teenagers she'd taught. But of course, she was complying with the board. Next semester they would be reading *Black Elk Speaks.*

Carnell closed his book and pulled out a spiral for today's grammar aerobics. In twos and threes, students were trickling into class.

"Ms. Jordan, you've got to come to the computer lab today. I've found more web pages and links that you can use in your search. I'll show you how to get there and you can explore on your own. It's cool. You've gotta see it!"

"OK, Carnell, you've captured my curiosity. I have to go by the administration office after classes, but I should be able to meet you by about four. I may be a lost cause. I don't think my parents want me to find them, or I would have heard something." But even as she spoke, Clara felt a flame of hope in her heart. For so many years, she had wondered and waited.

As the bell signaled the beginning of the academic day, Clara wrote on the blackboard, "Grammar aerobics - one ticket per correct answer."

Because her students placed a low value on such fine points as subject-verb agreement and the difference between restrictive and non-restrictive clauses, Clara had devised what she hoped were motivational tools.

From merchants around Santa Fe and Albuquerque, she had received gift prizes ranging from tennis racquets to CDs. When she'd explained it was for AIA, most people she talked to were receptive.

Instead of calling it a grammar auction, she called her project "communication enrichment."

All semester, students could earn tickets through various exercises that reinforced grammatical fine points. After they returned from Christmas break, Clara had scheduled a festive "grammar auction," in which they could use their tickets to bid on prizes.

She had asked her friend Annie to be the auctioneer. The shy, soft-spoken librarian assumed another personality once she got on the auctioneer's stand. Annie's auctioneering skills were in great demand by clubs and organizations in Santa Fe, so Clara lined her up many months before the auction was scheduled.

Clara entertained the class with a book called *The Transitive Vampire*, a clever book for teaching grammatical fine points with wit and funny line drawings. She translated the author's illustrations into examples more meaningful to them. Every right answer earned a red ticket.

By the end of the day, Homer had 83 tickets; Dorothy was runner up with 75; Jarvis and Deena tied for third with 52. This project was going well, Clara thought. The kids couldn't see the value of discussing pronouns and antecedents, but they loved accumulating tickets. Winning prizes appealed to them.

The final bell jarred through the late afternoon drone of activity. Together, they'd made a lot of progress. Clara was exhausted but pleased.

"Computer lab at four," Carnell said as he walked out. "Don't forget."

Clara had forgotten. "Oh, right. If I'm late, just keep surfing the net until I arrive. I've got an errand beforehand. Thanks for following through on this."

"Later," Carnell yelled out as he sauntered toward the lockers. Of all her students, Clara thought, Carnell would go furthest. His natural charm and good humor, combined with his sharp mind, creativity and enthusiasm drew people to him, herself included. He had an underlying humility that seemed to keep the other students from being jealous of his academic success.

It had been nearly a month since Speckled Horse's death and her attempt to go back to Virginia to see her parents. Clara had reservations to fly back East for just a week. This time, Annie would drive her to Santa Fe, where she would catch the shuttle to Albuquerque.

So many things to think of at once made her crazy. She needed to pack, she had to talk to Wren (would she be hired back next year and what would she do if not?), and there were still lesson plans to do for the rest of the week. If only she could clone herself, she laughed grimly. Clara the teacher; Clara the devoted daughter, tending Will and Louise; Clara the distance runner; Clara the Internet expert, searching for her roots on the World Wide Web.

She stuffed too much in her brief case for one night, the grammar plans for tomorrow, a workbook on *Old Man and the Sea* (which they'd be reading before the year ended), three sets of papers (pop quizzes, eleven-sentence paragraphs, a test from last week) -- roughly, five hours of work, when at most she would have an hour. Her brief case was so heavy that her shoulder would ache from the load, but no matter what she did, she never could streamline.

Just as she was about to lock her classroom and leave for the Administration Building, two things happened. Jerome Naranjo appeared at the door and she remembered the note she'd found right before Speckled Horse died. She'd been planning to mention the note to Jerome soon but was waiting until she unearthed it in the maelstrom of her paperwork.

"Oh, hi, Jerome. What brings you to AIA? Any news on the Speckled Horse case? I was just going to see Dr. Taggert. Do you want to walk there with me?"

Jerome smiled warmly and held out his hand, oddly formal. As they were shaking, he said, "Glad I caught you Ms. Jordan -- Clara. Yes, I am still working on leads, even though the Santa Fe police think they've narrowed it down to Johnnie. Somehow I just don't believe that's the answer. It's too easy to blame someone who's not here."

"I was going to wait to tell you this, but I found a note right before the murder that seemed to be about a meeting in the afternoon. The names meant nothing to me, but it might have something to do with it. Problem is, I can't remember where I might have stashed it."

It was one of those deceptive afternoons, warm and sunny, more like October instead of nearly Christmas. The huge cottonwoods that graced the campus still had a few golden leaves clinging to their branches. As they neared the Administration Building, Clara had a sense that Wren wouldn't be in. She was sure that the arrogant Interim Headmaster did not want to talk with her, but she had to keep trying. Not just her fate, but that of Will and Louise depended on her keeping this job.

Jerome stopped walking and stood to face her. She'd forgotten how tall he was. "Please, Clara, you must try to find it. From what I've gathered, the murder was tied in with something that was supposed to take place that afternoon. That might have been a meeting that Joe attended right before his ill-fated trip to your classroom. If I can find out

104

who the other people at the meeting were, we might unearth what really happened."

Clara looked right into Jerome's dark eyes. "You know, I thought of that when I found it, but everything that happened afterwards made me forget. It's got to be somewhere. I know I didn't throw it away. I promise I'll search."

"That would be great, Clara. I don't want to harass you about this. I know everyone just wants to put this behind them, get on with life, but I'm just not convinced that this student -- Johnny -- did it. It's too easy. There is more to it. Your note just might give us the information we need."

"It's just misplaced. I will look, trust me." Briefcase, purse and coat draped over her arms and shoulders, Clara locked the classroom door and was heading in the direction of the Administration Building. "Look, Jerome, I don't mean to be rude, but I've been trying all week to talk with Wren Taggert, and I'm supposed to meet with a student at four. I'll catch you later."

"No problem. Later." As Jerome headed out the side doors of the Communications Building, Clara realized she didn't have his phone number or know how to reach him. Not that she expected to find the note right away. She'd been distracted when she found it. Was it in her windbreaker pocket?

Once again, Wren's office was locked. Clara hated the uncertainty now enveloping her job, and she badly wanted to talk with the interim headmaster. Even if Wren wouldn't reconsider her decision not to hire her back next year, Clara needed to make sure she'd write her a recommendation. Maybe a letter would be the best approach. She could compose one in the computer lab after she looked at the web page Carnell was so excited about.

This day was too long. It would be much better if she could just go home, heat up some of the *posole* she'd made to last the week, and curl up with Oscar and a good book. It was highly unlikely that this Internet business would lead anywhere, but she would go though with it anyway just because of Carnell.

She loved that kid. Next to Annie, he was her closest friend in Red Mesa, her strongest link to the rest of her students, someone she could relax with and be herself. Carnell knew about her longing to find her Native American roots and her fear about actually making the connection.

Lost in thought, she walked to the Macintosh Lab, a room that doubled as an after-school hangout for the school techies. When an AIA student was enrolled in computer science, he or she had an e-mail address. They logged in to check their e-mail before surfing the net.

Theoretically, the kids were using the Internet for research and background material for their courses, and most of them did eventually use it for that purpose. One problem, Clara would point out to them, was that much of what they found was not accurate. A lot of so-called information was just opinion, unsubstantiated and sometimes just plain wrong. She tried to teach her students to discriminate between bogus and valuable information, to recheck their findings in the library, and to look at the sources. But it was not easy to convince them that data from the Internet might not be reliable. The Internet was magic. Clara realized they would rather believe in it than listen to her dire warnings.

"Oh, hi, Ms. Jordan." Carnell was already at a Mac, the screen ablaze with color. Next to him was another work station, obviously saved for her.

"Here we are. I've already logged you on."

Clara sat down next to Carnell and looked at her screen. It matched Carnell's screen, blank except for the hard drive icon at the upper right hand corner, menu titles across the top, and apple in the upper left-hand corner.

"We're starting from scratch," Carnell told her. "I want you to be able to come into the lab and search on your own. First of all, you have to go online. Just click on the apple icon and pull down the menu, then scroll to "Netscape Navigator.""

Clara followed Carnell's example, and the Netscape Navigator icon appeared at the center of her screen, shooting stars falling across the indigo blue backdrop. The symbol was intriguing, full of promise, and Clara wanted to say "Way cool!" just as one of her students might. Instead, she refrained and waited for Carnell's next commands.

This was exciting. Her initial skepticism evaporated as they entered the World Wide Web. Carnell showed Clara how to find a uniform resource locater, which he referred to as a URL, and also how to use a search engine.

"I usually go with Yahoo," he explained, "but you can always try Alta Vista or even Magellan. They all offer something a little bit different. You might think of it as shopping in different department stores." Carnell showed Clara how to start a search, how to make the request fairly specific and how to bookmark web sites to which she wanted to return.

At last they came to a web site titled "Lost Deer Homepage." Clara had expected bright colors and graphics, but it was plain, informational, black and white. At the top was a line drawing of a young Native American woman.

My name is Lost Deer Naomi, and I welcome you to the Lost Deer Homepage. I've been working for a long time on this, trying to compile all of the information that I was asked to include on this page. Then I couldn't figure out how to properly transfer all of these typed pages, and my desperate confusion was solved by Mark Williams whom I will always be grateful to.

Clara was riveted. Whoever this Native American speaker was, he or she was speaking directly to her. This was the first time in many years she had felt any hope about finding her real parents. As she read on, tears filled her eyes.

I'm hoping that this page will become a major resource for all of those who are trying to find their original families. Currently, I'm looking for people from various tribes who may be able to help those adopted children, who are now adults, find their biological families.

That's me, Clara thought. I'm one of those adopted adult children trying to find my family.

The writer went on to mention the Indian Child Welfare Act (ICWA): *This page is about the adoption of Indian children by families from other cultures. Before 1978, when Congress adopted the ICWA, there were literally thousands of adoptions of American Indian children by white families. Often this happened without the consent of the biological parents. Most of these adoptions were carried out by social workers who were taught to undermine the self-esteem of the new mother. The social worker's purpose was to convince Indian mothers that they would be incapable of taking care of their children, while white families would be able to satisfy all the child's needs. If the mother or father was unable to take care of the child properly, no considerations were ever given to the other members of the family as to whether or not they wished to adopt the baby. American Indians had no rights, no voice, no say as to what happened to their children. ICWA was created to put a halt to this adoption policy and to give American Indians the same rights everyone had when it came to their children and their families. However, there were people who found ways of getting around this law. Presently, there are many cases in which ICWA, a FEDERAL LAW, is being ignored.*

The thought of her mother's grief at having her, a blood-related daughter, taken away filled Clara with anger. How could she stand it? Why hadn't she found her after all these years? When Clara was very young, they had moved many times. She had never wondered why until now. Could it have been to keep her birthmother from tracking them down? Despairing thoughts engulfed her.

"Pretty cool, huh?" asked Carnell. He showed Clara the links that could lead her to individuals who, like her, were searching. Of course, it seemed unlikely that her birthmother would be connected to the World Wide Web, but on the other hand, she never thought *she* would be surfing the Internet.

It was nearly six o'clock and she had to get home to feed Oscar and herself. She made a printout of the Lost Deer Page, thanked Carnell, and headed into the chilly night air.

Some of the links -- such as "Resources for those looking for their biological families," "Geneology Links," "Lost and Found - Parents looking for their children and children looking for their parents" -- looked very promising. She would definitely return to explore them when she had more time, maybe even tomorrow night. At least this re-ignited the hope that died a long time ago. Maybe there was a light along her path after all.

Carnell left to get dinner at the cafeteria. She made a few notes on how to reach the Lost Deer Page, clicked her way offline, and started toward the door of the computer lab.

She was nearly out of the room when Henry stepped out of the small office just off the computer lab. He stepped in front of the door, blocking her way.

"Hi there, stranger. Where have you been hanging out?" Incredibly, he acted as though they were still going together. Maybe in his mind, they were, but she wanted nothing to do with him. Ever since the Thanksgiving debacle, she felt she couldn't trust him.

"I'm surprised to see you here, Henry. I really don't have a minute to talk, and besides, I think it's better if we just act like we don't know each other." She tried to brush by him but he moved from one side of the door to the other. Despite her antagonism toward him, she couldn't help but notice how handsome he looked. He was wearing the blue sweater she gave him for his birthday, and he smelled faintly like Dial soap. The aroma dredged up unwelcome memories, warm and disturbing.

"I've really missed you, babe, and I want to see you, even if all we do is just have dinner and talk."

108

"No Henry, it's all wrong. We don't have anything to talk about. We never did. It was a big mistake, and I don't appreciate your spying on me. I should be able to come in and use the computer lab like everyone else."

The students scattered around the lab were beginning to stare at them. Henry stood right in the middle of the doorway, an irritating grin on his face and a twinkle in his eyes. Clara hated him for coming back into her life like this. She had enough to think about with her students, Will and Louise, and the Lost Deer Page. Why couldn't he just leave her alone?

Henry blocked her second attempt to get out the door. She felt short of breath. It was best, however, to feign calmness and indifference. Henry would take advantage of her fear, and even though it was probably impossible, she needed to hide it from him.

"Hey, look, Henry, nothing against you, but I've got to get home right away. I'll talk with you over coffee at the Downtown Java Joint this weekend. We've never really ended things, and there are things we need to go over. Just let me by."

Henry pulled her close to him, pressing his body next to hers. "OK, I take that as a promise. I'll be calling you. Soon."

She finally escaped from the computer lab, ran to her car, locked all the doors tightly and roared along the pitted dirt roads to her cabin. The last thing in the world she wanted to do was start up again with Henry. She hadn't meant to give him any encouragement, but there hadn't been any other way to get out.

In five minutes, she was back on her street and up the driveway at the front porch. It was pitch black. She groped her way up the steps. Feeling for the keyhole, she unlocked the door and let herself in. Oscar, who always brushed up against her, purring, the minute she was inside, was nowhere to be seen.

Clara felt uneasy. Even though she had grading to do, she could think of nothing but curling up in bed with her latest magazines. For the next hour, she called for Oscar. He must be pulling one of his all-nighters. Surely he would be at her door mewing the next morning.

She took a hot shower and put on her favorite flannel pajamas. When she went back to her bedroom, the answering machine was blinking. She never heard the phone when she was in the shower. It was probably that pest, Henry, she thought, but when she played it back, there was nothing.

13

The Spider's Web

The sun was completely up when Larry Butt pulled onto Henry's unmarked road just off Old Santa Fe Trail. After driving 100 miles an hour from the Albuquerque International Airport on I-25 to the Old Pecos Trail Exit, he'd managed to reach Henry's cabin with five minutes to spare.

He'd nearly wet his pants after drinking so much coffee on the plane. After parking the rental car behind a clump of trees, Larry hid between the trees and the car to take a leak. Damn, he felt nervous. The sweat he'd developed during his break-neck drive was now, in the freezing morning air, causing chills. His stomach was churning and he felt a cramp rage through his bowels.

No time for nausea. It was now two minutes before eight. Henry's cabin was just a few feet away, boarded up as though abandoned. He must have been losing it, as he had crossed through the barbed wire when he remembered the brief case. Running back to the car, he opened the trunk, drew out the case, and bolted toward the cabin.

Set on a ridge across an arroyo, Henry's place looked abandoned. The windows were boarded up and there was no sign of life anywhere around. In fact, it looked as though the cabin lacked even a door. Larry, however, had been here before, and he knew the circuitous route to Henry's lair.

Near the cabin was a tool shed, even more dilapidated than the main structure. It was bordered on one side by an immense stack of pinon logs that had been there so long they were turning to sawdust.

Larry pushed open a door that creaked loudly, as if in complaint. The tool shed was empty except for a large credenza, intricately carved and probably antique. Larry pushed the credenza aside to reveal a trap door. Obviously no stranger to the procedure, Larry opened the door, descending a ladder into the musky depths, and began groveling along a low, narrow tunnel. It was Henry's subterranean passage, or, as Larry thought of it, "the path to hell."

He'd been here once before, when he went to work for Henry a year ago, and it had been even worse, as he didn't know what awaited at the end of the tunnel. Even though he'd crawled this way several times since then, this was just as bad as the first passage. The Eastgate heist was his first big job for Henry, and he was afraid he'd blown it.

The air was fetid and the cold, rough floor of the passage was making mincemeat of his hands. But time was running out, so Larry crawled faster. At last the tunnel grew smaller and came to an end. Sure enough, overhead there was the wooden door.

Remembering the code Henry had given him, he raised his bruised right hand to tap it out. Two taps far apart, then two close together, and two far apart.

No answer.

Larry took some deep breaths, sickened by the air's foulness, and tried again. Two far apart, two taps together, once again two apart. Cramped and miserable, he waited for an eternity. He resisted the urge to tap again, for Henry grew furious when nagged.

A crack of light above Larry's head revealed Henry's impish expression. It gave Henry great pleasure to see Larry Butt crawling like the worm that he was.

"Come into my parlor said the spider to the fly." Henry opened the trap door all the way. "I hope you brought the pot, because if you didn't this door is slamming down so hard it will give you a concussion."

"Yeah, Man, I've got your treasure, and the witnesses won't talk because they're dead." Larry was beginning to pant. "Just let me out of this hell hole. Please."

Henry lowered a rope ladder for his guest. "You know, I don't have many visitors, so you'll have to pardon the lack of formalities."

Clawing his way out of the hole in the floor, Larry stood up in the cavernous room that served as Henry's den. There was a huge fire roaring away in the fireplace and three small overstuffed chairs around a glass kidney-shaped table. Other than that, the room appeared empty.

The only light came from two aluminum Torchere lamps with harvest gold bases and bowl-shaped glass shades. Art Deco from the 1950s, Larry thought. Thelma had spent $1,000 on a pair of them, money they didn't have, right after Bobby disappeared. Larry remembered how angry Abe was at so much money being spent on lamps. He'd taken his anger out on Larry, beating him nearly senseless. Where had Thelma been? These lamps were so much like Torchieres from his past, they might have been the same ones.

The walls and floors were a dark, glossy wood, a cross between black and brown. The wood reminded Larry of church pews that he'd seen once before, when Thelma was in her brief religious phase, right before the Abe years.

He sat in a chair with his back to the fire. Henry was seated directly across from him, the flames reflected in his glasses, his long jeans-clad legs splayed out to either side. While most furniture in the outside world was too small for Henry, it seemed odd to Larry that here in his customized den he wouldn't have a chair spacious enough for his lanky frame. Surely it wasn't because of expense. Supposedly Henry was making a fortune from his illegal wheeling and dealing in artifacts.

Henry was staring at him, grinning expectantly. He placed his fingertips together, arching his long, bony hands together like a cave. "Well?"

Larry unzipped his briefcase and tenderly removed the gleaming black pot from the clean undershirt that served as its shroud. Ceremoniously, he handed it over. "Just like I promised, here it is -- in perfect condition."

"Ah, yes." Henry held the pot up as if studying its geometry and then placed it in the center of the glass table. The reflection, highlighted by flames from the fireplace, glowed around the pot's base.

Neither man spoke. A log in the fireplace dropped, sending up a crackling of sparks and further igniting the other logs. It was roasting. Henry felt his back scorching, and he started to scoot his chair further from the fireplace. For an exhausted moment, he imagined he was being torched by flames from the Eastgate mansion as it went up in flames.

"Do not move unless I say so," Henry boomed out harshly. "I want you to tell me how you came about this little beauty. Then and only then will you get your money."

Henry removed his jacket. Good. At least Henry would let him do that. He knew he'd better start talking soon, before the phony good humor of his boss faded and the true nastiness just beneath the surface emerged.

"You'll love the way it went. Smooth as silk, no witnesses, the Eastgates silenced. Just about perfect." Larry felt a rush of blood come to his face, as he saw, in his mind's eye, the flames licking the Eastgate's front porch. He gritted his teeth, trying to appear calm. He had erased that morning with Bobby so long ago: he could erase this.

What fire? There was no fire. If he could just remember that it hadn't REALLY happened, the fire would leave his mind entirely. In the meantime, as though some invisible hand had added fresh logs, the fire at his back grew hotter.

Henry's smile grew thin, and Larry sensed an undercurrent of menace. The long fingers were dancing along the sides of the black pot.

"Well?" the deep voice asked. "Just ABOUT perfect? About? What wasn't perfect? You'd better tell me because you know I'll find out anyway. I find out everything." The smile grew wider and deeper. The flames were reflected perfectly in Henry's round gold rimmed glasses.

Larry knew how to survive. Suddenly, despite the inferno at his back, he felt cool, calm and collected. "The pot was just where you said it would be and I spotted it early in the evening. The problem was a dinner party. Those fuckers were having a damned dinner party. I had to hide in the closet. When I crept out, the husband heard me and I blasted him. I hear this bawling and screeching upstairs so I go up and finish her, then I leave. Everything was perfect, like I said. The only thing that went wrong was that I had to wait so long in the closet. That's what I meant. I coulda got here earlier if it hadn't been for that."

Henry's smile looked pasted on his face. Instead of eyes, Larry was staring into glasses with their reflected flames. "So you got rid of the Eastgates, packed up our little treasure here, and then what?"

Larry saw himself leaving the Eastgates. He packed the pot carefully in his brief case, turned off all the lights, set the bolt so the door would lock after him, and carefully walked down the front sidewalk into his getaway car. It was still as death, the only sound a distant siren.

"Well, like I said, I silenced the Eastgates, slipped out quietly, jumped into the rented Tempo, caught the plane and came back."

Henry sat across from Larry as if waiting for more. He pressed his lips together and worked his fingers like a cage, back and forth. "Hmmmm. And what about the Tempo? What did you do with it before you caught this oh-so-smooth flight back to Albuquerque?"

Larry remembered that in La Mesa he'd been John Sanders, the identity he used for his towing business, the same person he'd been when he towed Henry and Clara out of the ditch before Thanksgiving, after the "accident." Usually, he was a sort of *dummkopf* working clod when he was Sanders, wearing lumberjack shirts and backwards baseball caps. Normally Sanders had a crew cut hair style, one of Larry's many wigs. But this time, he'd been pressed for time. Henry gave orders an hour before he had to leave.

When he'd rented a car in Albuquerque, he'd been Don Fallows, the nondescript business man who always wore a polyester brown suit and could disappear into any crowd. While Sanders had a big, childish handwriting that slanted forward with regular, schoolboy letters, Fallows' writing was erratic and jagged, sometimes forward and sometimes straight up and down, occasionally leaning back.

Larry had studied graphology and he knew which letters gave away the writer. He carefully shaped different "t's" to go with each persona. He'd studied acting in his two years of college at the College of Santa Fe, and he knew how to change his voice and posture.

113

Larry snapped. Lapses gave Henry time to read his mind. He talked fast. "Oh yeah, I am kinda foggy. A kid cried the whole way back to Albuquerque and I didn't get any sleep."

Henry yawned and said nothing.

"John Sanders turned the car in at LaMesa Budget Rental Car. I took a nearly deserted shuttle to the airport. You remember Sanders, that bloke who picked you and Clara up in the Thanksgiving snowstorm." He tried unsuccessfully to chuckle, but it came out more like a choking. Larry swallowed and took a deep breath. "Like I said, everything smooth as silk."

The fire died down. Not that Larry could see it, but his back was no longer baking, and the crackling had dwindled. Instead, a hissing, sizzling, settling down kind of sound came from the fireplace. The fire was dying. Oddly, as the room grew colder, it also grew brighter.

Larry thought maybe the Torchieres had been turned up. He remembered how enchanted Thelma had been with the three-way bulbs. Mongolion bulbs, or some such name. But Henry hadn't moved for the last half hour. Could the Torchieres have lit up on their own? Maybe Henry had them rigged. *Careful, careful,* he scolded himself. *You're losing it.*

Still not moving from his chair, Henry put a stack of bills on the table, next to the gleaming pot. "Here, all 20K. You've earned it, and in fact, I have another assignment for you. Now, listen carefully. "

Henry took off the gold-rimmed spectacles and pulled his chair closer to Larry. Larry took the rubber-banded stack of bills, wrapped them in the shirt that had covered the pot and carefully placed them in the briefcase. His fatigue gave over to exhilaration.

"I'm all ears."

"As you know," Henry began, "I used to date Clara Jordan. She got too interested in my business, so I cut her off. Of course you know, you towed us out of the snowbank last month. That was the last time I've had anything to do with that little busybody."

"Sure, I remember that you needed to keep an eye on her. That's when John Sanders started his towing company and we rescued you from freezing." It gave Larry a lot of satisfaction to remember how easily he'd slipped into the role of Sanders.

Henry continued, a crease furrowing his brow and his blue eyes turning into slits. "Clara seems to be nosing around again. I watch her through the two-way mirror in the adjoining office to the computer lab. She's spending a lot of time surfing the Internet with some student of hers. A few days ago, after the student left, I checked out the hard drive and the printer queue found the Eastgate address. It had been printed out.

"Now why do you suppose anyone would be interested in some address in LaMesa, California? And what would anyone do with the information? I deleted everything, but I'm not sure that kid...Carmichael, Carnell, something like that ...didn't take the address with him. Even if he didn't print it out, he may remember it.

"Dammit, Butt, you were supposed to keep an eye on Clara and make sure that she was too busy worrying about her own safety to pry into my business. Here's the plan. As John Sanders, you are to fill in for John Herrera, the custodian. Herrera is going to be out for back surgery and I've already told Taggert that you'd be perfect for the job. That way you can lurk around her classroom and the computer lab to make sure that she and what's his name aren't learning anything they shouldn't be. I've tried to make a date with Miss Busybody to see what's on her mind, but I need extra surveillance by you. Your mission is to do whatever is necessary to keep my cover. I take the pottery to Amsterdam in four days, and I need absolute security. Is that clear?" Henry was almost friendly. Now that Larry had proved himself.

It was clear, but Larry had a few questions.

"I understand, boss. I'll show up as the janitor tomorrow. I doubt if anyone even notices. We're both named 'John'." Thinking it might raise Henry's opinion of him, he added, "I've already been trailing that Clara dame. I gave her a little scare too, cut her cat's ear in two. Just a warning, to mind her own beeswax. How far should I go? Do you want me to get rid of her?"

His boss had only two modes: beneficent or irate. Larry wanted to ask about the money, but he was afraid that Henry's good humor would vanish, and he needed for Henry to be mellow. He needed to stay on his good side.

"You said it, I didn't." Henry smirked. "I have just a few days to make arrangement for the Ackerman deal, and I sure as hell don't need Clara's meddling. Do whatever you have to do."

This was the first Larry heard of the Ackerman deal, but he didn't let on. He relished the idea of trailing that bitch. She was dense, he decided. After he cut her cat's ear, she didn't catch on, and the next time he saw that grey dust mop of a cat slinking around, he'd wring its neck. The remains would be strewn in the cave where Clara liked to hang out, next to the petroglyphs. She'd find the carcass. It was just a matter of time.

Henry stood up and opened the trap door for Larry's ignominious exit from his lair. Larry strapped the briefcase to his chest, put his suit coat on and buttoned it up. Somehow, during the last part of their talk, the room returned to semi-darkness.

115

Still energized, Larry could hardly keep from grinning. He stepped down into the dark hole beneath Henry's log cabin floor.

"Yeah, boss, whatever it takes."

14
Retrieval by Internet

The alarm clock dragged Clara from a troubled sleep. Six a.m. If she was going to run and still make it to school on time, she had to swing into action right away. It was upsetting to have Oscar still missing. She was used to his prowling around her head in the morning, often purring in her ear, behavior that almost always saved her from having to rely on the alarm.

She went to the front door, expecting him to be outside, waiting impatiently to get in out of the cold. He sometimes pulled all-nighters like this, out hunting no doubt, but he always came home by morning.

But today there was no Oscar on the front porch. Shivering in her blue robe, she stood at the door and called him for several minutes. No response. In the distance, some coyotes were howling. She hoped Oscar hadn't become their dinner.

"Poor kitty, you'll use up your nine lives," she said to herself.

She would call him on her run, taking the ridge road this morning and then going toward the village on tomorrow's run. He was still a young cat, less than two years old, and she'd heard of cats being at the top of trees or houses and afraid to climb down. Oscar could be really dumb.

Clara pinned the house key to her waistband and stepped into the freezing pre-dawn darkness. If Oscar was anywhere in the vicinity, she would find him. She strained her eyes to see where the porch steps were, feeling her way along. Once she reached the dirt road in front of her cabin, it would be easier. She knew the road in front of her cabin so well that even in the dim half-light, she ran steadily.

The air felt damp, as though it were going to snow at any minute. As Clara's eyes adjusted to the dim light, she could make out the black silhouettes of trees bordering the left side of the road. A few hundred yards ahead, she spotted the tall ponderosa that signalled the beginning of her path up the ridge.

"Here Oscar, here kitty, kitty, kitty. Heeeeerrrre, Oscar," she crooned as she ran. Maybe he was injured. She stopped to listen for a mew or rustle.

Nothing but a wintry silence. Turning up the path to the ridge, Clara thought about the injury to Oscar's ear. Could it be that whoever did that had catnapped Oscar? Suddenly all the weirdness of the past month overwhelmed Clara and she started to cry. The death of Speckled Horse, her adoptive father's illness, the neverending search for her

117

biological family, phone calls with nobody on the other end, and now this. Deep wrenching sobs wracked through her as she ascended the craggy path to the ridge. She could hardly breathe, but she kept running.

This was a run to look for Oscar, not to wallow in sadness, Clara reminded herself. Besides it was too cold to cry. After using her bandanna to dry her face and blow her nose, Clara resumed her calls for Oscar.

A weak sunlight filtered through the ponderosas and the sky took on a pinkish glow. Despite her sadness, Clara was struck by the beauty of this place, the delicacy of the winter light. She stopped once more and listened for any sight or sign of her cat.

Instead of Oscar, she heard another runner coming up behind her. Her alarm gave way to relief, when she saw that it was Jerome. She remembered that he was also a morning runner. But what on earth would he think, after hearing her screeching for Oscar and her uncontrolled sobbing? That is, if he heard her.

"Aloha," he called out. "Hi there, Clara, mind if I run with you?"

"I'd love the company, but I don't want to hold you back."

"This is a light day for me. I ran 12 miles yesterday, getting ready for the Avenue of the Giants Marathon. It's not until May, but I'm building up my mileage slowly. If I add miles too fast, I always get injured."

They'd reached the end of the ridgetop and were now running downhill in the last part of a three-mile loop. The newly-risen sun glinted on the pine needles. It was turning into a beautiful morning.

Clara was happy not to be alone. She explained the situation with Oscar and told Jerome how worried she was about him. He adjusted his pace to hers, and they ran smoothly together. This was the first time since the school year started she'd had anyone to run with, and it felt nice.

As if reading her mind, Jerome began, "I don't mean to be sticking my nose in your business, Clara, but is something bothering you? It seems that you're upset."

Clara felt the blood rush to her face. She must have sounded idiotic, screeching for Oscar and crying. She proceeded to tell him everything, beginning with the quest for biological parents, having to spend the night in a cave during the recent deluge, the weird hangups on the phone, Oscar's disappearance. She didn't tell him about Henry and his unpleasant behavior. She really didn't want him to think she was still involved with someone else.

But it turned out that Henry DiMarco was who he wanted to talk about. The dirt path had widened enough so they could just barely run side by side. Clara watched her footing. To the right was a steep drop-off ending in a mountain stream.

"I'm still working on the Speckled Horse case, along with the sheriff's office, as you probably know," Jerome said. "We are hitting a lot of blind alleys, but there is one person who seems to have some connections, and we're working to learn as much as possible about him. I think you used to date him."

"Oh, you mean Henry?" Of course that's who he meant. Henry was the only man she'd dated in the two years since she and Hugh parted company. In the past, the mention of Henry's name would have brought pleasant thoughts and a warm feeling. Now it caused a mild wave of fear. Ever since the snow storm episode...

"Do you have any reason to think he's trailing you?" Jerome asked. "We think he may be involved in an artifact smuggling ring that could have involved Speckled Horse. If he thinks you know something about him, you may be in danger."

Clara recalled her terror during the aborted trip to the Albuquerque airport. She felt uneasy around Henry ever since then. Not that she'd interacted with him very much. Except for the latest unpleasant encounter at the computer lab, she'd hardly seen him. The two-way mirror that separated an office from the computer lab might have provided a hiding place for Henry to spy on her, but that was ridiculous. She dismissed the thought as paranoia as soon as it entered her mind.

"All I know about Henry is what everybody knows, that he was with an investment firm in New York, a really important, high-paying job, but he got sick of the rat race and moved back to Santa Fe to live with his parents. After a month of that, he said, he built a cabin on some of the land they own off Old Santa Fe Trail. I've been to his cabin once. It's surrounded by pinons and looks out across a broad plain at the Jemez Mountains. He told me he got involved with the school because his parents are on the AIA board. Apparently they've given hundreds of thousands of dollars to help it get started.

"Henry and I are finished, and I wouldn't even say we're just friends. But I seriously doubt that he has any reason for trailing me. I've heard that he's going with Wren Taggert now. That's according to my best friend Annie."

"Hmmm. Did you ever trace the call after there was a hang-up? Does anyone else have the keys to your cabin? Have you ever seen any signs of anyone coming in when you weren't home?"

"No to all three." I wish I could help, Jerome. But I just can't see Henry having any interest in what I do. If there is anyone stalking me, I don't think it would be Henry." She didn't tell Jerome her feeling that Henry was interested only in sleeping with her. She was another notch in his belt, and once he had her, he was ready for the next conquest. Remembering how used she felt at the time made her angry all over again. If she hadn't been breathing so hard trying to keep up with Jerome, she would have sighed.

As they neared her cabin, the sun hid behind a cloud, and the promise of good weather faded. More clouds were gathering -- dark, heavy harbingers of snow. Clara thought she saw something move on her front porch, a gray, shadowy form. Could it be Oscar?

"Here, kitty, kitty, kitty," she called out once again. With Jerome at her side, she sprinted up her driveway. To her disappointment, the porch was empty. As tears spilled from her eyes, she turned away. She didn't want Jerome to notice. Taking her key from her waistband, she fumbled for the lock.

"I'm sorry for carrying on like this, but Oscar was my best friend. We've been together for ten years. And it's not just Oscar, it's everything. I've just been terribly worried lately."

Jerome wrapped his muscular arms around her and rubbed her back as she wept. She was too distraught to pull away but instead, buried her head in his chest while he stroked her hair.

After a few minutes, she felt her tears were used up. She pulled away gently and looked up into his sympathetic deep brown eyes. Snowflakes were beginning to drift through the air.

"I feel like such a fool, and we're both freezing. How about coming inside for some hot coffee before you finish your run?" She was surprised and pleased at how natural it was to be enfolded in Jerome's arms.

"I'll see you in, but I think I'll take a raincheck on the coffee. My route has five more miles, and if I get too warm and comfortable, I may never finish. I'll see you inside, and then I'd better get back in gear."

Once they were in Clara's cozy living room, Jerome gave her another hug. "Let's meet again, but not by accident. As soon as I make some progress on the Speckled Horse case, I'll be calling you. For now, I've got to follow through on some of our leads. Please call me if you notice anything strange. And I promise to call Oscar wherever I run."

He handed her a card that read "Jerome Naranjo, Private Investigator/ Santa Clara Pueblo/ Route 229, Number 34/ Phone (505) 950-3446. E-Mail <Jerome@santaclara.com>, put on a windbreaker he had tied around his waist, and left to finish his run.

Clara felt happier than she had in weeks. She peeled off her clothes and jumped into a steaming shower, patted dry, wrapped herself

120

in her blue fleece robe, and twisted a towel around her long black hair. She patted moisturizing cream on her throat, cheeks, and forehead. Normally she did not wear makeup to class, just a dash of lipstick and a dab of blush. But today she was going to go all out.

She smiled at what seemed like the height of foolishness. Any man would have done what Jerome did, comforting her when she was upset, making sure she got in her house, making pleasant small talk about getting together. He was just being polite. Still...

She had just put on a blue corduroy jumpsuit and laced up her Doc Martens when she noticed a blinking light on the answering machine.

When had someone called? She knew it had to be after she left to go run. It might have been when she was in the shower. She pushed *Play*. A long silence followed by a click. Could it be someone letting her knew he knew when she was gone?

She felt so alone and vulnerable. This couldn't be happening... If only she had checked the machine when Jerome was here.

Twenty minutes later, as she drove into the parking lot of the communications building, she tried to put the hellish morning out of her mind. Her students needed for her to be all there, and furthermore, she and Carnell were going to work in the computer lab during the lunch hour. The more time she spent with Carnell, the closer she felt to finding her roots. Despite everything else going on around her, the search for her biological family had never seemed more promising. Hope burned inside her like a pilot light.

Her students never failed to snap her out of whatever low mood she happened to be in. Deena had been writing poetry on her own, at Clara's suggestion, and today she handed in five new creations with a handwritten note on the top sheet:

Dear Ms. Jordan, These are poems about my grandmother, a potter who worked into her eighties and made a pot the day before she died. I plan to enter these in my book, but before I make them final, I would like your suggestions. Thank you.

Your student Deena

"I really like what you're doing with your family history, Deena. I'll put these in my brief case and read them when I have time in the next couple nights."

She took attendance. Christine was absent for the fifth day in a row. Some of the kids had told her she was pregnant and her parents had sent her to relatives in Arizona, but others said that was just a rumor.

Treena volunteered to take some homework to Christine's family when she went home this weekend. Treena, like Christine, was from Laguna Pueblo.

Descriptive writing was today's emphasis, and Clara had the class begin by sketching and making notes about their favorite places in nature. After twenty minutes, she called on various students to read their paragraphs in front of the rest of the class. Then, after the presentations, she had them pair up and do peer reviews. They were to check each other on spelling, grammar, vocabulary and interest. The reviewer made notes as he or she reviewed, and the notes were to be labeled and handed in along with the essays.

She had them well-trained, and they were good at working on their own. This was a process they'd done since the beginning of the year. In a rare moment of inattentiveness to her class, Clara reached in her briefcase for a manila folder that contained the Lost Deer Page printout. Carnell had said something about hypertext or clicking on "links" that apparently would take you to more information, kind of like uncovering a box within a box within a box. She thought she understood, but they'd had to stop before getting to them. That was the first thing she would ask Carnell about during their lunchtime session.

She looked up, prepared to interact with the class if necessary. However, everyone was writing, and it looked as though peace would reign at least for another five minutes. She read more of the web page text.

What does Lost Deer mean?

Lost Deer means a child who will be lost to his or her family, heritage, spirituality, ancestral history, and language forever. This was a name given to a little Pueblo girl when she was taken from the arms of a Grandmother and placed in the arms of a man who belonged to the Dominant Culture. As he pulled the little child out of the Grandmother's arms, the Grandmother began calling to her, "Lost Deer, Lost Deer!" The Grandmother knew that this child would never be able to find her way back to her People, she would always be lost.

That's what she was, a Lost Deer. If only this page had some of the "links" that Carnell told her about, she might be able to connect with someone who could lead her back to **her** people. It wasn't that Will and Louise, who had raised her with such love and care, weren't wonderful parents. That wasn't it at all. She loved and respected them, and she always would. She was fiercely loyal to them. But another part of her longed to be in her other Mother's arms, to be with parents who shared her dark skin and coarse jet black hair, who had her high, chiseled cheekbones and widely spaced teeth. They had to be out there. Clara felt in her heart that they must know she was searching. Surely they would respond to her hand stretched out across time, distance, and years. And the Internet would provide the atmosphere for this reaching.

Just as her students were finishing up their writing and reviewing exercise, Clara caught a line of the Lost Deer Page she'd overlooked. In blue boldface letters was the phrase **Resource for those Looking for their Biological Families.** If there were a link that would lead her anywhere, surely this was it.

Usually she was there for her students, but this morning, Clara could think of nothing but the web page for "lost deer." Automatic pilot, that's what Will used to say about Louise when her mind was occupied with a new dress design or beading project. She would go around for hours at a time cleaning house or fixing meals while mentally she was back at the sewing machine or beading table. The right kind of sleeve or color of bead would occur to her and she would leave Will and Clara abruptly to get back to her "real" work.

Maybe that's why Louise didn't seem to notice as Will grew increasingly vague and absent-minded. Or maybe she knew all along that his mind was going and her zealousness for crafts was an escape, a form of denial.

Clarissa Quick-to-See raised her hand. "Ms. Jordan, you said you'd give us an idea of the auction prizes. I've got 200 tickets and I'd like to know ahead of time what we're going to be bidding on.

"Of course. I forgot all about it. The bell's about to ring, but I'll give you at least part of the list. If I'm interrupted, I'll finish the rest tomorrow. Ok, here goes. Calculator; tennis racket; 10 certificates for ice cream sundaes at Mom's Ice Cream (they're 10 separate prizes); gift certificates for dinner for two at La Choza, Diego's, Tiny's, Maria's Kitchen, Cloud Cliff Bakery, Tecolote Cafe, and Souper Salad; a pair of cross country skis and poles; a tape recorder; a portable CD player; and gift certificates at several sports stores and bookstores.

The lunch bell interrupted her catalogue of prizes. "Ok, students, I'll finish the list first thing tomorrow. Revise your essays tonight and we'll read them out loud to one another. Practice reading to your roommates. Ask them for suggestions about projecting your voice, using eye contact and pacing yourself. Have fun with this, and I'll see you tomorrow.

Classes were dismissed early today so students could participate in the annual pre-Christmas dorm cleanup. This was a tradition started by the retired Ms. Fine, a much-loved language arts teacher, who discovered that her students were incredibly stressed by the demands of school at this time of year and that when their parents came to pick them up for the holidays they were not packed and ready.

Eight years ago, the tireless Ms. Fine had supervised the entire cleanup herself. Since then, the school had more than doubled, and now the event was supervised by dorm parents. The teachers were supposed to use this time for making lesson plans, but she had already mapped out her classwork through the end of January, so she was going to work with Carnell on Internet. As an honors student, Carnell, along with two other top students lived in an on-campus apartment. For honors students, the cleanup was optional.

When she arrived at the Macintosh lab, Carnell was already seated at a monitor, engrossed and clicking away with the mouse. He was browsing on Native Net, looking up personal web pages and expanding his already vast e-mail correspondence pool.

"Oh hi, Ms. Jordan, I got here kind of early cuz my uncle and aunt and cousins are here from Dulce and they want to take me shopping with them at the factory stores. I have an hour we can work together, and I can show you all you need to know to search on your own. We'll go over how to send and receive e-mail and I can help you get connected up at home in the next couple days. Clara had ordered a modem card from a mail order computer warehouse but she didn't want to take any chances on connecting things up improperly. She would wait until Carnell could come over to help her.

Clara sat at the monitor and Carnell moved to the seat beside her. They browsed through the news groups on Native Net and entered into some online chats. While interesting, nothing led anywhere valuable. Everyone in the so-called "rooms" had bizarre nicknames: Gomerpyle, LUV2rite, Catgirl, Mindhead, IdeaPete. Clara amused herself with imagining who was behind each name. The conversations were inane, aimless and often just plain dumb.

"Let's get to something more meaningful," she suggested to Carnell. "These people -- whoever they are -- don't seem to have a life. I think it's amazing that they spend all this time trying to talk with people they don't even know."

Even as she said it, she realized that she was about to do just that. But this was different: she was trying to find her roots, the mother who had given her life.

"Yeah," Carnell agreed, "I was just thinking that. Let's return to the "Lost Deer Page" and check out the links you were interested in.

They went to the web sites Carnell had bookmarked from earlier work they'd done together. Clara clicked on Lost Deer Home Page and scrolled down the side for something that might get her back on track with her search. ICWA (Indian Child Welfare Act) was in blue lettering, so she clicked on it. Sure enough, this was a link.

"You're a good teacher, Carnell," she said. "I'm learning to tell what links are and how to access them and how to, how do you say it? to navigate."

Carnell beamed. Unbeknown to anyone, he had a crush on Ms. Jordan, even though Sharon Cheraposie, a Tesuque Pueblo girl, was going around telling everyone that they were going together.

Clara clicked on a link. Here, just as she remembered it, was the Indian Child Welfare Act. Her earlier assumptions were correct.

If the mother or father was unable to take care of the child properly, stated the act, no considerations were ever given to the other members of the family as to whether or not they wished to adopt the baby. American Indians had no rights, no voice, as to what happened to their children.

ICWA was created to put a halt to this adoption policy and to give American Indians the same rights everyone had when it came to their children and their families. However, there were people who found ways of getting around this law.

Clara scrolled down the web page, reading about several cases in which ICWA was being ignored.

Carnell's uncle Jake and three cousins appeared at the door of the computer lab. "Your Aunt Millie is out in the Trooper waiting for you, guy." Jake was a smiling, portly man wearing corduroy slacks and a Dallas Cowboys sweatshirt and the cousins, who ranged from seven to twelve, were adorable. She could tell how much they loved Carnell.

"Opps, gotta go. Sorry to leave so suddenly, but we promised the kids that after shopping in Albuquerque, we'd take them on rides at Uncle Cliff's Amusement Park."

Clara felt a pang. For a moment, she wished she were going on the outing instead of continuing with her search. After Carnell and entourage left, she returned to her task with a mixture of determination and weariness.

Why not just go home and see if her cat had returned? She was tempted to just give up. There wasn't a snowball's chance in hell, as Will used to say, that she would find her roots through the Internet, and yet it seemed that she had exhausted other possibilities.

But chances were that Oscar wouldn't be there. She had a sinking feeling about it. If he were alive, hunger would have called him back home by now. Clara would just stay here in the computer lab until the school day was over at 3 p.m. Even if she found nothing, it was better than facing the disappointment of an empty house.

Aimlessly, she clicked on various lost deer links, reading about more legislation, more myths about the lost deer, a tale of Zintkala Nuni and the Wounded Knee Massacre of the Lakota people.

She was not paying close attention when suddenly she came to a link titled "The stories of thirteen modern day lost deer." Clicking on the addresses, she began reading the lost ones' postings.

"CWacon" wrote, *Today I received the sad news from my friend that her nephew, who is Navajo, would not be returned to her family. The child was placed with a 'white' family after his birth. This adoption has broken two laws in particular which I pointed out in my previous post. This news has devastated all of us.*

"PaulaNotHelpHim" wrote, *I received the most shocking and unbelievable words that one could possibly ever want to hear, that our case to bring my niece home had been decided and that she will remain with Leonard and Betty Linstad. My breath was taken away for just a second, I had to swallow hard for a couple of times to keep the grief, the hurt and the tears from coming. The grief and hurt were momentary, the tears will always be there, but for joy when my niece comes home.*

She clicked her way through twelve of these messages, calls from cyberspace, vignettes of the pain and suffering caused by separation from sons and daughters, some tales of children looking for their real parents. It was nearly three p.m., when she could legitimately leave school. But why, she thought, leave the last message unread.

She clicked on the final link of the "Modern Day Lost Deer" section. GSuina wrote, *My daughter Lucy was taken from me so long ago, but it seems only yesterday. The tears I have cried since I lost my beautiful daughter could make a river or an ocean. It has been 30 years since I last saw Lucy. The social worker took Lucy, who was ill, away from me because she said I could not care for her. This was an icy place in the road of my life but I recovered. A white doctor who worked at the Santa Fe Indian Hospital and his wife took my Lucy illegally and moved far away. I was poor, with no family support, and I could not trace them. My husband, a German immigrant, was not liked by my people, San Ildefonso, and I think my family was actually glad when he died in a tragic car accident. But all that is water under the bridge. I am out of tears, but I have become strong. I am posting this because I want to find my daughter, to reconnect with her. Josephine Gurule, who designed this web site, encouraged me to post this search. My daughter should*

126

remember her grandmother Antoinette, the illustrious potter, whose trademark was the arrow of life. My daughter, though she was very young, would spend long hours by her grandmother's side as she potted. She was a very artistic child who would draw arrows with her crayons. This is how you will know if you belong to me. Lucy, if your are out there, please e-mail your mother.

    Clara felt blood rushing to her cheeks. It couldn't be, but then again, it just might...she remembered that the name on the file had read "Baby Lucy." She definitely remembered drawing arrows when she was quite young. In fact, she was sure about the arrow memory when she'd been trapped overnight in that hidden-away cave. Yes, arrows had been in her past. And she knew in her heart that Greta must be her mother.

    Clara stayed late at the monitor, writing and rewriting her response to Greta. Basically, she said that she would like to establish an e-mail correspondence and if they both felt comfortable about it, to meet sometime in the future.

    Annie came by the lab to see if she wanted to go out to dinner, but Clara told her friend only that she was finishing up some work and they could maybe go out tomorrow night.

    Though it seemed completely deserted in the computer department, Clara was not alone. In the office, watching her through the two-way mirror, sat Larry Butt.

15

Something wicked this way comes...

Ruth Holland, a semi-retired petroglyph expert and writer, was having trouble writing the conclusion for her weekly column in the Mesa Monitor, "Confessions of a Rock Hound." She'd had a quiet Thanksgiving, and decided it would be best to go to bed early and finish her writing job in the morning. A firm believer in the adage "Necessity is the mother of invention," when she had to come up with ideas, she always did.

A soft-spoken, well-read and extremely articulate woman in her early sixties, Ruth could truly say that she enjoyed her now single state. She preferred the company of Max the cat to that of her ex-husband Nicholas, who had -- in predictable style -- thrown her over for his secretary, a blond 25-year-old with remarkable breasts, good legs, a passable face, a head with little in it but limitless admiration for Nicholas.

After their daughter Jill graduated from college and was launched with a good job and a fiance, Ruth had nothing to keep her in Santa Fe, New Mexico, where she'd been a high school English teacher. Even during her marriage to Nicholas, even before he abandoned her, Ruth -- previously bisexual -- discovered that she preferred women to men. When her college roommate Andrea, with whom she'd had a brief affair, invited her to a visit to La Mesa, she gladly left Santa Fe. She went in July a year ago, fell in love not with Andrea but with the town itself, packed her entire house, and moved to La Mesa.

She was reading in bed when she first heard a disturbance coming from several houses away. Maybe it was a domestic squabble. Never one to meddle in the business of others, Ruth tried to ignore the screams. Finally they stopped, and she went back to her reading. She heard a car leaving fast, and opened the window. She instantly recognized the roar of flames and ran to the phone to call 911. The fire department spent the rest of that hellish night battling the inferno. A crowd gathered around what had been the Eastgate mansion, but Ruth hadn't joined them.

Along with the rest of La Mesa, California, she had tried since that chaotic night to make sense of the grisly murder arson in their midst. Every day, the *Monitor* reported more of the story, but as the details piled up, the mystery deepened. The Eastgates, wrote a *Monitor* reporter, made wealthy by both inheritances and successful high-level careers, were well liked and respected in the community. No one knew of apparent enemies. They were known for their philanthropy and their collection of rare and precious artifacts from all over the world. Clarence and Lanie Boynton, who were the last friends to see them alive, told the reporter about a piece of black Indian pottery, their latest acquisition, that the Eastgates proudly displayed to them earlier in the evening.

"I remember that real good," Lanie gushed to a *Monitor* reporter, "cause as soon as Dan held up the pot, my little Jimmy, who never in his short little life'd rolled over, rolled off the bed onto the floor in the next room and screamed bloody murder. I downright hated that pot 'cause it seemed to put a curse on that sweet baby. Thank goodness, he seems OK now, but... " The reporter cut her off, needing more relevant information from the Boyntons.

However, Ruth, who was collecting all the newspaper's stories about the Eastgate tragedy, made a note of the pottery. She would e-mail her good friend Hollis Bentley at the Santa Fe *New Mexican* about the pottery. Detectives on the case had given the *Monitor* an artist's sketch from the Boynton's verbal description, and Ruth thought that perhaps Hollis might know something about the pueblo the pot might have come from. She liked the idea of using her connections to help police close in on the villain.

Following La Mesa's Thanksgiving disaster, Roberta Logan, manager at the Dairy Queen, was reading the *Monitor*. Roberta, a platinum blond somewhere between 30 and 45, possessed a kind of brassy prettiness, and a deep, throaty voice that men found irresistible. She'd risen through the ranks at Dairy Queen, starting out as a dishwasher and advancing in just two years to the top position.

"Couple Dies in Fire," blazed the newspaper headlines. A photo of the gutted out Eastgate home was accompanied by reporter Bryce Walker's account.

In the quiet La Mesa neighborhood of Altavista, Walker began, *it seemed like a peaceful holiday. Dan and Carol Eastgate, a retired surgeon and his writer/professor wife were entertaining their friends Clarence and Lana Boynton. After a dinner of turkey and stuffing, said Mrs. Boynton, they looked at the Eastgates latest acquisitions, including a black San Ildefonso pot. The Eastgates are well-known folk art collectors. Her baby fell off the bed as they were admiring the pot, Mrs. Boynton related, and shortly after the show and tell, they went home.*

Roberta shuddered as she read "Thanksgiving from Hell." Something was floating around in the back of her mind, and it had to do with Thanksgiving. Most of her colleagues at Dairy Queen had families or at least children, but since she was alone in the world, she had volunteered to work during the restaurant's abbreviated hours.

On that Thursday, it had been practically deserted. Nearly everyone was home with loved ones. She was the kind of person who didn't mind being alone, kind of enjoyed it. She and Josie, the cook, joked about it in the morning. "Now, who would be coming in here on Thanksgiving? Only people who didn't celebrate the holiday. But since it didn't have racial or ethnic overtones, maybe it was kind of innocuous, like Valentine's Day or Halloween. Not really offending most people's philosophy or religion.

Roberta loved games of chance, and she loved to bet. She bet Josie five dollars that they would have fewer than 30 customers all Thanksgiving day. During the morning hours, only five or six customers straggled through, most of them drivers on their way somewhere and wanting coffee. It looked as though she would win, Roberta told herself. She started planning what she would do with the five dollars. Maybe go to a matinee of the new Stephen King movie at the Roxy, maybe buy the latest suspense novel by her favorite writer Jann Arrington Wolcott, maybe buy a new lipstick at Suzie's Discount Beauty Supply.

When a nondescript man in a brown suit ordered a hamburger and coffee at one o'clock, Roberta chalked him up as customer number seven. She was not happy to see him. Maybe Josie was right and business would pick up toward evening and they'd be swamped by three or four in the afternoon.

She remembered how nervous the man seemed under a veneer of calm, and how he appeared to be killing time. Most people bought their food, wolfed it down, and escaped from the plastic, melamine and stainless steel atmosphere as quickly as possible. But this guy ate his hamburger slowly and deliberately. He got three coffee refills, and he read the *Monitor* page by page, even the classified ads. At one point, Roberta thought he was trying to flirt with her, but then he went back to the newspaper's crossword puzzle. Several kids came in and got ice cream cones, but the man in the brown suit didn't seem to notice them.

What was it, she asked herself, that seemed dangerous about him? It wasn't just his presence at the formica topped table, his lingering over the *Monitor*'s crossword puzzle or his frequent looking at the time. In her years of working the fast food places, Roberta was used to customers using the restaurant as a kind of holding pattern, a way station. When you didn't know where else to go, you could always kill some time at the fast food joint.

Clearly, Mr. Nobody was filling up his afternoon, just waiting. But unlike others who hung out at Dairy Queen, this guy was tense, coiled tightly, clearly waiting for something specific. His anonymous outfit was too neat and new looking, his shoes weren't scuffed, everything was in place. He reminded Roberta of one of those replicates in science fiction movies. He might have been an alien from another planet disguised as a person or a human who'd been given an implant, maybe in his left ear.

She wanted to get back to *Deathmark,* the thriller she was devouring, but with Mr. Brown Suit Nobody lurking around, she had to pretend to keep busy. She polished the formica counters for the nth time, made fresh coffee, replenished all the styrofoam cups, plates, and straws; filled all the bins with packets of salt, pepper, sugar, artificial sugar, catsup, mustard, and mayonnaise; made sure the napkin holders were full.

Her attempts at conversation were met with silence, although once she caught him looking at her with a cold stare, a reptilian look that sent chills down her spine. Best to avoid eye contact, she quickly decided.

Definitely bizarre. It was four p.m. when Clo, the late shift clerk reported for duty, and Roberta was relieved to escape. Her heart beat faster when she had to walk by this creep, and the minute she hopped into her 1999 Honda Accord, she locked all the doors. The horrible thought passed through her mind that maybe he was interested in her and that he might leave and follow her home. Instead of taking a direct route to her apartment on Orange Street, she turned right three times to throw him off track and then got on Interstate 5, the long way home. No one seemed to be following her, but she would not breathe easily until she got home and locked the door tightly behind her.

16

Death Trap

The telephone's sharp ring pierced through Clara's dream of running in a grassy meadow. She reached toward the nightstand next to her bed and fumbled for the receiver. Lately she'd been afraid every time the phone rang it might be the mysterious silent caller who simply breathed; it might be Louise calling with more bad news about Will's condition; or it might be horrible Henry.

To her relief it was Annie. "Hi, sorry to call so early. I'm having car problems and I wonder if we could work something out so you could pick me up and we could still keep our dinner date tonight."

"Sure. I keep telling you that green bomb will be the death of you. That thing needs to be junked, not fixed. It's beyond therapy." Clara stifled a yawn. "But sure. I'll be glad to pick you up, and yes, we can still go out. But it's not even six. Let me wake up and I'll call you right back."

The air was freezing, the cabin floor like ice. Clara threw on her robe and turned up the thermostat. If he'd been around Oscar would be yowling to be fed. With the colder weather, he demanded more food. Despite the veterinarian's warning that Oscar should lose a couple of pounds to avoid developing feline diabetes, Clara nearly always gave in to his pitiful laments. He was getting roly-poly, but when the weather got warmer and he could frisk around outdoors and climb trees, Oscar would slim down to a healthier weight.

But Oscar was on a permanent vacation or else gone forever. She had to get over it. Clara ground Italian Roast beans and brewed a small pot of coffee. She was definitely going to cut down on her caffeine intake, but now was not the time. After her second cup of strong coffee laced with half and half, she sat down at the small table in her bedroom. A dog-eared, day-by-day calendar showed her agenda for Wednesday, December 11. She was taking her classes to the library so they could develop topics for term papers that they'd begin next semester after the break. Good. She'd have a chance to fine-tune her schedule to mesh with Annie's so they could get together for dinner. That green disaster of a jalopy had to go. The best thing that could happen to Annie was if she couldn't drive it at all. Then she'd have to buy a new car. Clara kept telling her that the green car was really a monster.

It was too late to run, and she couldn't go at noon because she wanted to try to see Estrellita during her lunch break. This was the third day in a row she'd had to miss, and not running put her in a foul mood.

Trying to be upbeat nonetheless, Clara chose today's clothes with care. She put on waffle-soled, black, lace-up boots, a white lycra and cotton turtleneck, some red and blue beaded earrings one of her students had made, and a long black wool jumper, A-line.

She opened the door and yelled out for Oscar. "Here, kitty, kitty, kitty...here, kitty, kitty, kitty." Of course, no Oscar appeared. By now, he had probably starved or been eaten by coyotes. Clara blinked back tears. For nine years, Oscar had been her faithful friend. When she first got him, she used to carry him around in her jacket pocket. Even though it had been a week, she wasn't ready to admit that he was gone for good.

Cold, dry winter wind whooshed through the treetops around her cabin. Clara stood gazing up at the sky and trees as though she could make Oscar materialize. When she finally looked down, a piece of gray fluff in the corner of the porch caught her eye. She leaned over to pick it up. My God, this wasn't fluff, it was a severed, fur-covered leg. "Oh no," she screamed. "Oscar! Who did this to you? My poor kitty, who killed you and tore you apart?" Clara stuffed a fist in her mouth to keep from crying.

She felt sick, but she wasn't going to let herself become hysterical. School was about to start, and besides she had to pick up Annie and make car arrangements. As she put the leg in a small box and set it on the floor of her hall closet for later burial, she entertained a brief moment of hope. Maybe Oscar had lost a leg but was still living. No, that didn't make sense. If his leg had gotten caught in a trap or bitten off by another animal, why would it end up back on her porch? She laughed grimly. Maybe the leg was trying to get back home even in the hope that the rest of Oscar would follow. No, that was too crazy. Someone must have killed her pet and put the leg on her porch as a kind of warning.

She was just washing her hands after taking care of Oscar's leg when the phone rang.

"Oh, hi, Annie. No, I didn't forget. I was just about to call you when I found the most hideous thing outside my door. It was a piece of Oscar. His leg. I know, I know...I'll be right there. No, I won't need my car until after school. We'll play it by ear. I'll do whatever I need to do to help you with transportation. Yeah, I'll be right there. Ciao."

A bizarre beginning to the day. She hoped things improved. Her students, most of whom she liked a lot, usually had a calming effect on her. No matter what was happening in her life, Clara was always there for the kids. She started up her Cherokee, put on the emergency brake, then dashed up the steps to make sure the front door was locked.

Annie was outside her house in the driveway when Clara drove up. She must be really late, thought Clara, as her friend absolutely hated to wait outdoors. She was usually pretty laid back about when she got to school, as there were no classes ever scheduled for first period in the library.

"Can you believe it?" Clara asked as Annie hoisted herself into the Cherokee. Finding the cat foot was so gross and horrible. Who could do something like that? I've heard of people shooting cats because they didn't like them, but dismemberment? Talk about a sick mind..."

Conversation stopped when they arrived at school, but Clara and Annie would talk throughout the day. After the Cherokee was parked in the teacher's parking lot, Annie walked to the right, the new multi-media library, and Clara to the left, the large adobe communications building. The bell was starting to ring as Clara walked into her classroom.

Almost perfect attendance. Amazing, in light of the fact that Christmas break would start in less than two weeks. She'd heard from other teachers that with all the different pueblo feast days, it was almost impossible to teach anything at this time of year.

"We're too busy taking attendance, finding out who's attending what feast day celebration, and filling out attendance reports," eighth grade science teacher Darryl Wright had complained to Clara just yesterday in the teacher's lounge. "They might as well just declare a holiday from December first to January fifteenth."

But Clara's students were there except for one or two, whom others said were sick with the flu. She wasn't sure how she rated it, but whatever the reason, she was happy about it.

"I'm glad to see all your smiling faces here today," she began. "We've got a lot going on, and what we're doing today will actually help you get a head start on next semester. First of all, I want Carnell to give you an update on our collaborative book."

Carnell rose from his seat in the back of the room. With a new haircut and a red and yellow AIA sweatshirt, he looked spiffy. From a shy, awkward guy at the beginning of the school year, he'd turned into a poised, articulate student leader. His popularity was soaring, and yet he maintained that edge of humility and the endearing quality of being able to laugh at himself.

"Well, you'll all be disappointed to know that we won't be getting our copies of *MEMORIES OF JOSEPH SPECKLED HORSE* back from the printer until after Christmas vacation. Paper Tiger is doing a fantastic job, but they had too many Christmas invitations, cards, programs, stuff like that to do before ours."

Groans arose from the class. "Oh no, I promised my Mom I'd bring our book home for Christmas," said Deena. "We got it to the printer in time. Let's use another company," groused Homer.

134

"They can't do this to us," complained Dorothy. "Boo," "We want our money back," "Fire the printer," grumbled others.

Carnell, ignoring them, continued. "The cover will be yellow, with blue, white and black. We picked out three drawings from the contest to decorate the front: Paul's turtle, Bernadette's snake, and Deena's hummingbird. We used all the other drawings to decorate the essays and poems on the inside. Guys, it's really going to be worth waiting for. You'll see."

The grumbling died down. "Thanks, Carnell," Clara said. "You've done a lot of work, you and all the rest of your committee. We'll all get a free copy and I've talked to Ms. Taggert about possibly selling them in order to earn money for a spring field trip. Paper Tiger donated the printing and I got a grant for the paper, so any money we make will be all profit.

"But that's for next year. Back to the present. Remember at the beginning of the year when I said we would all be learning how to do term papers by actually doing them. Well, this morning at the library, you're going to have time to actually start your research. Ms. Archuleta is expecting us at nine. I have index cards for you to list references. Before we go, I want you to list at least five possible topics that you're interested in, and when we're in the library, you should try to find five books about each topic as a beginning to your research."

If only her students were as enthusiastic about coming into her classroom as they were about leaving it, Clara reflected. All kinds of excuses popped up when the bell rang and they came straggling in for first period, but when it was time to leave the classroom, they were punctual, having all their notebooks and writing implements in order.

Ah well, she'd been told when she first started teaching at AIA that the main thing was keeping the students in the classroom, that they didn't like being confined. A collective mentality seemed to rule them. They reminded her of restless birds, flocking and swooping from one attraction to another.

By 9:15, after she passed out Xeroxed copies of "How to Choose a Term Paper Topic" and "Research Basics -- Library, Internet and Interviews," she directed her 25 students to the library, where Annie was expecting them. They exited room 210 and ambled over to the Kiva Building, which housed the 5,000-book collection of AIA. It was a source of pride to Annie that the present library had grown from a mere 300 donated books, from parents of the kids and the board, in just one year. Part of the school's plans included a new building to house not only a more elaborate computer center but a bigger and better library.

135

Annie and others were at work on a grant proposal for broader funding than presently existed.

Unaware that the library they were entering was soon to be expanded and upgraded, Clara and her students invaded Annie's domain. It was kind of like a field trip, Clara thought to herself, even though it was no further than the two tenths of a mile from the Communications Building to the library.

Annie wore her professional look, looking very svelte in an olive wool suit with split skirt and long double-breasted jacket. Her long black hair was pulled back in a French braid, and she wore rust pumps.

Clara sat down as Annie stood facing her restless but seated 25 students...Annie passed out sheets of notebook paper. "If you haven't already done it," she began, "please write down five topics that you might like to research. Then we'll share them." After that, you need to choose one and find books that will tell you about it. Never mind if you change your mind. This will set you in the right direction, and when we come back from Christmas break, you'll have a very important part of your work almost done."

Homer wanted to write a term paper about The Grateful Dead. Because his favorite uncle, Teddy, was a Deadhead, he'd grown up hearing Dead music, had even gone with Teddy to some of the concerts, and wanted to know how the original group formed and how their music had evolved. Christina chose to research the loss of rainforests and what was being done to reverse their devastation. Deena selected the Tarahumara Indians of Mexico.

After they had shared their topics, the class still had 30 minutes to locate references that they could use to flesh out their ideas. Clara went around the room from table to table, making sure that everyone was with it so far. The library session was going far better than she'd thought it would. She hated to admit the fact that Annie just might be better with the kids than she was.

The class seemed to be on automatic, with the students bustling around looking through the card catalogue, taking books out of shelves here and there, writing notes. Clara realized that there was nothing she had to do just this minute, so she sat down at one of the tables and began grading a set of papers.

Deena came up to her, eyes shining brightly and a shy smile gracing her usually somber face. "Ms. Jordan, you won't believe what happened. First of all, I've got my paper all set. It's about the use of the yucca plant throughout Native American cultures of the Southwest. But guess what, Johnny Tsosie came back to Mr. Wright's first period class. He was on a vision quest, just like we've all been saying. He brought

136

back the three answers that the old ones asked him a year ago. This proves he couldn't have been responsible for Speckled Horse. Everyone's acting like he's a big hero, and his family is having a big celebration tonight, all for Johnny."

Clara gave Deena a big warm smile. "Oh Deena, I'm so happy to hear that. We all knew that Johnny was innocent. His family and friends all believed he was just on a vision quest, but there were doubters, people who just wanted someone to blame. They would have pinned Speckled Horse's death on anybody."

"Johnny's brother Ronald told me about it this morning," Homer chimed in. "It was really cool, Johnny said, and he said he'll never be the same again. When we told him about the suspicions about his being gone, the connection to the death and all, he could hardly believe it."

With the excitement of Johnny's return, it took the rest of the morning for Clara's class to select their term paper projects. Deena volunteered to Xerox all the index cards of lists for Clara to keep. That way she would know what people planned to write about and could help them keep on track.

By the time the lunch bell rang, every student had at least one term paper topic. Clara was pleased that despite the excitement of Johnny's return to school, they had managed to get their task accomplished. Her students never ceased to amaze her.

But because suspect number one was back, accounted for and therefore not responsible for Speckled Horse, the mystery festered anew. The grief that had come to visit Clara when the heinous event first happened had never really gone away. Instead, it lodged itself inside her and had taken up permanent residence. All the joy felt at her students' good performance drained out of her, as she realized what Johnny's return meant.

If he didn't do it (which she never believed anyway but like others had come to accept at least the possibility as a sort of out), then someone else did. The horrific truth came crashing down on Clara and somehow reminded her directly of Oscar's disappearance and mutilation. Though she couldn't say why, she felt these two facts were somehow related.

"Come on, Clara, you look like you just heard that Christmas vacation was cancelled," Annie joked. "I know we both decided that a trip into Santa Fe for dinner would be too much for our budgets, but let's go down to Dina's Diner tonight for enchiladas. I heard they're *muy rico*. Someone's got to support Red Mesa's one and only restaurant or it will go out of business before we've even had a chance to try it. I know you're depressed about Oscar and your poor father, but Dina will be so happy to see us, you'll snap out of your funk. You know how yakky and overjoyed she'll act. Here's our chance to support the local economy and make someone's day."

"Yeah, Annie, you're right. I just can't get over how I was like everyone else, thinking secretly that Johnny might really have done it. Obviously, I didn't let on to the kids, but the longer he stayed away, the more I started to believe that he was on the run. Lately there have been so many loose ends, missing puzzle pieces, dangling questions. I kind of thought I'd go see Estrellita in the afternoon because she was going to be in the clinic. You might have to wait a bit. You don't have the bomb, so I drive, right? Not that I mind, I don't mind at all."

By three that afternoon, the weather had turned mean. While giving her sixth period class their assignment for the next day, Clara noticed splats of rain against the big classroom windows. The sky had turned from blue to gun metal gray, the dark was more than just winter. A storm must be brewing, and what was now rain would be snow before the next morning.

Clara shivered, sorry she hadn't worn a heavy sweater and wool slacks. Why had she thought the nice weather was going to continue forever? She had to wait to coordinate the evening's plans with Annie before she went to see Estrellita.

She looked over the term paper topics, filing them in a folder that she labeled "January 2001." They might have one more chance to visit the library before Christmas break, but basically, they'd get underway after school resumed next year.

Just to pass the time, she got out her attendance book and started averaging the grades so far. For the 25 in her home room, she went through and crossed out the lowest grade for each student. It was no more than what she'd promised them, but she felt as if she were giving them an early Christmas present. So far, Anita had an A-, Donald a C, Chris a B, Leroy just barely a C-...Suddenly Clara was overcome with fatigue. She put her head down on the desk, her mind a whirl of questions...

Since Johnny was free and clear of suspicion, just who killed Joseph Speckled Horse? What happened to Oscar? What would her meeting with Greta be like? Would she like her long-lost daughter? More importantly, would her daughter like her? Clara fervently hoped that neither of them would be disappointed. After waiting all these years, it would be ironic if they couldn't stand each other. But somehow Clara knew that wouldn't happen. She had a completely open mind, if only Greta did...

"Yoo hoo," Annie called from the door. "Am I in the right room? This looks like it's been converted to the Sweet Dreams Hotel."

"Oh my God, I can't believe it's already four fifteen," Clara said after struggling to wake up. "I must have been asleep for an hour, and I told Estrellita I'd be at her office by four-thirty. But you're all ready to go out." She looked at Annie with a furrowed brow. "I feel like I'm losing control of everything."

"Don't worry. I've got it all figured out. See, I've got to go check on the green bomb and they must have taken the phone off the hook because there's no answer. So, you go ahead and pay a call on Estrellita and in the meantime, if I can drive your car, I'll check on Ernie's Garage in person. Then I come back, we go out, and if the bomb is repaired you can take me by after we have dinner. Don't you think it's a perfect plan?"

"Well, sure, I guess so. I have to go right now if I'm going to catch Estrellita in. Here are the Cherokee keys. Remember to let it warm up for at least two minutes. I'll just be in Estrellita's office."

"Great. It shouldn't take me more than 45 minutes round trip. Before I go, I'll try phoning again, but I'm pretty sure they aren't answering. If only they're still open by the time I get there."

"I know how you drive," Clara quipped. "I have no doubts about your getting to Ernie's in more than enough time. It's 3:15 now. I'll go to Estrellita's now and probably stay no more than an hour. I'm sure you'll get back sooner than that unless Ernie needs to dissect the car for you. Why don't you just hang out in the library and I'll swing by and get you for our night out on the village. Here are the car keys."

"Sounds great. If the bomb is well, I'll have Ernie leave the key under the mat and after dinner you can swing by the garage and I'll just drive it home."

"You're a peach, Clara. I don't know what I'd do without you."

Annie hugged Clara. Keys jingling in one hand, she scurried down the hall and out to the teachers' parking lot. Clara locked her classroom and went upstairs to Estrellita's office, the room she occupied when she wasn't working at the Indian Hospital.

The older woman's face lit up when Clara appeared at her door. She was a vision in deep tangerine velvet, a broomstick skirt and turtleneck top. Thickly stranded coral heishi around her neck and matching earrings completed her elegant look.

"Ah, *mi hita*," you are a sight for sore eyes. Come in, come in. Take a load off your feet. Can I fix you a cup of herb tea?"

Clara sank into a blue velvet upholstered easy chair that looked as though it began life in the 1950s.

"Yes, I'd love some tea, whatever you have is fine." Estrellita made Clara feel as though her visit was the highlight of the day. She realized how much she'd missed her, and remembered the scented glycerine soaps that she'd bought for Christmas. She was supposed to have wrapped and brought them to this meeting.

As if reading her mind, Estrellita slid open a desk drawer and whisked out a package wrapped in red metallic paper with a green satin bow.

"I know you're probably going to be headed back to your Virginia parents before long, so I wanted you to have this before you go. In fact, you can just open it now."

Inside the layers of pale lilac and magenta tissue paper were two delicate yellow and black feathers bound in leather around the bottom of the quills and backed with a pin and clasp. The feathers were about two inches long. As Clara looked at them more closely, she detected some fronds of green and blue mixed in with the yellow.

"Oh Estrellita, they're beautiful. So colorful and fanciful. And a pin in the back so I can wear them! I have really never seen anything like this."

Estrellita beamed. "But, you are asking yourself, what are they? Don't feel bad. Unless you grew up in my family, you wouldn't know their significance. They are from a rare bird that is seen only in the spring. I'm not sure what they scientific name is for the bird, but we have always called it the *Pajarito Nino*. We never stalk or kill these small creatures for feathers but instead study their habits, learn where their nests are and collect whatever stray feathers we can. Children are best at finding the feathers.

"We save these special gifts from nature to make protective amulets and these special feather pins. Some years there are hardly enough feathers to make pins and amulets for our own families. Other times, we have an abundance, and we are able to share these special gifts with others who are dear to us.

"The pin will protect you and can even save your life. Wear it near your heart and next to your skin, not where the world can see it. You do not need to wear it every day, but only in times of stress or when you feel vulnerable or are about to face a situation that may be dangerous. And keep it in a safe, consistent spot.

"It is said that the feathers will fly away on their own, just as if they wanted to rejoin the spirit bird from which they fell. I have given these pins -- just a few, for there are not many in the world -- to people who didn't follow this advice. They wore them for awhile and their fortunes improved, but then they carelessly let them drift away. After that their lives sank. Some died in tragic accidents. Others just deteriorated. It was all proof that the feathers were the real thing."

Clara looked at the delicate yellow feather pin in the palm of her hand and thought about the creature that had originally worn the feathers. Some dead bird, feeding the fantasies of humans. She respected Estrellita, however. Whatever she said couldn't be too far from the truth. At one level, she thought Estrellita's feather story was a fanciful myth. But at another level, she thought it just might be true, this magical power of the feathers.

"I'm pinning these inside my sweater right now, Es. I need all the help I can get, from feathers or wherever. Maybe they'll help me when I meet my real mother."

Estrellita raised her dark eyebrows. "Ah, you mean your biological mother? You didn't tell me you'd found her."

Smiling with delight, she hugged Clara. "I am so happy for you, *mi hita*. This will be a chance to fill in the missing puzzle pieces. It is wonderful...but tell me, how did it happen? Did she find you or did you find her? Have you talked with her? How do you feel about this?"

"Well, believe it or not, I found her online. You know my student Carnell Dorame? Well, he was helping me surf the Internet to look for web pages that might lead to parents looking for their children, family members who have fallen through the cracks, "lost deer" who have been abandoned or adopted. I came across E-mail messages from Greta Suina, whose story sounds like I could be the daughter she was forced to give up for adoption."

Estrellita looked puzzled. "I don't really know what you're talking about. What do you mean by "surfing" the Internet? What are *web pages?* All this jargon gives me a headache. You're saying that while you were looking for your mother she was also looking for you?"

"Yes, you've got it! You don't have to know about cyberspace to understand what happened, Es. The main thing is that instead of hiring a private detective, instead of traveling all over the Southwest, instead of sending out a mass mailing, I just went on the Internet. Or, in a way, I did do a mass mailing. Not through the post office or snail mail but electronically."

As the light in Estrellita's small office grew dimmer and the day waned, Clara tried to explain her Internet search in simple terms. What Es was really interested in, however, was not electronic communication but how Clara felt after all these years about meeting the mother who bore her.

"Aren't you angry at her for giving you up?" Estrellita queried. "Don't you feel rejected? Don't you wonder why she has waited so long to try to find you?'

Clara sighed. "Es, you're such a skeptic! I know, I know... it's not easy to understand why a mother would wait for 33 years before contacting her daughter. But it could have been a lot of things. Maybe she'd agreed with Will and Louise that she wouldn't try to come back into my life. Maybe things were hard for her and she didn't have the energy to try to be a Mom. Maybe she did try to reach me but was never able. We can't judge her: we just don't know."

They talked about Greta Suina, who neither one knew, for another 30 minutes or so. All of a sudden, no one had more to say on the subject. Clara felt a chill around her shoulders as she looked at her watch. An hour had passed since Annie had left the school to check on her car. She should have been back 20 minutes ago at the latest.

"What's wrong?" Estrellita asked. "You look as though you've just seen a ghost."

Clara felt the blood drain from her face. Her hands were cold; she was sick to her stomach. "It's just that, well...it's Annie. She was going to the car place and then coming right back. She should have been here by now. Something is wrong."

Estrellita put an arm around Clara. "I can see why you're worried, *mi hita,* but there's probably some logical explanation. Maybe the car got a flat tire. Or possibly the repair people weren't quite finished with working on the car. You've been pushing yourself too hard, and I think your imagination is running away with you."

"But Annie knows how to change a flat tire. And she wasn't going to pick up her car right now anyway. She just needed to see if they'd finished it today like they promised. Besides, if she had made it to the car place, she would have called me to let me know if she was going to be late. She wouldn't have wanted me to worry."

"Could she be waiting for you at the restaurant? Where was it... Olive Garden? Want me to call and see if she's already there?" Estrellita was on her feet now, pacing. Her usually smooth brow furrowed, a look of despair in her dark eyes.

"Something horrible has happened, I know it," Clara gasped. "Annie would have called me if she'd changed plans. She wouldn't just leave me wondering." Huge, wrenching sobs made it impossible to talk. Estrellita rushed across the room and put her large, strong arms around Clara.

Neither woman spoke. A distant siren pierced the silence. Together they rushed into the uneasy dusk outside Estrellita's office.

17

Down the Slippery Slide

Larry had to do something before the shit hit the fan, but he would allow himself just this one night to decide what. Juggling a bag of food from Taco Bell, three six-packs of Tecate, a carton of cigarettes, and two movies from the new x-rated video place in town, he struggled to unlock the door to his hovel. He'd seen better digs, but with his recent activities, it was best for him to move around, and to live in the *barrio,* where no one knew him and all the neighbors kept their doors and windows tightly shut and their business to themselves. Hell, no one even looked you in the eyes in this dump of a neighborhood. Perfect for someone like himself.

Larry downed three beers and a burrito supreme before settling down to watch the action flicks he'd selected for the evening. He'd finish the six-pack as the first movie got underway, a special effects car race. The movie would be lame, but at least it would take his mind off what he knew he was going to have to do. Damn Henry, he'd never be able to just slither away, as he always had before when he got into these tight spots. Henry could see right through him; he knew right away when he was lying; he could sniff out the slightest flicker of disloyalty from miles away.

No, Larry's life wasn't his own. He'd given up being a free agent long ago when Henry bought off the judge in New York who was going to convict him of statutory rape. Larry made the mistake of getting involved with the secretary who worked for Henry's firm. She'd asked for it, begged for it, then afterwards, she claimed she'd been forced. Damn little liar, turned out she wasn't even 16.

Henry took care of the whole thing, smooth as silk, and Larry didn't have to sweat it out for more than a week. At the time he made it clear that Larry now owed him one, and it was then that they fell into what turned out to be a master/slave relationship. Henry gave Larry a big cut of the profits from his Internet artifact business, but more important was the feeling of being important, needed, damn near indispensable.

Up until he became Henry's right hand man, Larry felt he had been regarded as nothing but a pest. He was always second fiddle to his brother Bobby, and then, even after Bobby's "disappearance" he was not number one. His mother just minded his interference in her long, steamy catalogue of love affairs. When he wiped out the Eastgates for Henry, *erased without a trace* was how he liked to think of it, Henry's faith in him skyrocketed. Now, everything they'd built together was threatened by that high-falutin' broad Henry ended up dumping.

He swilled another Tecate and then did a line of coke. Another nice perk of being in Henry's employment was a steady supply of any drugs he wanted. The boss was ascetic; he neither drank, smoked nor snorted...but with his underling, he was the soul of generosity.

Yeah, this was fine, but it wasn't the real world. As Larry put the second video, *City Singles,* into the player, he started to feel rotten again. What would he do when Clara started putting two and two together? If only she'd gotten it when he killed her cat; if only she could see the photos he'd taken of her when she was about to sink into her bubble bath; if only she knew he followed her on the running trails. But no, she didn't have a clue. She'd ignored all the warnings and was now making things less than comfy for him and the boss man.

The *City Singles* "sexcapades" flickered on. Larry drank more beer, wolfed the rest of the tacos, chomped down several Snickers and Mars bars, then snorted another line of coke. As his head tingled and he was filled with energy, he beat off in a vain effort to ignore that nagging thought: Henry would demand an accounting; Henry wanted Clara shut up, no matter what it took.

Slouched down in his red bean bag chair, legs splayed out, surrounded by the trash of his pig-out, Larry nearly fell asleep. But suddenly on the screen, there was a big explosion. He woke up from his semi-slumber with a start, and started watching the video again. Angela's enemy, a nasty woman named Jennifer (wife of Angela's latest boss), had just been in a car crash.

A light bulb went on in Larry's dulled brain. Why hadn't he thought of it? Clara would die in a car crash, and Henry's worries, like Angela's, would be over! He knew the red Cherokee well, and he would pay a secret visit to the parking lot where it stayed while she taught. Yes, that was it, the perfect solution. Like the Eastgate inferno, no one would ever be able to trace Clara's little "accident" to Larry Butt.

Congratulating himself, Larry snorted another line of coke. Henry didn't give a flying fuck for Clara, he'd told Larry so more than once. He'd be damned grateful to have her out of the picture. No more meddling, no more snooping around the computer lab with that fat Indian kid Carnell Dorame. Henry had explained to Larry that Clara and Carnell might be able to trace his activities online.

Larry pretended to understand as Henry explained how he'd received the Eastgate's address by E-mail from his bosses, who he called "the big guys," and how he'd tried to print out a hard copy but couldn't because of a paper jam. He'd taken care of the glitch, but he wasn't sure how many copies of the address he'd sent before he got the printer message.

"See, that Dorame kid was at the printer, fiddling around, when I went over to fix the jam. Who knows what might have come out. I asked him if he'd seen any documents in the last ten minutes, and he said no but why would he tell me the truth? Besides, something might have come out later. I erased the address from my hard drive, and I looked through the recycle bin for a week afterwards."

Larry hadn't wanted to talk about the Eastgates, as Henry might find out about the fire if they pursued the topic. He focused instead on phony reassurances that the computer lab didn't offer a threat.

"With all the crap printed in that room, who would notice some address in California? It's like thinking the garbage collectors go through the eggshells and cat litter looking for credit cards. Hey man, I'll keep a close watch on Clara, Carnell, and the computer lab. You don't need to stay awake nights worrying about a stray piece of paper."

Henry had seemed reassured. He gave Larry some dope, patted him on the head, and told him to go have a good time. "Do whatever you have to. Just keep that bitch Clara Jordan out of my business. I don't want to hear of any leaks, understand?"

Larry understood perfectly. It was clear as a bell, clear as the water had been when he and Bobby hung over the rock looking for magic fish. Like Bobby, Clara could disappear. No one could say Larry Butt wasn't resourceful. He even learned from the movies. When the explosion poofed away that movie bitch Jennifer, his problems were solved. There was an answer right on the screen. Hell, he might even find the chemicals he needed right there in the school's laboratory, saving himself the trouble of going to stores in Santa Fe.

Looking around in disgust at the mess he'd created, Larry rewound the videos, cleaned up the cans and greasy food sacks, and spent the rest of night frantically scrubbing his hovel. Ajax in the sink, Mr. Clean on the patched linoleum, Endust on the 50s motel vintage furniture. More coke, using up the last fleck, he finished the housework.

It may not be much, but no one could say his place wasn't clean. Larry felt like he was being a model assistant. He would make Henry's life smoother, and he'd even send Thelma a Christmas card this year. She wouldn't believe her eyes. It had been three years since he'd let her know his whereabouts. Exhausted but self-satisfied, Larry fell asleep at five a.m. His last thoughts were of the bomb he'd set under Clara's car. It would be set for twenty minutes, time enough for her to get home. She lived in that cabin near the ridge, no one around for miles, no one to discover her right away. By then, Larry would be visiting pals in

Espanola, gone for the holidays. Henry would hear about the "accident," and Larry felt he would know it was a custom Christmas present, from Santa Claus to Henry. Then, hanging out with Leonard and Manny, druggie friends, he would wait for the big guy to find him. Henry always knew where to find Larry, and when he did, it was always to give him orders.

Larry called Frontier Mining Explosives in Santa Fe and talked to a helpful clerk named Stephen. Yes, they had RDX. Yes, they knew where he could find a detonator and a small metal container with iron magnets. They recommended a product called Primacord to attach the explosives to the timer.

By the end of the conversation, Stephen was Larry's new best friend. Yes, he could pick up everything by noon tomorrow. No, he wasn't going to blow up anyone. He'd had a problem with gophers and other rodents in his cellar, and he'd given up on traps and poisons.

"You see," Larry lied, "I'm quite a gardener, and the damn rats are eating the roots of everything. I'm tired of playing games. By the time I finish with them, there won't be a rat, mouse or gopher for miles around."

"Whatever," laughed Steve. He'd seen a lot in the five years he'd been with Frontier, but this mad gardener was the nuttiest. After the order was logged in, Steve looked for his boss Connie to tell her about it. When he couldn't find her, he went out to the parking lot to sit in his car and smoke a joint. By the time he came back, it was time to go home and he forgot all about the episode. Weirdos everywhere. It wasn't his job to report them.

18

All the News that's Unfit to Print

Since the Eastgate murders and the fire that consumed their home, Ruth Holland had taken extra security measures. She no longer went to the movies at night, a pastime she'd frequently enjoyed. The relationship with Andrea hadn't worked out, so Ruth's social life had dwindled to an occasional Sunday brunch at Friendly's Cafeteria. Her friend in Santa Fe, reporter Shelby Melton, kept sending her suggestions for getting out and meeting people. She also sent Ruth a subscription to *The Santa Fe REPORTER.* the newspaper she'd switched to recently.

For weeks, Ruth let the *REPORTERs* stack up in her study untouched, but this week's edition had a feature story that caught her eye. "AIA's Afflictions -- Native American School faces Tragedy".

The cover displayed a full-color spread of the school campus. Taken in the summer, the expanded photo showed the rose garden, the rolling green hills surrounding the low, stuccoed academic buildings, a view through some cottonwood trees of the school library with its wooden arch handcarved by AIA students.

When Ruth noticed that her friend Shelby had collaborated with another reporter to write the story, she picked it up and began reading.

For the American Indian Academy in Red Mesa, NM, last year's halcyon days seem to be gone forever. After opening in 1999 with great fanfare and strong financial backing, it seemed that American Indian Academy was the answer to many educators' prayers. But Fall of 2000 began the mysterious on-campus death of AIA Headmaster Joseph Speckled Horse. Police have not ruled out the possibility of foul play.

The shocking news brought a wave of grief and fear to AIA students, faculty and administration alike. According to interim Headmaster Wren Taggert, "Only a supreme effort by teachers and staff has managed to keep the situation in control. We have been dealing with the loss and grief of students in constructive ways, and we are striving to maintain a 'business as usual' atmosphere, hard as this is. We will always remember Speckled Horse as the great leader and true educator that he was, and when our new gymnasium is built, probably around 2005, the plan is to name it in his honor. Having a proper gym for our students was always one of his dreams."

But it will take more than a new gymnasium to heal the wounds. To compound the mystery, the very night Speckled Horse was apparently murdered, a rare Santa Clara pot, crafted by the legendary Gregorita

Suina, was stolen from the school's private collection. Suina's works, which went for thousands in the 1990s, have quadrupled in value since the potter's death in 1998. Santa Fe police have speculated that there may be a connection between the pottery heist and the Indian educator's death, but so far have no concrete evidence.

A sharp ring of the phone interrupted Ruth's perusal of the AIA story. It was her editor at the *Monitor*, Vivian Gonzales.

"Hey, Holland, what about that column you were going to get in by this morning? We gotta have it." Vivian was originally from Los Angeles but had earned her journalism degrees in Chicago, and she talked with a Midwestern twang. She always made a point of telling Ruth about the excellent response *Monitor* readers gave to the weekly column "Rock Talk" and she tried in vain to convince Ruth to let her use a small mug shot by the title. Ruth didn't care for the recognition, but she did love the fact that she might be inspiring potential rock hounds to develop their geological inclinations.

But this time, there wasn't a shred of flattery in Vivian's nasal voice. "I KNOW you do the column as an afterthought, I know you don't care about your career as a journalist, but you gotta think of little Jimmy or Sally out there, the budding young rock collectors. What will they think if you let them down? And didn't you say that you had a really good idea for this week's "Rock Talk," something about the crystal formations at the cave near Diablo Bridge? Come on, Ruthie, you can't let your readers down, not to mention your pal Vivian."

"My God, Vivian, I spaced the column this week. You know how careful I am about deadlines. Tell you what, stop the presses if necessary. I'll write a quickie conclusion, and fax the whole thing to you to you ASAP. I sure wouldn't want to be on the *Monitor*'s shit list."

What Ruth didn't want to tell Vivian or even admit to herself was the real reason she forgot the column. She was distraught by the Eastgate affair, worried about her safety, rethinking the decision she'd made to move to La Mesa. After all, the house was just rented. She could last out her lease, pack up and move back to Santa Fe. It would not be the end of the world.

But it wasn't like Ruth Holland to be intimidated. She was not a quitter. Her family back in Enid, Oklahoma, had all wanted her to get married like her sisters Peggy and Phyllis. But she had gone to Oklahoma State on a full scholarship and earned her Ph.D. in geology at Stanford.

She quelled her thoughts of moving, brewed a pot of Earl Grey tea, booted up her computer, and brought her Rock Talk column to a masterful conclusion. Never let it be said that Ruth Holland didn't meet her deadlines.

By 4:00 p.m., Ruth was happy with her column. She'd ended with an invitation to the readers to come to the geological society's January lecture on crystals, including contact names and numbers. After trying several times to send her article by email, she decided to deliver her column in person. She had been too much of a shut-in lately, and she enjoyed Vivian's crusty but warm-hearted repartee.

Backing her 1997 Ford Taurus down the hilly driveway, Ruth could feel her spirits lifting. Her gloom was dispersing like La Mesa's morning fog. As she drove by the wreckage of the Eastgate's house, she deliberately turned her attention elsewhere, fiddling with the radio to tune in the local talk show, "Mesa Moments" on KFLM, 1290 AM. Her friend Margaret Johnson was talking about indoor gardening.

Why, she asked herself, would she want to leave a place where she could turn on the radio and hear her friends? She would not fall victim to fear! Traffic was building up, so she was glad she hadn't waited until five.

The *Monitor* office, unlike most businesses on Central Avenue, had a spacious parking lot. Ruth parked the Tempo next to a big red van and sailed into the reception area.

Dolly Lucero looked up from the classified section.

"Oh, hi, Miz Holland. Miz Gonzales had to leave at three for an appointment. She said she was sorry to miss you but you could leave your article with me. I'll see that she gets it first thing in the morning."

"Great. Thanks." She handed Dolly the hard copy and disc with her column and turned to go. It was disappointing not to have a chat with Vivian, who always made her laugh. The *Monitor* lot was even emptier than when she'd arrived. No doubt the weekend workers had met deadlines and escaped for at least a night off. She respected the journalism profession. Overworked and underpaid for the most part, they had to love what they did. Certainly they weren't doing it for money.

It was by now five o'clock in the afternoon. Ruth sighed heavily as she steered the Taurus out of the *Monitor* parking lot. The sky was leaden. Maybe they would get the rain that forecasters had been predicting for the last week.

Ruth passed by the Hollywood Video Emporium, resisting the urge to check out some movies to watch tonight. Even though she had nothing she absolutely had to do, she would feel better getting something constructive accomplished rather than being a spectator.

A few splats of rain on the front windshield made her decide against stopping to buy groceries at the Piggly Wiggly. No point getting

149

caught in a deluge, when she could just as easily shop tomorrow morning.

On the other hand, she was hungry. She hadn't eaten anything since this morning's leftover coffee cake. The Dairy Queen right next to Piggly Wiggly seemed like a good idea. She would have a cheeseburger, fries and a milkshake and go home to work on her book proposal. Ordinarily, Ruth would never think of going to a fast food joint, but this was no ordinary time. "I deserve a break today--" she thought to herself, "no shopping, no dishes, just get dinner out of the way and save time."

A noisy family with four children sat in a booth eating french fries and sucking on soft drinks. The children, ranging from three or four to about ten, were arguing loudly, and their mother kept threatening to leave.

"Now, Peter, if you don't quit teasing Robin, we're going to march right out whether you're still hungry or not. She's only a baby, just let her grab your food. If she takes it all, I'll buy you more. If you can just get along, I promise you can have ice cream cones. Todd, just quit pinching Rebecca. What has she done to you?" Rebecca, at the mention of her name, began screaming loudly. Todd glared at his mother and slyly kicked Rebecca under the table. The frazzled looking father, a portly man in a too small jogging suit, looked pained but said nothing.

"May I help you?" Roberta asked. She was surprised to see someone like Ruth at Dairy Queen. A middle-aged single woman, well-heeled, in gray flannel slacks and a cotton turtleneck, stylishly cut short salt and pepper hair. She looked as though she might have stepped out of the pages of J. Crew for Seniors. Why would she be here, eating alone, at a Dairy Queen?

"Hmm, let's see," said Ruth, with the air of someone who did not often find herself at a fast food counter. "I'll take a cheeseburger, large fries and a chocolate shake. And water, I'd like a glass of water."

Roberta repeated the order back to Ruth and punched numbers into her register. She handed a register-produced slip to a uniformed teenage assistant then, turning back toward Ruth, smiled pleasantly. "That's $8.47 please."

Ruth gave Roberta a ten dollar bill. "I can remember when that would have cost half that. It wasn't that long ago. Oh well."

"And it probably wasn't here. La Mesa has always been known for sky-high prices and rock bottom salaries," Roberta said. "We pay as much for goods and services as San Francisco, and most people barely make minimum wage. I should know, I'm at the bottom of the bottom. Here's your order, Ma'am. Enjoy."

150

Ruth sat down as far as possible from the obnoxious family. The father bellowed, "When I was your age, young man, I would have been overjoyed to go eat french fries with my family. My father never did anything with us. We didn't have the luxury of eating in restaurants. We were lucky even to have food on the table."

More hitting, more screaming. The baby raised the volume of her high-pitched screaming. Ruth tried to finish the *Santa Fe REPORTER* article as she nibbled her cheeseburger. She was sitting as far as possible from the family without moving to the restaurant's outdoor tables.

Her food was growing cold, but the messy, chaotic noise polluters robbed her of what little appetite she'd had. Finding her place, Ruth stuck her fingers in her ears and finished reading the Santa Fe *REPORTER* article.

Clara Jordan, the teacher in whose classroom the body was discovered, agreed that the school is keeping the situation under control. "There's still some unrest," said Ms. Jordan, "but my students are coping surprisingly well. At first it was really difficult, I mean being in the same room where their beloved headmaster had died. The first few days, we had a so-called grief therapist in the class and I guess that helped some of the kids. What helped the most was a project we came up with. The students wrote poetry and essays, some did drawings, to express their feelings about the death of Joseph Speckled Horse. I have some wonderful writers and some really talented artists. We're putting everything together in a book titled THE WIND'S SHADOW: Memories of Joseph Speckled Horse. We hope to get it put out by a small publishing house in Santa Fe early next year."

In the meantime, Santa Fe police, working in conjunction with a private detective, are running out of leads. The family of Joseph Speckled Horse and friends of the school are offering a $3,000 reward for anyone who has any information leading to the arrest of the person or persons responsible for the crime. For information, call 1-800-786-7746.

Ruth unpugged her fingers from her ears. The family had left and Roberta had come out from behind the counter and was looking down at her.

"Ma'am, you haven't touched a thing. I apologize for the Adams family. Every now and then we get rude people like that, and as much as I'd like to tell them to take their business elsewhere, company policy doesn't allow it. Let me bring you another burger and fries."

Unbelievable, Ruth thought to herself. Niceness and civility where one would least expect it. "Well, I know it's not your fault. It's just that it's been a rough day at the end of a rough week. Sure, if company policy allows it, thanks, I would love a fresh dinner."

As she was finishing the last french fry and sipping the last of her chocolate shake, a sudden whoosh of wind rattled the plate glass door of Dairy Queen and brought gusts of rain. Ruth grabbed the car keys from her purse, swooped up her briefcase, and headed to the door. She called back to Roberta, who was clearing the table. "Bye, and thanks again."

"Drive safely," Roberta yelled back. As she cleared the table, she noticed the *Santa Fe REPORTER* article still open at the end. Her eye caught the last paragraph and its mention of the $3,000 reward. She looked out the window to make sure Ruth had driven away, tore out the article and stuffed it quickly in her apron pocket. Three thousand dollars would just about pay off her credit card bill. The whole world passed through the doors of Dairy Queen. She would just recall Thanksgiving Day. What the heck, someone had to win the reward.

19
Running Into Trouble

The moon shone bright as day through the cabin windows. Shadows of the junipers and pinons danced on the wooden floors. Sleeping fitfully in the queen-size gel bed next to the lightest window in her tiny cabin, Clara tossed and turned. Anticipating a long training run in the morning, she'd gone to bed at eight p.m.

It was always a mistake to go to bed too early, Clara should have known. Ordinarily, she slept no more than five or six hours. By three a.m, Clara was wide awake. After fifteen minutes of trying unsuccessfully to go back to sleep, she got out of bed and stretched.

Ever since she'd decided to train for the Bandelier Mini-Marathon in March, it was no problem getting up early to run. This was a little ridiculous, but what the heck. She'd been planning to start at four a.m. anyway, running from then until six a.m. Getting up now would allow her to run a lot further than planned. She could even make it to the cave and back. That would be a three-hour run. It might be crazy, but she felt strong enough to do it, and since the death of Oscar, long runs were the only thing that brought her any solace.

Clara did her usual yoga *asanas* -- *Salutation to the Sun, The Cow, the Cobra* -- and then put on polypropylene longjohns, a cotton turtleneck, a GORE-TEX running suit, wool socks, her new Reeboks, a wool stocking cap and ski gloves. She might be too warm after several miles, but she'd learned to start a run being comfortable. It was always possible to layer down, tying shirts or jackets around her waist, putting extra gloves or caps in the fanny pack she always wore. But once she got a chill, she could not get warm enough no matter how far or fast she ran. Today's workout would be slow and steady. It would be the first really long run she'd taken since her foot was better.

After securing her new runner's headlight, pinning the house key inside her waistband, adding her pepper spray mini-cannister to the mints and handkerchief in the pack, and locking the front door, Clara stepped out into her porch and breathed in sharply. The thermometer by her door read fifteen degrees, and it was always warmer next to the house.

She hadn't really thought much about where to go, but wherever it was, she'd better start now. Why not try going to the cave where she'd found the petroglyphs? There was something about them, a memory awakened. If she kept visiting them, she might be able to remember more about the time when she was still with her natural mother. Crazy to

153

start out like this in the middle of the night, but she just might make it. The moon was full, and she would be able to see. Besides, her feet knew the way.

The sooner she started moving, the better.

20

New York Connections

At five a.m., it was dark as night. A moonless sky made the stars seem even more brilliant than usual in the inky New Mexico sky. A shooting star, tail end of a meteorite shower known as the Sagittarids, flashed across the pre-dawn sky and was gone. The tiny adobe at the corner of the red clay plaza was the only house with its lights on.

Jerome Naranjo was on the phone with his cousin Michael Fonseca, up and coming New York painter. The two had grown up together at San Ildefonso, both attended American Indian Academy, ran for the "Runnin Braves" cross country team, graduated two years apart, Michael first. Jerome went to the Law Enforcement Academy, an extension of State University of New York. Michael went to the Manhattan School of Design. During those days, they would meet in the Village for drinks or dinner. They had never been very close at AIA, but during college, they became best of friends.

Michael's career began in Santa Fe, when he was featured as one of the few painters in the SITE Santa Fe show during the nineties. He found himself going to New York so often, he moved there in 2000. Jerome moved back to his home in San Ildefonso and worked as a private detective for a Santa Fe investigation firm. He was very active in tribal affairs, seeming to bridge the gap between the two cultures with grace and ease. He missed Jerome, who was like the big brother he never had, and the two talked from time to time and kept in touch by email.

In the fading light of a wan New York afternoon, painting toward the end of his usual eight-hour work day, Michael was putting the finishing touches on his latest cat. This one was titled "Fritz on skis." A large, Sylvester style black and white cat, slightly rotund, heavily whiskered and wearing a mischievous grin, was standing in a grove of Ponderosa pines on a pair of cross country skiis. One paw was holding a ski pole up in the air, as though Fritz was on the verge of shooshing down a snowy slope.

The cat series commanded $4,000 and up, for each painting. This one, because of its large canvas and because Fritz was new in the catalogue of cats, would go for as much as $7,000. Michael had been working since the first light of dawn, as he hoped to have Fritz ready in two weeks as part of his opening at the trendy new gallery, *Light of Day*. One of his collectors, Melissa Beihl, was coming from Dallas just for this show.

The phone's insistent ringing broke his concentration. Damnation, thought Michael, why the hell hadn't he turned on the answering machine? In a foul mood, he finally answered.

"Yeah, waddaya want?" he barked.

"Hey, Mike, old buddy. Is that any way to talk to your old buddy Jerome? What if I'd been your girlfriend?"

"Hell, I don't have a girlfriend," Michael said, the iciness melted away from his voice. "Man, it's just that I've been working like a dog. It's good to hear your voice. Watcha got on your mind?"

Jerome hardly knew where to start. The last time he'd talked with Michael was three months ago when his friend came back for some feast days. For old times' sake, they shot baskets and ran together. Summarizing with broad brush strokes, Jerome told about the murder of Joseph Speckled Horse and the troubled air that surrounded the Indian academy. Without going into detail, he told Michael about Clara and the death of her friend Annie in a car explosion.

"The car had been wired, and it obviously was meant to kill Clara rather than her best friend, who just happened to be driving it. I think I know who was behind it. This person used to live in New York, and that's why I'm calling..."

"So who is this Clara?" Michael interrupted. Sounds like you have quite an interest in her. I'm no detective. I'm an artist."

"Just cool it, Michael. I don't expect you to be a sleuth. I may need to get in touch with your brother Fred. He's with the New York Police Department, right? I remember your saying once that he'd busted an art smuggling ring. I have strong reason to believe that the creep who's trying to kill Clara is tied in to the Joseph Speckled Horse murder and a pottery theft at the school at the same time as the killing."

"Man, you lost me," Michael said. "I'm just an artist...I deal in visions, colors, cats. You got some bad stuff coming down out there. This Clara, I can tell you really care about her, and hey, even though I don't know what the hell is going on, I'll do anything I can to help. So what's the alleged killer dude's name? I can ask Freddie about it in the next couple days and I'll get right back to you."

"Marco. Henry DiMarco. He's about 6 feet four, thin, dark curly hair. He was kicked out of a New York investment company, I think it was Smith and Becker, for illegal use of their Internet provider. Came back to Santa Fe with his tail between his legs and lived for a time with Mommy and Daddy, *ricos* who gave the school a major endowment. Passes himself off as a computer scientist, which is why the school hired him, that is in addition to Mommy's strong influence."

Michael interrupted. "Is DiMarco in this alone?"

"No, we think he is probably not the actual killer but working with an accomplice he controls. We got a lead yesterday from California about a dude named Larry Butt, also goes by the name of Laurence Jacobs.

"Ya gotta be kidding. Larry Butt? Sounds like some kinda pond scum."

"He's the prime suspect in the murder and burning of a retired couple, Dan and Carol Eastgate. Broke in on Thanksgiving and waited in a closet until that night. This Di Marco is apparently part of an art smuggling ring and we think he sent Butt to steal back some pottery that was stolen from the school. The fucker has a habit of selling things, stealing them back, reselling them. He has a ticket for Zurich, where he deals with a Jonathan Ackerman, multi-millionaire whose recent interest is black San Ildefonso pottery.

"Ackerman came to Santa Fe for Indian Market, spent $100,000 on jewelry and pottery, which apparently just whetted his appetite for more. He communicates regularly with DiMarco on the Internet. One of the AIA students, bright kid who's in Clara Jordan's class, has been tapping their E-mail. He also found the California couple's address in the computer lab where DiMarco had been doing some work.

"Here's the hooker. His ticket is for two days from now, on the 18th. We suspect that Clara might be his next target. She used to go with him, and she knows too much."

"God, what a mess," Michael exclaimed. "Hang up and I'll call Freddie right away. He's connected. If this DiMarco fucker had any kind of criminal activity at all when he was here, he'll know or he'll find out faster than you can say Henry DiMarco."

The two cousins hung up the phone and Jerome lay down on his narrow bed to rest. His bedroom, like the rest of his simple, utilitarian adobe house, was austere, simple, monklike. The day had been exhausting, but at last some progress was being made on this DiMarco/Butt case. He closed his eyes and drifted off. Half asleep, he began to dream of walking along the river with his grandfather Jimmie Quick-to-see. His grandfather had been gone for years now, but in the dream, he was a young man.

They were walking along the river. Jerome was twelve. It was spring and all the leaves in the thick brush along the shore were budding. A few patches of snow sparkled through the young green leaves. Jerome followed his grandfather, listening intently while the strong, handsome man explained where the birds found food and made their nests.

"This is old, old growth," he was saying. "Good for the grosbeaks and flickers. They feast on these rosehip berries and use the low growing

157

elms for shade and protection. We must protect these areas and never remove anything from the home of these birds. Mother Earth's wisdom must be honored and respected. We are here as guests. Our job is to protect the order that Mother Earth has ordained. We are the custodians."

Jerome could feel the warmth of early spring sunshine on his head and shoulders, and the love of his grandfather enveloping him. They stayed by the river for a very long time. Whenever he began to grow impatient, he would feel his grandfather's hand on his shoulder and his breathing would become more even. He was learning to just wait.

Just as Jerome was beginning to relax, the phone's harsh ring crashed through his consciousness. He bolted into an upright position and grabbed the receiver.

"Ola, Mr. Naranjo. It's Carnell. I'm calling because Clara Jordan isn't here this morning. She didn't come to her first period class, and no one knows where she is. Ms. Taggert sent someone to her cabin, but she wasn't there either. Everyone is saying that she may have been upset about Annie Archuleta's death and done something rash. They've started a search. I called you because you used to run with her and might know where she could have gone."

Jerome's blood ran cold and his heart started to beat faster. Sure, he knew where Clara was likely to run, but so did Larry Butt, and he was probably trailing her as they spoke. The noose was closing, and there was no time for a false move. He should have known when the car explosion got the wrong person, Butt would not give up.

"Stay right there, Carnell. I know where Clara might have gone and I want you to come with me. She is in danger, and we're going to have to run like the wind to save her."

21

A race for life

The night air felt warm compared to when she'd left her cabin. A bright moon lit Clara's path up the ridge to the rocky area where she hoped to rediscover the cave. Towering ponderosa pines scratched the sky, their trunks dark sentinels lining the way.

Clara was panting as she powered her way up the steepest part of the trail, toward the end of her first mile. There was no way she wanted to be late for class, but her strong desire to see the cave this morning overrode every other impulse. She was making excellent progress. Surely there would be time.

The keening of coyotes echoed off the surrounding foothills. This time of year, they were driven by hunger. Packs of them roamed about looking for prey. For the first time, Clara considered the possibility that poor Oscar might have been dinner for a coyote, an awful thought. On the other hand, she had found his severed paw on her doorstep, and that wouldn't have been the work of a coyote. No, something human had killed her beloved pet.

Clouds passed over the moon, making it harder to see boulders and roots along the trail. Some bushes near her rustled as though a small creature had just run in or out. A bird's warble sounded through the night air.

On she ran, racing against time, imagining the arrows on the cave wall, hoping that a bright dawn would allow her to discern them. Even if she wasn't able to see any artwork in the cave, however, this would still be a magnificent workout. Her students wouldn't believe it when she told them she'd already run ten miles this morning.

As she ran, she thought about Greta, her newly discovered mother. They would meet soon, but for now, their acquaintance had been just by phone and e-mail. Greta had told Clara about Dorothy Suina's pottery. Dorothy was Greta's mother, Clara's grandmother. Because most of Dorothy's pottery, according to Greta, had an arrow motif, Clara felt compelled to get back to the cave. Though she didn't know how, she could sense that her Grandmother the potter and the cave were connected.

Pottery was the cause of Joseph Speckled Horse's death, she mused. Though nothing was proved, Jerome had told her that the AIA headmaster was killed because of his involvement with a pottery smuggling ring.

"In over his head," was how Jerome put it. He said that Speckled Horse was pilfering away much of the school's heritage, its private collection of pottery crafted and donated by talented relatives of AIA students.

"Of course," Jerome had said, "he thought he was doing a good thing. Where do you think the new gym came from, the landscaping, the uniforms for the cross-country team? Speckled Horse was making illegal money from selling off the school's treasures and converting them to perks for the school."

Clara remembered their conversation during a run they'd taken together. It had been on this path, come to think of it. They hadn't made it to the cave that day, as it was threatening rain, but Clara had told Jerome about the petroglyphs she'd found there and he promised to go with her sometime in the near future.

The clouds drifted by the winter moon and it was once again light enough to see the path clearly. Clara quickened her pace. The faster she ran now, the more time she would have in the cave. Ever so subtly, dawn was approaching and the earliest lightening of the sky made it possible to discern the rocks ahead.

Clara tripped on a log across the path, twisting her ankle and knocking the breath out of her. As she was falling, she thought she heard a small click, like a camera. As she lay on the ground assessing the damage to her ankle, she listened in mild terror.

Having been a runner for twenty years, she was used to the sounds of nature. Animals, the wind, water, and birds...she recognized the rustles and whispers, the calls. But this was a mechanical, metallic sound, not a sound of nature. It sounded most like a camera. But why would anyone be taking pictures here, out in the middle of nowhere?

What was there to do but to keep running? She tried to move as silently as possible...Maybe she could outrun whatever it was before she reached her destination.

After scrambling to her feet, Clara ran faster. No more clicks or mechanical sounds, the forest around her was silent. The earth under her feet was sandy and shifting, which meant she'd reached the rocky incline that led to the cave. Her path, between two rock walls, was so narrow that she could touch grainy rock on either side. Around a curve and then up a series of crude natural steps, she was nearly there. The path seemed to end abruptly, but Clara remembered that this was where she'd had to climb up several tiers to higher terrain.

Time was running out. She had to hurry. Hugging the boulder above her head, Clara swung herself up for a foothold. She managed to get to the top of the rock outcropping, but scraped her hands and knees as she scrambled across to the continuing path. Once the boulders were behind her, she resumed an upright position and ran. The sky was lighter now, pale silvery gray, and she could see the trees that grew around the cave's entrance. Almost there.

As she turned around the last bend before the final stretch, she didn't notice the shadow moving through the trees behind her. She didn't hear the deep breathing of her pursuer. Her thoughts and her eyes were directed ahead toward a grove of silver-barked aspen. If her memory served her, the cave was just beyond the last slender trunk. She would find the petroglyphs, trace them with her fingers, commit them to memory, and then draw them when she got back.

Reddened eyes, filthy hair and clothes, the killer prowled after her like a hungry beast. Knife in hand, ready to use if there was another false step, another fall, or to wait until she was inside the cave with only one way out. As he grinned hideously, his teeth, unseen by anyone, glowed in the first pre-dawn light.

The thought of Clara -- caged, caved, cowering -- turned him on. He could have some fun before he brought out the knife that would shut her up forever. And Henry would be pleased. The only leak would be stopped...no more meddling, no more using students to snoop around on the Internet. No way in hell Clara's nosy little plan would continue after she was gone. He nearly laughed out loud at the thought. It would be his doing, helping his master.

Stealthy footsteps trailed her light-footed tracks, but Clara didn't notice. At the end of the line of aspen, she slowed down to a walk and stretched her arms and legs. She'd been running for over an hour, and it felt good to stop.

Ah yes, here was the grotto that led into the cave. Unfortunately, the opening faced west, not east, as Clara had remembered. Even wearing her headlamp, it would be difficult to see much once she walked in more than a few feet. But she wasn't going to run all the way here and go home with nothing. She could walk along the right side of the entrance, trailing her hands along the wall, until she came to the arrows. Instead of using her eyes, she would use her hands to trace the carved areas. She knew she could form a mental picture to carry when she ran back to quickly shower, change, and meet her first period class.

She would make a sketch even before she saw her students, and then show it to Greta when they finally met face to face. She felt a strong connection with the petroglyphs, as though she had seen something like them before. Despite having to feel rather than see them, she would have no trouble remembering.

Slowly, slowly, she made her way along the cave wall. The petroglyphs were somewhere between waist and shoulder high, so she walked cautiously along with her right elbow bent and her hand trailing against the wall. So far, her splayed fingertips passed along smooth rock, a little grainy here and there but nothing deep enough to be a carving.

Jerome drove his red pickup to the Communications Building. He'd been asleep when Carnell telephoned, and he was still struggling to fully awaken. He now wished that he'd stopped at the truck stop between his house and the school for a cup of coffee. Even though he was alarmed at Clara's disappearance, he was groggy and sluggish.

"Thank God you're here, Naranjo," said Carnell. Clara's favorite student was anxiously waiting in front of the Communications Building. "I started the class like Clara said, but Ms. Taggert came by and she sent everyone to study hall. She told the class some story about Clara's being called away on an emergency."

Jerome's truck was parked right by the building front. "Hop in, kid. I know the trail that Clara probably took, and we're going to run after her."

Carnell looked down at his big floppy high-topped sneakers. "Can we stop by my dorm room? I need to change into sweats and grab some running shoes. These clodhoppers slow me down."

"No problem. We're going to need to be fast on our feet." Jerome's truck needed new shock absorbers, and they rumbled so noisily along the dirt road to the senior honors apartments that conversation was difficult.

Carnell raised his voice several decibels. "I don't think it was any emergency that took Clara away. She told me she was planning to run ten miles before class. I remember her saying if she didn't get back on time, I could be the teacher for the day and just start without her. We laughed about it because sometimes I think my ambition is to be a teacher of Indian kids. She said I could count it as student teaching."

Jerome frowned. The death of Annie Archuleta, Clara's best friend, pointed to the strong possibility that the car bombing's intended victim was Clara, not Annie. Alone on the trail to the cave, she was extremely vulnerable. If she was being stalked by a killer, she could hardly have made it easier.

After the truck was parked, Carnell ran inside his double-storied cabin and changed clothes. His housemates were in class, so with no explanations to give, the change didn't take long. He emerged in maroon sweatpants, a black windbreaker emblazoned with the AIA logo, a gold and white shield and crossed feathers.

162

The change took less than five minutes. Hoisting himself back into the passenger side of Jerome's truck, Carnell waved his right foot in the air. His floppy sneakers had been replaced with newish blue and white Nikes. "See these feet, made for running."

Prowling along on hands and knees, he could smell the lagoon. Long ago, he'd explored this cave, and he knew that there was a bottomless hole in its bowels, a pit that would be perfect for disposal of the body. He needed to catch up with his prey before the dumb bitch walked right into it. She would still be gone. She wouldn't be a thorn in his boss's side, but he would miss the satisfaction of watching her terror, seeing that sexy body squirm, maybe hearing her beg for mercy.

Unlike Clara, who was like a mole in a dark tunnel, the killer could see in the dark with these special glasses Henry had given him before the Eastgate visit, the better to do his dirty work.

The only mercy the bitch would get might be something to remember him by between her legs before he slit that creamy olive-skinned throat and threw the garbage into inky waters where no one would find her for weeks or years. And long before they found her, he would be somewhere else in the world with the master, who even now was on his way to Zurich. The master was carrying the treasure he'd stolen back from that human offal. Disgusting yuppie maggots, they'd deserved to burn.

Clara had found the first of the carved arrows, and even though she couldn't see them, she was memorizing the shapes with her fingers. Tracing along the wall, she imagined what each arrow looked like, how long it was, how thick. There were zig-zags at the end of the arrows, perpendicular. She felt and memorized those as well.

Three...two...two, she repeated the configuration to herself, so she would retain it until she was back at AIA near paper and pencil. Three long arrows shooting forward, two shorter ones aimed toward the top of the cave, and above both of those arrow clusters and slightly ahead were two zig-zag lines, horizontal to the arrows.

In the pitch black, Clara trailed her fingers along the cave walls, tracing the delicate etched lines of stylized arrows. She didn't have to close her eyes to imagine what they looked like. Now that she was walking rather than running, the cave felt colder than ever. Shivering but feeling triumphant, she used both hands to give the petroglyphs her full attention. She would be able to take back a mental if not a visual picture.

Breathing hard, pumping their legs at an agonizing pace, Jerome and Carnell ran toward the cave. The footprints they followed weren't Clara's. From many runs together, Jerome knew the waffle pattern of her New Balance running shoes. These were the prints of a man, the would-be assassin of Clara.

"I'm going ahead," Jerome said hoarsely to Carnell. "We don't have much time. You just follow, and don't kill yourself trying to keep up."

With that, Jerome surged ahead, up the ridge that led to the narrow, rocky path to the cave. He propelled himself faster by swinging his arms on either side, pumping them in unison with his legs. His mouth was abnormally dry and his lungs ached with the effort of running anaerobically. Normally, Jerome was a fast runner. He competed in Pueblo footraces, always coming in first in his age group and often beating out men half his age. But at his fastest, he ran seven-minute miles. Now, he was doing six twenties and thirties, one mile after another. Sweat poured from his brow into his eyes; his body gleamed with moisture, his corded muscles, reflecting moonlight, shining like silver.

Above in the winter sky, a meteorite flared. A coyote keened in a distant canyon and was soon joined by its fellows. Carnell was now a full mile behind Jerome, running his best but panting and cursing the extra five pounds he'd been meaning to lose. Excess baggage, he would shed it before the next full moon. He twisted one foot and caught himself on a boulder before careening entirely sideways. Pain shot through his ankle, but Carnell chose to ignore it.

"Careful," he advised himself. "Quit worrying about your fat, can't do anything about it now. Think of Clara, catch up with Jerome. Clara needs both of us."

Carnell thought of Clara's excitement when she'd found Greta, her birthmother. He had been part of her search, and Clara told him that when she and her mother met face to face, he would be the first to meet her. Thoughts of the future propelled him forward. It was unthinkable that something could happen to his beloved teacher before her dream was realized. He could tell she was in great danger now, maybe even fighting for her life. He forgot about being tired and locked into a fast but bearable pace. Mentally, he sent strength and speed ahead to Jerome.

As Carnell ran, he found his mind roaming through the past weeks, ending up in the computer lab. After he'd found the Eastgate address and stuffed it in his pocket, a strange man, no one he'd ever seen before, was walking by in the hall. He was wearing a cheap brown polyester suit and a bowl-over-the head haircut, the kind Carnell's mother used to give him when he was seven. When Carnell asked if he could help him, the man said no thanks, he had an appointment with Ms. Taggert. It was only later that Carnell remembered that Ms. Taggert was out of the office all that week. Whatever the man's business was on campus, it was not to see the acting headmaster.

Later, when he'd gone on some errands with Clara, one of them to get her directional signal fixed on the Cherokee, he's seen someone exactly like the strange man at LaMesa's back yard maintenance garage. He remembered everything about that afternoon. "Shade tree mechanics," Clara had mumbled *sotto voce* to Carnell, "but they can handle something like a directional signal." This time the stranger was dressed in a plain gray cotton jumpsuit and wore a backwards baseball cap over his greasy hair. The cap was emblazoned with a Cities of Gold logo. Carnell was struck at the similarity of the two men and was about to ask if he had a twin at the school recently looking for a brother.

"Nah," the mechanic drawled back. "An nevah go near books and classrooms ef ah cun hepit. Think I'm allergic to'um. I had a brother who was a real brain and he did enough school for the both of us. Me, I hated schools and everythin boutum. Learn more in a car hospital, on the street, in the forest...anywhere but in a fuckin school." With that, he'd spat out the wad of tobacco he'd been chewing.

Despite the cap and the drawl, Carnell was almost positive this was the same guy who'd been lurking around the computer lab. And all of a sudden, Carnell knew the man who wanted to kill Clara.

This was the same creep who was stalking her now, if only he could tell Jerome. Carnell lifted his arms higher, lengthened his stride, increased his pace. By now his accelerated heart rate did not make his chest ache. It was intense but bearable.

Ahead, looking white in the increasing light of morning, loomed the rock outcropping right before the cave. Jerome was probably already there, hopefully right behind Clara and whoever. Carnell raced toward the last part of his journey, praying that it would not be too late.

Shivering in the cave's darkness, Clara explored the petroglyph by hand. Even though she couldn't see anything, she could picture the carvings in her mind's eye. In addition to arrows, she traced a round sun-like shape with scallops around the inside, a four-petaled symbol for the seasons, steps to the kiva, and the T-shaped drawing for land, air and water.

She went over and over the wall until the mental picture was firmly in place. It hadn't been easy, but she felt confident that she could draw everything after her run back to the school was finished. She

165

needed to hurry, as her students would start arriving in about an hour. She'd told Carnell she might be late to class side, and she could trust him to keep everything under control.

Just as she was about to draw her lingering fingertips from the petroglyphs, an icy hand grasped hers. Terrified, she heard herself scream, a harsh sound that seemed to come from somewhere outside. Afraid, angry, her heart pounding, she wrenched her hand away and started to run fast into the inky darkness that must have been the cave's center.

"Come back, you goddamn bitch. I just need to ask you some questions." The voice sounded vaguely familiar. Where had she heard it before?

Terror gave her running an extra boost. Running rapidly but with extreme care, Clara came to what seemed to be a dead end. Not far behind her, her pursuer tripped, cursed and started up again.

Clara groped frantically for a hole, a cave within the cave, a tunnel...anywhere to hide. Behind her was an opening that seemed to lead to another path. She slipped quickly around the corner and started on the new tunnel or path, whatever it was. The dim semi-light of before had given over to inky darkness, total and unrelenting. She slowed to a light-footed jog. There might be a drop-off right ahead of her or, something she'd heard about but never seen -- the cave's hidden lagoon.

Stopping, she listened. No sound of anyone walking or running; no sound of anything except her own shallow and exhausted breathing. Maybe it was OK to rest a minute; maybe HE had kept straight and she'd lost him, at least for now.

Leaning against the rough stone at her back, Clara sank to a crouching position. She fought back the tears that burned her eyes. Her position was ridiculously vulnerable. Even if she'd lost her pursuer, she didn't know how she would get out of wherever she was.

Waiting, waiting, Clara kept listening intently for a telltale sound, a footstep, a distant voice. Nothing but silence. Both her legs were cramping badly. Crippling knots of pain gathered in her calves. Despite the fact that she'd vowed not to get to comfortable, to stay crouched so she could run at an instant's notice, she slumped further to a seated position and stretched out her aching legs in front of her and began vigorously massaging her calves.

She had no idea what time it was. No doubt her students were gathered in the classroom wondering where she was. Carnell would have the situation under control by now. She imagined him in front of the classroom, taking attendance and making excuses for her. No doubt Wren Taggert had gotten a whiff of what was going on and disapproved.

So, maybe she'd be reprimanded, maybe even fired, At this point, she didn't care what happened. If only she could get out of this hellish nowhere alive.

Clara clapped her hand over her mouth to keep from screaming. She felt afraid once again. Now she knew when she'd heard that voice she kept remembering. It was during the aborted Thanksgiving trip to the airport. Harry, Larry, or something like that, the tow truck driver that had come to pull them out when she and Henry had skidded off the freeway into a snow bank. His mission this time was not rescue, and there was little doubt that Henry was behind that episode just as he must be masterminding this one. Despite the damp chill, she began to sweat.

22
To sleep, perchance to dream

Carrying a single black suitcase, Henry DiMarco rode an airport bus to 42nd Street and Grand Central Station briskly toward the Cornell Club, where he would use his uncle Leonardo's membership. A spring in Henry's step matched the buoyancy of his mood. Tomorrow morning he would leave for Zurich on a one-way plane ticket.

Friends back in Red Mesa would hardly have recognized this version of Henry. His usually wild black curly hair was shorter, slicked back in a forties style; his beat up Nikes had been replaced with gleaming black leather Italian pumps, hand-tooled on the toes and around the heels; his jeans supplanted with a lightweight wool suit with faint pinstripes and an off-white silk shirt, open at the neck. He strode confidently, with an air of professional insouciance.

Everything was as planned and on schedule, even with that bumbling Butt doing his best to screw it up. Tucked safely in his bag, Henry had the pottery that the Swiss couple, millionaires several times over, requested. They would get it the day after tomorrow and he, Henry DiMarco, would get a cool 500K. It had been so easy, "like pickin peas," as his Virginia-born father used to say -- when they were on speaking terms.

Henry loved New York. These streets felt familiar, as if he'd never left. Cold, gray concrete everywhere, towering buildings, elbow-to-elbow people. The smell of car fumes and roasted chestnuts, the sweet violin music of a blind musician playing for quarters and dollar bills, the uncollected garbage...it was as all just as he remembered when he worked for Forbes and Pennycook in their administrative data section. Damned bastards for going after him. He hadn't done anything wrong, just a temporary financial adjustment that he planned to make up for later, when his stocks rose.

It was only Uncle Lennie's intervention that kept them from canning him for absconding with funds. Instead, Leonardo DiMarco paid off aging, half senile Donald Forbes and had Henry released rather than fired. Someday he would make them sorry; he'd show Forbes and Pennycook Investments up for what they were -- hypocritical frauds.

He reached 44th Street, turned right, and walked to #4, the subdued, classy entrance to the Cornell Club. Uncle Lennie had told him he could use it anytime he was in the city, but Henry hadn't asked him ahead of time, hadn't made a reservation. He just hoped that Lennie didn't already have someone else using his membership.

Henry pushed open the heavy glass door and strolled across the marble floor to the reception desk. He concentrated on acting as though he knew the Cornell Club intimately, although it was only the second time he'd been here. The other occasion had been when Uncle Lennie had put Henry up for the night before he was to be interviewed by Mr. D.H. Forbes. The data manager position with Forbes and Pennycook was a sure thing and the interview was, they both knew, a mere formality.

Actually, he would have liked to call Uncle Lennie, invite him the to Cornell Club lounge for a drink, but he refrained. No one could know he'd even been here until he was airborne. He was sure he'd covered his tracks completely, but he would be truly free only when he was safely on the other side of the Atlantic.

After checking in, Henry walked into the empty elevator and punched nine. His room, 920, was at the end of a long, green-carpeted hall. Dark, elegant, the room enveloped him. Heavy cream colored satin curtains closed it off from the street sounds eight floors below.

Henry took off his shoes and stretched out on the king-sized bed. No one knew he was here, and he liked that anonymity. Exhausted, he closed his eyes and tried to sleep, at least for five or ten minutes. But it was no use. He had worked too hard and too long for this moment. He felt the turbulence he knew must be roiling in Red Mesa, even as he was preparing to vanish from the town's reality.

No one would imagine him here in the heart of New York City, about to embark on a new life in Europe. This was a moment he'd imagined for a long time. In his imagination, he would be called an *importer*. His Santa Fe connections, after taking their cut, would supply him with whatever artifacts were in demand.

The Ackermans had promised to put him up until he was able to find an apartment in Zurich. They assured him that a host of their friends were eager to begin their Southwest collections. He was going to be in great demand. His years of being the black sheep of his family, the ousted corporation employee, the supernumerary at a school who hated him and everything he stood for...those days were soon to be gone forever.

As refreshed by these thoughts as he would have been by an actual nap, Henry sprang up from his half slumber. Realizing that he hadn't eaten all day, he decided to go down to the Cornell Club Bar for a sandwich. He remembered sitting there four years ago with Uncle Lennie, hearing about the fame and glory of Cornell in the old days, how they'd gone downhill after the sixties and student rebellion, but how much he still loved his Alma Mater. Uncle Lennie would grow more nostalgic with each gin and tonic he put away. It was a pattern familiar to Henry, who had learned to sit very still and patiently during these trips down memory lane. And he was richly rewarded for his patience. The Fifth Avenue apartment that Uncle Lennie had paid for, the job at Forbes and Pennycook, the expensive silk shirts and classy business suits.

"Can I take your order, sir?" The cocktail waitress, with a heavily made up face under a beehive of red hair, spoke in velvet tones. How long had she been standing beside his table?

Henry eyed her full, taffeta black mini-skirt and long, shapely legs. Not bad. But, no. He was on a business trip, maybe one that would save his life and make his fortune at last. "Sure, I'd like a gin and tonic and a pastrami on rye."

The waitress scribbled on a tablet and swished away, her shapely hips seeming to wag at Henry. He hadn't been so turned on since Clara, before he realized she would betray him. Ignoring his growing erection, Henry sank back into thoughts of the past.

He'd been Leonardo's surrogate son, consolation to the old man since his only son Beau was killed in a plane crash at age 40. And for a while the relationship worked. He was the bright young up and coming executive; he provided lots of bragging material.

After the blowup at Forbes and Pennycook and the accusations that Henry had been using their clientele for illicit sale of Native American sacred pottery and artifacts, as well as embezzling funds, Uncle Lennie cut him off. If he'd learned nothing else during his dubious academic career of junior colleges, the University of Phoenix, and computer hacking, it was how to cover up his tracks on the Internet.

Henry did most of his soliciting and selling through a provider in Moldova, making it almost impossible to trace his transactions. So the charges against him were never quite verified. Forbes and Pennycook, calling it "downsizing," let him go. Before he moved back to Santa Fe to his parents' house and the nebulous job at the American Indian Academy, Henry had done his best to make amends with Uncle Lennie. Dinners, apologias, listening to the old man reminisce about Beau and what a wonderful son he'd been.

Henry hadn't spoken to his real father for ten years and regarded their non-relationship as a mutual loathing society. Uncle Lennie was the closest thing to a father he had. He wished Uncle Lennie were here now to hear about his plans. Of course, he would have to disguise his "importing" business, but Henry was good at disguise.

His drink and sandwich were on the table. Funny, he hadn't even noticed the redhead bringing them. Eating and drinking abstractedly, he continued thinking about the chapter of his life that was ending. The

170

sandwich was tasteless. Dry bread, pastrami that seemed to have the herbs and spices omitted. No matter. He drank several more gin and tonics and paid his bill.

Before going up to his room, Henry walked around the wood-paneled bar and looked at the black and white photographs of Cornell students from years past. Here was the rowing team from 1928 in their baggy Bermuda shorts and tops that looked like undershirts. Many had mustaches and hair parted in the middle. They reminded him of Charlie Chaplin or Groucho Marx. Some were holding long paddles in one hand, like a shepherd's staff. They were all dead now, an eerie thought.

Just up from the 1928 photo was the track team of 1947. They were dressed much like the rowers, baggy shorts and undershirts. The hairstyles looked less dowdy. Not so many Chaplins and Marxes. The third runner from the right on the front row, if he remembered correctly, was Uncle Lennie. His handsome face looked out at Henry from across the years. Deepset eyes, a crinkly smile, slicked back hair, and a slim, well-proportioned body, the young Leonardo reminded Henry of himself some 15 years ago.

He studied the legs of the 1947 running team. Long, slim, powerful. He imagined them carrying the then-young men over hills and across the unspoiled terrain of upstate New York. He could hear their yelps of joy, sense their youthful exuberance. Now they were old and decrepit.

An unwelcome vision of Clara passed through his mind. He once thought she would be a suitable partner but when he realized that she was convinced she was part Indian, she would never help him in the acquisition of sacred artifacts to sell. When Henry told her they were mostly worthless junk made of mud and feathers, she had lit into him with a diatribe. He didn't need that, and from then on, he realized that she was potentially an enemy.

After the redhead asked him a couple times if he wanted another drink as he perused the photo gallery, he decided it was time to go.

Locked in the snug quiet of his room, Henry unzipped his suitcase, peeled off a layer of socks and underwear and took out the package. He unfolded layers of tissue paper and gazed tenderly at the sacred prayer pipe, onyx, marble, and wood with inlays of turquoise, brass and silver; the gleaming black turtle with a star-shaped geometrical design on its back, a rare early piece by the late New Mexico sculptor Daniel House; and the wedding gift that Speckled Horse had given him in return for a roofing job on the freshman dormitory.

The wedding gift was the greatest treasure of the lot. Black, probably Santa Clara, the pot stood seven inches tall, shaped gracefully

171

like a pear standing on its small end. The decorations around the side were fine, sharp and delicate. Speckled Horse, who was reluctant to part with the pot but wildly anxious for the new roof, had explained them to Henry: a sun, stylized turkey feathers, corn sprouts, a four-petaled flower shape representing four seasons, the land, air, and water bar with perpendicular lines hanging off the side, and finally, the steps to the Kiva.

Henry was sorry that Speckled Horse had to be eradicated; the Indian leader had reminded him a little bit of Uncle Leonard. On the other hand, it was a relief not to have to keep supplying him with perks for the school. Wren Taggert, the acting headmaster, would now be sending him artifacts in exchange for a cut of the profits. Funny how easily he found a replacement for Speckled Horse.

Henry worked fast. After he realized Clara was his enemy, he seduced Wren. Though she wasn't as physically exciting as Clara, she was in many ways a kindred spirit. However, he reminded himself, their union was strictly for business purposes.

Henry called the front desk for a wakeup call at five a.m. He checked his ticket for the third time. A ten-thirty a.m. flight on TWA for London, then on to Frankfurt and Zurich. He laid it on the nightstand by the clock radio, as though it were a gun he might need if someone broke into his room.

After a long, hot shower, he lay naked in the luxurious bed and watched the tail end of the ten o'clock news. Everything depended on his making the flight to Europe. Larry, with his slavish adulation of Henry, would make sure Clara didn't do anything to screw up his plans. He'd promised Larry that after the business was established he would be needing him here, but of course there was little chance that he would.

Just a few thin hours separated Henry from tomorrow morning, and his mind was on fire. His whole life had come to this, and now everything had to work perfectly. To stop the thoughts whirling through his mind, he imagined having the redheaded waitress, whom he decided to call her Zelda, in his room. Before ten minutes passed, he fell into a deep sleep.

23

On the Trail

After the call from his brother Michael, Freddie Fonseca spent several hours asking questions at Forbes and Pennycook, Henry DiMarco's former employer.

Like his brother, Freddie had grown up at the Pueblo. He became interested in law enforcement after working for summers as a student intern at Los Alamos National Laboratory with Johnson Controls. Winner of the prestigious Neufeld scholarship, for Native Americans interested in police work, he trained in a special program at the Seneca Law Enforcement Institute in upstate New York, landed a job with the New York Police Department, and worked his way up to private detective.

Unlike Michael, who was slender and of average height, Freddie was a huge man. With his burly physique, his NYPD uniform, his long black hair worn in a single braid, he created a minor sensation as he went through the guest sign-in at Forbes Towers.

To increase his chances of getting unpremeditated answers, he deliberately avoided calling ahead, made no appointments. He sought raw reactions to the name "Henry DiMarco." He would not start at the top of the corporation. His plan was to interview randomly selected employees, mainly in the data processing department where Henry had worked for nine months.

Right at the outset, however, Freddie's hopes of keeping a low profile were dashed. Bradley Tove, the security guard, phoned upstairs to alert his niece Barbara, a secretary, about the Indian detective's arrival. Barbara told Gwen Warren, receptionist for Data Processing, and Gwen alerted her boss Sue Collins. Sue told her personnel manager Norman Joyce, and he informed Will Blackwell in accounting. By the time Freddie took the busier than usual elevator to the tenth floor, everyone knew that an Indian was going to be coming around asking about Henry DiMarco.

Sue was Freddie's first stop. Almost as large as he was, dressed in a man's suit, Sue spoke in a deep, rumbling contralto. Her chestnut brown hair was cut in a short bob, her black eyes were lively and intelligent. Less mannish and fifty pounds less, thought Freddie to himself, and she would have been an attractive woman. He laughed almost out loud: that was a helluva lotta "if's."

Clearly the top honcho of the tenth floor, she sat ensconced in her expensively furnished office. Dark wood everywhere, the walls lined with books, deep green plush carpeting, black leather covered chairs, a huge brass-trimmed desk.

"Hiya, pleased to meetcha." Sue rose slightly from behind her desk and offered her hand. Despite the stuffiness of the office, her manner was warm, friendly, informal. Freddie took note of her deep Texas accent, her firm handshake. He half expected her to offer him a cigar.

"Let me guess," he ventured. "You're from West Texas."

"Nah," Sue laughed. "Tulsa. I grew up on my Daddy's ranch, decided the last thing in the world I wanted to be was a cowgirl, came East and became a business woman instead." She looked around her office fondly, her eyes caressing the fine furnishings and paneled walls. "Yeah, a tycoon. But Mr. Fonseca, what can I do fer yah?"

Freddie shifted his weight uncomfortably in the oversized leather easy chair. "Well, I'm here to inquire about a former employee, Henry DiMarco. I think he was with your firm from 1998 to 1999."

"Oh yeah, that guy from Santa Fe." Sue's forehead was knit with concentration, I really didn't know him. He was a legacy from a close friend of Oliver Forbes. Yeah, someone he owed a favor to. Like I said, I hardly knew the guy."

Freddie stayed silent, looking at Sue expectantly. It was always better not to say too much.

"Well, yeah, he seemed pleasant enough, but he never really fit in. We decided he was too much of a cowboy type to ever become a city rat. Oh yeah, now I remember. He had a reputation as an expert on Native American pottery, and he went through all the single women who work here, some married ones too from what I heard."

"Went through?"

"Yeah, dated, loved 'em and left 'em, used 'em up and spit 'em out. There was a rumor he got one of the maids pregnant and had to leave in a hurry. Yeah, that's what people said, but I always thought there was more to it than that. My data processing manager said that he was embezzling and using the company's Internet connection to sell pottery. Never proved it, though."

"So the accusation was just dropped -- or what?"

Sue paused, as if trying to think up a plausible answer. "Forbes probably covered it up. Can't keep track of everyone in a firm as vast as ours. Yeah, I think it was something really big, swept under the rug. Anyway, I thought 'Good Riddance.' Soon we all forgot DiMarco even existed. A mere blip on the Forbes and Pennycook screen. Yeah, DiMarco's gone and pretty much forgotten. Marky, we called him behind his back. Never to his face: the guy was humorless. He was

174

secretive, anti-social. No farewells, no luncheon when he cleared out. Business as usual. Yeah, Marky. Hadn't thought about him until just now."

Sue pushed her chair out from behind the huge executive desk and lumbered to the wet bar, cleverly hidden behind a false row of books, to Freddie's right.

"I usually don't have a drink at 11:00 a.m. but it's been a rough week. Ya care to join me in a nip 'o brandy?"

Freddie didn't drink. He looked at his watch. "Well, thanks, no. I need to talk to some of your other employees before everyone leaves for lunch."

Sue poured herself a large goblet of expensive brandy. Freddie thought he saw her hands tremble slightly. DTs? Nervousness? Laughing loudly, the Tulsa tycoon set down her glass, and shook Freddie's ample hand. Her grip felt damp.

"Damn short timers." She shook her head. "I don't think you'll be able to find out much about DiMarco. "He wasn't here long enough for anyone to get to know him. Yeah, a short timer."

Freddie saw himself out the heavy office door. He thought he smelled cigar smoke as it closed it quietly behind him. Something fishy there. Maybe Sue just had a *laissez-faire* management style but then again, maybe she was covering up.

As it turned out, Freddie had time to talk with three more people on the tenth floor before the mass exodus for lunch. Gwen Warren, a small, grey-haired woman with a pixie face, told him how much she disliked Henry. "He never stood up straight and he never looked directly at you. I was glad they got rid of him."

Norman Joyce, who looked as though he hadn't slept for a week, ran his fingers through thinning blond hair as he tried to remember the name. Tieless, he wore a glaringly white starched shirt. Finally, he said, "Seems like DiMarco made so much money selling things on the Internet he was able to quit his day job. Problem was, he was using our Internet. Scumbag. Everyone got micro-managed after he was canned. If you'll excuse me, I'm late for a date with my wife."

Will Blackwell was eating lunch in his office and surfing the Internet. When Freddie came to the door, he quickly switched his computer to the screen saver, a series of Impressionist paintings. An array of junk food littered the table next to his computer station. Of all his interviewees, Will seemed the most forthright. Freddie judged him to be in his mid-forties, a youthful smooth-skinned face juxtaposed with a half bald head. Freddie wondered when baldness was correctly called premature. Was 40 premature? How about 50? Will's golden-brown eyes gleamed with intelligence. Freddie guessed that he probably spent hours on the Internet feeding a private cyber-life far more interesting than the day job here at F&P.

"You know, I never believed the line they gave us about DiMarco's quick exit... When he first came, I was his one and only friend. We used to play racquetball during lunch. He showed me pictures of Santa Fe, invited me to come visit during ski season and stay with him at his parents' digs. Seems like the DiMarco's relative started a fancy Native American prep school, only the second of its kind in the Southwest. Marky was vague about the details. Big article about it in the *New York Times*, in case you saw that."

Not picking up on the DiMarco family gossip, Freddie got to the point. "Tell me about Henry's job. What, exactly, did he DO for the company?"

"Hmmm," mused Will, "let's see." He picked up a jumbo carton of french fries and after offering them to Freddie, who politely refused, wolfed down twenty or so.

"I frankly don't think Marky - I mean, Henry - did much of anything but surf the net. He had a home page with Santa Fe lore and culture, and he kept in touch with dozens of people by e-mail, people in New Mexico, Arizona, California, here in New York, Switzerland. Ostensibly he was hired as a sort of computer guru, a trouble-shooter, but when any of us asked for help, he wasn't around, or he was glued to the phone. Hell, he was some kind of favor that old man Forbes was doing for a cronie, a Leonardo somebody, some wheeler dealer connected to the mob. Maybe. Who knows?"

Will started on one of three Big Macs, gesturing toward the others. "Really, help yourself. I have to eat something now, got a racquet ball game at four. Tell you what, someone who really knows is this chick who worked as a custodian. Valerie Costello. She was putting herself through art school. Real looker. She and DiMarco were an item. She's not here anymore. After Henry left, she gave notice. Norm told me she's working at a topless place near 42nd Street. I'll write down her what used to be her address and phone number, maybe it still is."

He handed Freddie a card with the requested information scribbled in red ink. "She hoped DiMarco would take her with him, but I heard he made a point to avoid even talking with her before he left. Anyway, good luck. What did Henry do, get in a western shootout? Showdown at OK Corral?" Will laughed at his own quip and started on the second Big Mac.

"No, we're just checking his background in regard to an exporting business. Thanks for your help. Can I tell Valerie you sent me?"

"Sure. Just find out where she works. I used to tease her, said I'd surprise her some night when she was strutting her stuff. I woulda asked her out except Henry made it clear she was his territory..."

"Yeah, well thanks, Mr. Blackburn. I appreciate your cooperation."

"Blackwell, it's Will Blackwell. It's on that card. You be sure to tell Valerie I asked about her, ya hear."

Will turned to his computer, switched from his screen saver to Yahoo and clicked in "Ski resorts, California." He needed to get away, maybe meet some snow bunnies. He gobbled the last Big Mac and promptly forgot everything about Henry DiMarco and Freddie's visit except for a fleeting hope that with Henry out of the picture, Valerie just might decide she had time for him.

Valerie Costello lived in a rent controlled apartment at 3 Washington Square Village. Freddie decided not to call, instead taking the subway from Lexington Avenue to Greenwich Village on the off chance that Valerie might be at home.

A stunningly beautiful young woman in her mid-twenties opened the door to the fifth floor apartment. She'd been asleep, Freddie guessed, as her long wavy black hair was rumpled and there were pillow creases on her cheek. That fit in with the topless dancer story. Work all night, you have to sleep in the daytime.

After Freddie explained who he was and why he was there, Valerie let him in. The apartment was filled with large abstract paintings, huge geometrical blotches of color on white, work by Valerie, no doubt. Hardly any furniture. Some bean bag chairs, milk cartons for makeshift tables, cinderblock and board bookshelves. That fit in with the student story.

Freddie asked for a glass of water. Valerie didn't walk; she slinked. No wonder she was Henry's main squeeze, thought Freddie. Shapely hips outlined by skintight, low slung jeans, a narrow torso, large breasts that bounced freely under her black velvet turtleneck. Shoeless, she had purple painted toenails and several toe rings.

"Ms. Costello, can you tell me if Henry is currently in New York?"

"Hell, call me Valerie. I was trying to forget that Henry DiMarco existed. It's hard for me even to talk about that prick. He was supposed to be back around now but I haven't heard anything from him. I called this fancy club of his uncle's where he said he'd be staying but they said he hadn't checked in. Probably lying. He was a skilled liar, lied that he loved me, lied that we would go back to New Mexico together, lied

177

about how he was getting Indian artifacts to sell. He said they were gifts from his late grandmother and that he was supposed to save for his first house, but I know he ripped them off. He's a bastard. I hate his guts, and I'll do anything I can to get him screwed over. Like, he really fucked me over, fucked up my life."

Tears were trickling down Valerie's lovely young face.

"Just one more question, Ms. Costello, Valerie. If Henry were in New York, where would he be staying?"

Valerie wrote down the address of the Cornell Club on the back of the card with her address. "Mr. Fonseca, if you see that swamp thing, put a bullet through his black heart. Tell him it's from Valerie." She started to weep in earnest, and Freddie slipped out the door, closing it softly behind him.

He drove to the Cornell Club. When he showed the muscular dreadlocked black receptionist his badge, the young man said. "Yes, he's supposed to check in tonight under the name of his uncle Leonardo DiMarco. Shall I tell him you called?"

"No," Freddie said. "Just tell me when he's checking out."

"He said to give him a wake-up call at four-thirty a.m., that he had to catch a plane at six. I estimate he'd leave here at five. Said it was real important and gave me a fifty-dollar bill to make sure there were no mistakes. Also asked me to tell anyone who asked that he cancelled the reservation and wasn't coming until next month."

"Great. I'll be going now."

The receptionist looked worried. "There isn't any trouble, is there? You won't tell him I told you he would be staying here?

He made me promise not to, but I always obey officers of the law."

"No, I'm just making sure that there won't be any trouble. Henry DiMarco will never know you told me anything. You have my word." He shook the receptionist's hand. "Thanks for your information. You are not implicated in any way, and you should be perfectly safe." Freddie handed him his card. "Just be careful when DiMarco checks in. Don't look at him wrong."

24

No Exit

The nagging ring of a lemon yellow deco-style alarm shattered the chill morning air, but Freddie slept right through it.

After the clock had nearly run down, Rosie Fonseca, his wife, shook the shoulder of her sleeping husband and stared wearily at the clock. It was four a.m., an hour when any sane person would be asleep, but as Freddie liked to remind her, "the law never sleeps."

Freddie groaned, sat up, patted Rosie on the shoulder. "Go back to sleep. Forget this even happened, honey, it's just a dream." Barefoot, he padded to the kitchen to flick on the coffee maker.

Number one priority: going to the Cornell Club before Henry emerged. There would be no reason for DiMarco to suspect anything, but just in case, Freddie planned on parking the patrol car in a police lot nearby and waiting on foot. If it got too cold outside, he'd wait in the lobby.

The Fonsecas lived on Magnolia Street in Brooklyn, in an apartment. Now that Rosie wasn't working, monthly rent stretched their budget. To cut down on heating bills, Freddie turned the thermostat to sixty degrees every night, and though he'd turned it up this morning, the air still felt Arctic. He got into his black pants and green cable knit sweater as quickly as possible. It would be easier to talk with Henry if he were in plainclothes. Maybe.

Rosie was already back asleep. Lately, she was tired, exhausted. Maybe this meant she was pregnant. They'd been trying for over a year.

He paced from the bedroom to the kitchen to the living room. Too nervous to eat anything, he downed several cups of strong black coffee. He removed his sweater, strapped his gun and holster closer to his chest, and put his sweater back on. Something drew him back into the bedroom. His wife's blond hair fanned out over the pillow like golden flax. He gently kissed her cheek and resisted the temptation to take off his clothes and crawl back into bed.

At four-thirty a.m., Freddie's slow-moving patrol car offered the only sign of life on Magnolia. He radioed headquarters. "Closing in on DiMarco. Cornell Club right off Fifth at 44th. Be prepared to send support. DiMarco's a tough customer and I learned that he's hell-bent on leaving the country."

Jim Benavidez, his main back-up, promised a top alert. "If I can, I'll have someone over in the Forties by the time you're there. You'll be covered. Hey boss, we've gotten another report on DiMarco, this one from a Wren Taggert at that Indian school near Santa Fe. She confirmed the stolen artifact story. Over and out."

The pitch black sky to the East was slowly turned silver and some pink clouds graced an otherwise bleak scene. Sparse traffic. The concrete canyons of Brooklyn felt like a comfortable old shoe to Freddie, who'd lived here for the last eight of his thirty years.

Lost in thought, Freddie crossed over East River on the Brooklyn Bridge. He pressed down on the accelerator. He planned to arrive at the Cornell Club no later than five, the earliest, he figured, Di Marco would be leaving. Freddie had checked all international flights going to Zurich that morning. Henry was on the passenger manifest for United Flight 2064, scheduled to leave at eleven a.m., check-in at nine.

It was drizzling lightly when Freddie parked the patrol car and walked two blocks to the Cornell Club. An elderly homeless man, either an early riser or an insomniac, slouched in a doorway on Fifth Avenue. He was wrapped in brownish rags and several moth-eaten wool blankets. His wrinkled face spoke a timeless, universal fatigue. He would have fit in on the streets of Calcutta, Los Angeles, or Mexico City.

The man stuck out his skeletal, gnarled hand. "Got any loose change, Mister? I haven't eaten for three days. A quarter? A nickel?"

Freddie reached in his pocket, pulled out a dollar, and put it in the filthy hand.

"God bless you," the beggar rasped.

Briskly, Freddie hurried on. The pitiful wretch would probably spend it on something to drink, but it might help stave off some of his misery, at least for a few hours.

At two minutes after five, Freddie reached East 44th. Lights were shining from the Cornell Club's windows and the glass door.

Freddie stepped inside the unlocked front door. Even at this hour, the club reeked of subdued elegance. A silver coffee and tea service had been laid out. Nobody else in the lobby. Behind the reception desk, the young night clerk appeared to be making wakeup calls.

Freddie sat down and picked up a copy of the *New York Times*. Rather than reading, however, he reviewed his plan. He would try talking to DiMarco in the hope he might postpone his trip for questioning. Though suspicions abounded, DiMarco did not have a criminal record. Maybe he'd be reasonable. Even as he hoped for that, though, an inner voice said 'Fat chance'."

Time weighed heavily. Freddie walked back and forth across the marble floor. As his tension mounted, his pacing increased. Five-fifteen and no sign of DiMarco. No sign of anybody, for that matter. The desk clerk had disappeared.

180

Freddie's cellular rang. He reached inside and pulled out the sleek plastic phone. This was the force's new miniature version, small as a pack of cigarettes yet more powerful than any previous models. Myrtle at headquarters asked what the hell was happening.

"Yeah, still waiting," Freddie told her. "He should have been coming down by five but I've been here half an hour and..." The creak of the elevator alerted him. "I think he's here. Gotta go." He clicked the phone back together and thrust it in his jacket.

The tall, curly-haired man who stepped through the elevator's brass doors matched the picture of Henry DiMarco that Jerome Naranjo had Fed-Exed to Freddie. He carried a single black bag on wheels and frowned nervously at his watch as he emerged from the elevator.

He showed his badge as he confronted the man. "I'm Officer Freddie Fonseca with the New York Police Department. Are you Henry DiMarco?"

"Yes, but I've got to catch a plane and I'm really in a hurry."

Henry walked out the club door two steps ahead of Freddie. They strode along Fifth Avenue, Henry ostensibly looking for a taxi, Freddie questioning him every step of the way.

Henry walked fast, trying to wear out the heavier man, but Freddie was remarkably agile for his size.

"Do you know a Wren Taggert?"

"Look, I don't really have time for this. My plane leaves in just a couple hours."

"Are you currently carrying any pottery artifacts removed from the school that Ms. Taggert directs, the American Indian Academy?"

Henry turned around and glared at Freddie." Look, I don't know what you're talking about. I never heard of Wren Taggert or the American Indian Academy. You have no right to harass me. You can just go to hell."

"OK, fine, Mr. DiMarco." Freddie pulled a search warrant from his jacket pocket and held it up in front of Henry. "Uh, you won't mind if I make a quick search of your suitcase before you catch a cab. Just a formality. I know you're headed to Zurich, and I know all the departure times. You'll have plenty of time to catch your flight. I need to inspect the contents of your bag."

He took the handle of the black suitcase and tried to pull it from Henry's tight grip.

"Now, Mr. DiMarco, if you'll just cooperate, this will be easier for..."

Henry's cool demeanor slipped away. His face became a snarling mask of hatred. Yanking on his bag, he kicked Freddie in the knees.

181

"No ya don't, asshole...leave me alone. I got better things to do than waste time with a fucking search. How do I even know you're who you say you are? Now, get lost."

"I realize this seems intrusive, but we've had reports of Native American artifacts of the Southwest being smuggled and sold both within and outside the country. We have evidence that you are involved. If you have nothing to hide, this will take less time than arguing with me."

Henry pulled harder on the bag. With his free hand, he waved at a slowly passing yellow cab. But even at this lean hour of the morning, the cab driver wasn't willing to get involved in a fracas. Soon it would be light, and he'd find another fare.

Henry released the bag and ran up Fifth Avenue. Freddie picked it up and tossed it behind some uncollected garbage sacks in front of a Chock Full 'o Nuts and took out after Henry. He made a mental note to get back before the garbage collectors came by and before the shops opened, and then he darted after Henry. The race was on.

But Henry ran faster. Making a mental note of exactly where he'd pitched Henry's suitcase, which he was now convinced contained stolen artifacts, Freddie spotted Henry turning on Forty-seventh Street. He turned the corner seconds later, only to catch a glimpse of Henry scaling the fire escape of an old-fashioned brick building.

Slowing down to a fast jog, Freddie called his supporting officer, who'd traveled to this area as a backup. "Fonseca here, 47th, right off Fifth. Suspect climbed fire escape, entered what appears to be third floor. I'm following. Get here ASAP. Over."

Freddie shot ahead and catapulted up the fire escape to make up for lost time. Henry had smashed through the top of a glass door and disappeared from sight. Not wanting to make any noise, Freddie reached through the gaping, jagged glass and, using a wire that he kept for just such occasions, he unlocked the door from through the shattered glass and crept inside.

The building must be one of the downtown behemoths that the city had decided to renovate by 2005. It was old and shabby but not yet falling down. And Henry had to be in here somewhere. When his backup came, they would automatically cover all the doors, the basement, and especially the third floor exit that he had just passed through

He followed Henry up the fire escape, through the door, and onto the third floor. A stale, fetid smell assaulted Freddie's nostrils, and a huge gray rat scuttled by. He was in a dark hallway, lined with apparently abandoned offices. He listened hard. Complete silence. Had

Henry had escaped to another floor or was he hiding in one of the rooms on either side?

He decided to check into the rooms one by one, starting at the end closest to the fire escape. If Henry moved from any room further down the corridor, he would hear. His heart beat faster; they were closing in the scumbag who possibly had orchestrated the murder of Speckled Horse and who was robbing Native Americans of sacred heritage, their pottery.

Freddie turned on light switches, the old fashioned two-button variety, that were to the immediate left inside each door. The first room was a dust-covered office, with law books on the shelves, a disconnected phone, a desk pad dated 1997. Before leaving, he peered into the closet and an adjoining bathroom. Spiderwebs, a thick layer of scum in the sink, dirty coffee cups on a shelf above the toilet.

Methodically, Freddie inspected the rest of the vacated offices. Judging by the dust and spiderwebs, it seemed all rooms had been abandoned at the same time. There were footprints in the dust, but other than that, no sign of Henry.

Outside, the rain had stopped. Morning light shone feebly through the filthy windows, lighting up the dustmotes that now danced through the air. As Freddie looked around the last room on the hallway, a siren's approaching whine shattered the stale, musty silence.

Just as he was starting down the stairwell at the end of the hall, a bullet sang by, barely missing his head. He dove to the floor and reached for his revolver but before he could get it out of the holster, DiMarco pounced on top of him and pinned him to the floor in a stranglehold.

Henry shoved his face next to Freddie's. Eyes reddened with rage, he spit out, "You'll pay for this, you damn half-breed. I'll sue you for invasion of privacy and for making me miss my meeting in Zurich. This is a civilized city where ordinary citizens try to make a living, not some backwater vigilante hellhole like the godforsaken place you were hatched!"

Freddie struggled to throw Henry off, tried to get a stranglehold around his throat. He could hear the sirens approaching still closer and prayed that they were his patrol's. If he could just keep Henry talking, maybe he could stay alive until they got to the building and climbed up to the shattered glass door.

"Henry, you scum, we've known about you for a long time. All we needed was for you to make a move like this."

"You waited too long, you fat turd," Henry laughed. "I have other ways to get to Zurich. I have friends, you miserable dolt, and right now, they've made plans to get me out of the country. I just booked a commercial flight to throw off you goons. But by the time I finish with you, you won't even be conscious. I know where you left my bag, the one you stole." Henry traced the blade of his dagger along Freddie's throat, drawing a thin line of blood.

Freddie glared into Henry's narrowed eyes. "You stupid ass, I've got friends too, and they're on their way right now. If you'll come in for questioning, I promise you won't get hurt. We'll all be happier. Besides," Freddie lied, "we have a confession from someone who says he's responsible for setting up the theft of sacred artifacts from the AIA."

"Damn you, I haven't stolen anything."

The two men had wrestled their way to the top of the inner stairwell. More sirens blaring. *Mother Earth and Father Sky*, prayed Freddie. *May the patrol arrive any second.*

Knocking the knife from Henry's hand, Freddie rolled over and scrambled to his feet, running backwards toward the fire escape. Just as Henry started after him, Freddie pulled out his gun and aimed at DiMarco.

Henry pulled a thirty-eight from his suit jacket and aimed directly at Freddie's head. After ducking into one of the abandoned offices, Freddie peered from behind the half-opened door, aimed, and shot Henry in the shoulder.

Howling with rage and pain, Henry aimed back at Freddie with a shower of bullets. A frenzied exchange of bullets punctuated by door slamming. Wounded and bleeding, but still firing his gun in Freddie's direction, Henry staggered up the hall toward his enemy's side office fortress.

The fire escape clattered and clanked as an army of police officers approached. Just as Jim Benavidez burst through the door, the DiMarco luck -- wasted in illicit trading and misery making -- ran out. A bullet from Freddie's gun found its way to Henry's heart.

25

The Maze

Thirty minutes seemed an eternity. Clara's head was pounding and her legs were knotted with cramps. Her thighs ached from squatting and both calves ached with what Louise used to call *Charlie horses*. She'd been hiding out in her niche ever since she'd heard the sickeningly familiar voice of her taunter. Trying to forget her present misery, she thought about the carved arrows that attracted her to the cave in the first place.

What at first seemed pitch black, wasn't. As her eyes adjusted, she detected a dim light came from above, a distant fissure in the craggy, multi-layered rock ceiling.

Even though she wasn't religious, she prayed, *Dear God, please help me get out of this alive.*

After a few pleas to an unknown power, she continued reflecting on the amazing discoveries of the past few weeks. She knew now that she and Greta were connected by the arrows. And she knew that the same style of arrows that were carved in the endowment pottery, the bowl for which Joseph Speckled Horse had been slain.

She was Greta's daughter and the granddaughter of Running Woman, a legendary potter as well as a talented and tireless long distance runner. Greta had told her that much through e-mail.

If only I live to get to know her, to claim this part of my heritage. I can make it right with Will and Louise; I must escape from here to meet my birth mother, to see Carnell and my students, to run again with Jerome.

Where in the vast universe am I? Gotta stretch, get rid of these cramps. I'm a human pretzel: they'll need pliers to straighten me out. Gotta get out of here. I need air, daylight.

An inner voice directing her, Clara crawled out of a niche and tried to get some idea of the space around her. As she stood up, her head grazed the top of what seemed to be a tunnel. She spread her arms out on either side and touched cool, rough stone with her splayed fingertips.

Walk, don't run. Just keep going. Carnell, just tell the class I'll be back tomorrow. Greta, I'm going to live to see you again. Will and Louise, I will make it back for Christmas. Jerome, we'll run again...

Even as she forced upbeat thoughts, Clara worried that she might die. What if this route took her to the mouth of the cave, into her pursuer's snare or toward a drop-off? This was crazy, like being inside some sinister womb. Though it seemed dangerous to keep walking into oblivion, it was worse just sitting, waiting, hoping for a miracle.

A soft, dripping sound caused a tingle down her spine. Water. The lagoon that Jerome had told her about. This meant that she was going the wrong way, opposite air and freedom. Just as she was about to change directions, an arm wrapped itself roughly around her torso.

My God, he'd been following all along.

"Don't be afraid, I'm just the tour guide here in this little pocket of hell. You're going the wrong way." The man turned her around, and walked her toward what she supposed was the way out.

The dim light made it hard to see her assailant. Clara decided the best strategy was to humor him. The anger of his earlier taunt had been replaced by an obsequious, crooning tone. "Uh, yeah," she replied, "I was sort of lost. Haven't we met before? You were the tow truck guy when Henry and I went adrift in that snowstorm before Thanksgiving."

A long, low laugh. "Larry Butt, at your service. I've been a student of yours for a long time...or shall we say, an observer? I'm a disciple of Señor DiMarco. The master who taught me all I know. He did it with pottery, and I'll do it with you. When we get out, I'm taking you to a special place. You'll be blindfolded and bound, so you won't know exactly where it is. Then, when we're back, I'll ask for a ransom. When someone comes forward with it, I'll join your ex-paramour in Zurich."

Clara felt something hard and round in the small of her back, suspiciously like a gun barrel. Her legs were leaden. She was tense, afraid, exhausted.

A sheep being led to slaughter.

Between the echoing plod of their footsteps, Clara detected a faint dripping sound.

My God, the lagoon. The path must have curved back...or maybe there's a second lake. Chance for a getaway. Get Butt to the water. Keep talking so he won't hear the water. Push him in; jump in; anything...

Clara faked a jovial tone. "So what if no one thinks I'm worth your asking price? Maybe Henry would fly us both to Zurich. Maybe you can ask the school to buy me back. They could ask my students to take up a collection..."

The air felt damp. Even without seeing it, Clara knew there was water ahead. The question was, "How far?"

Dripping and splishing...We're getting close now. Does Butt not hear? Does he plan to drown me? Maybe this bastard can't swim...

"Shut up, bitch. Henry doesn't want you anymore. You're used up, a discard. The only reason I don't pull this trigger is that your parents -- the ones you tried to see at Thanksgiving -- have some bucks. What wouldn't they give to have their little girlie back safe and sound?" She felt the gun barrel's tip gouge further into her back. The dripping had grown into a torrent. How could Butt not hear it?

The thought of Will and Louise being threatened infuriated Clara. But she bit her tongue. She would pretend to be the perfect victim.

"Oh, Mother and Daddy...they'd give anything. Please don't hurt them. They adopted me when I was five, an orphan, really, and they've been so wonderful to me..."

Clara reached her right foot back and tripped Larry Butt so he fell face forward. She ran a couple steps ahead and dove into the lagoon. Her feet could touch the bottom, but she swam quickly away from the rough stony edge. What lay ahead could not be any worse than what was behind her.

The initial chill wore off as Clara swam quickly toward what appeared to be a grotto. Sometime, she couldn't quite place where, she'd heard that the lagoon led to a river or water passage. Or maybe she'd just imagined this. Did it really matter? Where else could she go?

Her prayers had been answered. Apparently Butt didn't know how to swim.

"Get back here, bitch. There's a drop-off. If you keep going, you'll die. Come back...I'm not going to hurt you." More shouting, gunshots...

The cave ceiling seemed to be growing thinner, a faint light glowing overhead. It had been at least fifteen minutes since she'd heard anything from Larry Butt. Limp from the exertion of swimming through icy water, Clara hoisted up a football shaped rock and scuttling, crablike, ascended a sloping boulder. Her right foot found purchase on a rock ledge above the boulder.

A voice inside her head directed.

Ignore that shivering. No time to wring out clothes. Gotta get out of this underworld while you have the strength. Thank God Butt can't swim. Larry Butt...the murderer of Joseph and Annie..., Henry's puppet.

It was growing lighter. When she could take her attention away from the next foothold or toe niche, she looked above.

Yes, yes...the sky. Three more steps and I can make it. Run...find the path, get back to the school. Carnell sent your class home. Go home; get dry.

Using what little strength she had left, Clara grabbed a ledge above the boulder where she crouched. Her soggy clothes seemed to weigh a ton and leached away her strength.

An odd vision of the New Mexican's headlines reading *Woman Killed by her Clothes* made Clara laugh in spite of herself.

She swung wildly from the ledge. Sky and earth were directly above her. Her hands ached; her fingers were growing weak. When she could no longer maintain a tight grip, her left foot touched something. Praying that whatever rock outcropping she'd contacted would support her, she slid her foot back and found a ledge. Using the perch for leverage, she pulled the upper half of her body to the earth above and elbowed up.

Feeling like a prairie dog emerging from its burrow, she crawled her way into bright winter sunlight. Compared to the dankness of the cave, it was like being in a sauna. She sat for a moment by the crevice from which she'd emerged, and thought about what to do next. This was the other side of the ridge where she and Jerome frequently went running. She felt certain she could find a path that would take her back to AIA.

A rustle emerged from a grove of pinons ten feet away. It was Larry Butt, his back turned to her. Clara froze, and then sank back into the crevice. Miraculously, her feet once again found the ledge. This time, he would not let her get away.

Like a soldier during warfare, Clara crouched in her meager foxhole. The minutes seemed like hours. Through sheer will power, she kept from moving or making noise.

At last Larry Butt wandered away. Clara pulled out of her rock prison into the bright sunshine. For a winter day, it was surprisingly warm. Her watch, which wasn't waterproof, had stopped at ten a.m. She guessed it was about noon.

After stretching, she removed her damp shirt, twisted out the moisture, and put it back on. She noticed a tear at the bottom of her shirt and a piece of material missing. That must have happened when she climbed down the boulder to begin her swim, that as well as the gouge on her hand. Despite strong sunshine, the air was cold. She needed to move, to run, to pump blood back into her chilly arms and legs.

Of course Larry Butt would still be tracking her, but instinct told Clara he was ahead rather than behind her. She jogged downhill on sandy terrain. Her plan was to find the mouth of the cave and the path that led back to the school.

When Jerome reached the lagoon, he decided to stop and wait for Carnell. His young friend was an amateur spelunker and more likely to know the cave's hidden passages and secret routes. Besides, he didn't want the two of them to get entirely separated. They needed to work as a team.

If there were other entrances and exits to these craggy depths, Carnell would know. Jerome directed his flashlight all around the lagoon's visible boundaries. No apparent paths leading elsewhere. The lagoon itself seemed not to end where the cave walls narrowed, but rather dwindled off into a kind of underground river. He lay down on a boulder overlooking the water and held his flashlight out over glassy surface. Yes, as far as the eye could see, the water seemed to continue.

As Jerome explored by flashlight, Carnell ran up, breathing hard. "I feel like I just ran the Ironman Triathlon," he gasped. "You go fast, man."

"Well, a real triathlon is running, swimming and bicycling. Here's your second leg, Carnell."

"Oh yeah, this is what we used to call the snake pond. When I was five years old, we came here with one of my uncles. The pond turns into a river that slithers and winds until you get to a place where you can actually climb out to the earth above the cave. I'd forgotten about it until now."

As Jerome was inching his way backwards into a sitting position, Carnell shone his flashlight on the boulder.

"Hey, what's that, Jerome? Did you fall?"

The two leaned down to examine a dark stain and a ragged piece of white cotto jersey next to it. Jerome licked the fingertips of his left hand and rubbed them across the stain. When he was finished, he examined his hand by flashlight.

Carnell looked at Jerome with a puzzled expression.

"Just what I suspected, this is blood. And this looks like it's torn from Clara's running shirt. Someone was after her, she fell down, and decided it was worth the risk to swim in the hope of finding a way out."

Carnell started rolling up the legs of his sweatpants. "There's an opening about a half mile away where you can crawl out of the cave to the ground above. I remember where the river comes out. We used to call it "where the snake meets the earth. Why don't I go the river route and you backtrack to the cave's mouth. That way, one of us is bound to meet her, and probably whoever is after her. I'm a strong swimmer."

While Jerome didn't like the idea of taking orders from a ninth-grader, he could think of no better course of action. He knew that Carnell was devoted to Clara and that Clara loved Carnell like a teen-age son.

"And if we meet that weirdo that's chasing Clara," Jerome said. "I have my knife and some rope, and we both have our wits. Watch for the sea snakes, little brother, and I'll run like the wind. If you don't see anything at that end, come back down to the cave's mouth and we'll meet there."

Larry Butt was in poor condition. Too many Jolt Colas and candy bars, way too much coke, and hundreds of nights in front of the idiot box had turned him into a marshmallow. Chasing Henry's bitch inside the cave was the most running he'd done since he and Bobby were growing up. The late Bobby.

When Clara was out of reach because he'd never learned to swim, Larry had doubled back to the mouth of the cave and then climbed the hill above it. He looked everywhere for another way out of the cave, walking within a few inches of the crevice but repeatedly missing it.

Cursing his bad luck, Larry stomped down the sandy hill where he'd wasted an hour trying to trap his prey. Maybe she'd drowned like someone else he knew. Like Bobby. Even though many years had passed since his brother vanished, the thought of Bobby filled him with a mixture of rage and fear.

But in case she hadn't drowned, he'd find Clara before she got back to Red Mesa. She'd slipped away for the last time. Larry fingered the gun in his holster. If anyone got in his way, he'd blow out their brains. He laughed maniacally.

Less than a mile behind Larry, Clara ran through the forest alongside the path. Running warmed her, and she no longer felt hypothermic. However, she'd made a serious mistake when she'd decided against taking off her running shoes and wringing out her soggy socks. The clothes she was wearing, lightweight and loosely woven, expelled moisture. Her heavy shoes and socks, however, retained most of the water they'd collected when she swam her way to freedom. The tops of her toes burned at the joints, a sure signal that blisters were forming. She tried to tune out the pain by thinking of her students.

Clara was sure Carnell would have told them something plausible, making sure panic didn't break out when she didn't appear. Today was shot, but she'd get back in time to recover from this misadventure and then she'd owe the kids an explanation.

It would be a good one. She imagined calling today "the run from hell," and she took mental notes of how, one by one, her toes were going numb. "Three down, two to go..." She could use this as a springboard for writing exercises. Nearly all her kids were heavily into sports and outdoor activities. The topic could be something like "My Worst Athletic Event" or "I Wish I'd Stayed Home."

190

She was just twenty feet uphill from the path that led to the cave when she saw the back of Larry Butt. He stumbled along muttering a stream of profanities and brandishing his gun in the air. Clearly, he'd lost it.

Clara slowed to a stealthy walk, making sure to keep hidden behind the pinons and junipers. Compared to the tall trees and thick growth of the Appalachian trail where she'd hiked in her youth, Clara thought, there was meager hiding space.

Another figure besides Larry loomed ahead in the distance.

My God, it can't be, but it is -- Jerome. Standing out in the open like a sentinel. Carnell told him I was missing and they formed a two-man search party.

Clara tried to send her thoughts ahead.

Please, please, Jerome. Look out. *There's a mad man headed your way.*

Jerome turned around just as Larry Butt sent a bullet his way. Fortunately, it was so badly aimed, it just whistled through a pinon next to him. Jerome disappeared from sight, somewhere behind the surrounding trees and boulders.

Barely breathing, Clara crept closer. Even though Larry probably didn't know Jerome, and he was after her, he would shoot anything in his path. He was just crazy and desperate enough.

"Where are you, bitch?" Larry bellowed to the trees and sky. He shot into the air. "You got away from Henry but you're not going to get away from me. You and me, we're going on a little trip. You're gonna be my ticket outta this shithole and if you're real nice, I might let you live...

"Come on, I know you're behind one of those trees. I can hear your breathing, and I can wait all night."

Raging forward, Larry stopped only a foot from where Jerome lay hidden next to a limestone outcropping. Clara watched in fascination as Jerome's arm reached out from a clump of bushes. He tugged Larry's leg and threw him off balance, then pounced on him with the full weight of his body. As Larry and Jerome wrestled in the dirt, Clara snuck forward and pulled the gun from Larry's side. By the time he realized it was missing, she was standing next to him with the gun aimed at his heart.

Jerome got a rope out from his waist pack and bound Larry's hands behind his back. "Well, every dog has his day, and yours is up, scumbag." Larry glared at him and spit, but Jerome deftly moved out of the way.

Clara kept the gun aimed at Larry while Jerome did the honors with rope.

"Hi, folks, no wonder I couldn't find anyone." Carnell, looking tired but relieved, was back from his watch. "I see we caught the skunk in his skunk hole."

"Yeah, it's going to be a long march back to Red Mesa. You get ahead of this rat turd, Carnell. I'll get behind, and just so he doesn't forget I'm here, I'll prod him every now and then with the gun barrel. Clara, if you feel like running, why don't you go on ahead and notify the Santa Fe sheriff."

Suddenly the exhaustion of this strange ordeal lifted from Clara like California fog at mid-day. She started jogging ahead of the three men and soon broke into a full-fledged run.

26

Reunions

The next day, Clara awoke at her usual 5 a.m. Light snow had fallen through the night, transforming the ponderosas around her cabin into green and white sentinels. After yesterday's ordeal, she felt drained. With Jerome at her side, she'd told her story to the Santa Fe police, explaining her suspicion that Larry had been responsible for blowing up her car and that he was linked to Joseph Speckled Horse's death. Butt was being held for questioning, which made her feel safer. She was ready to put the nightmare of the last two months behind her.

She couldn't quite bring herself to go running. Even with Butt in jail, there was something eerie about going where he'd been trailing her. Despite the fact that her legs ached, the foot that she'd treated with Estrellita's herbs was not at all sore. All her running in the past couple days amounted to a full-length marathon. A day off wouldn't hurt.

Back in her classroom, Clara felt light, cheerful, surprisingly energetic. "What was supposed to be a ten-miler," she told the kids, "turned out to be a marathon."

"Yeah, we already knew," said Rebecca. "Carnell told everyone. He said you got lost and he and Mr. Naranjo had to go running to look for you. In a secret passage. It sounds really cool. Can we take a field trip to the cave?"

Clara was relieved to hear nothing of Larry Butt. Carnell had promised not to say anything other than "Ms. Jordan got lost." As always, he'd kept his promise.

"Has anyone been lost in a cave?"

No hands went up.

"Have any of you ever been lost?" Six out of the twenty students raised their hands.

"Take out your spiral writing journal and pencils. I want you to write about the scariest or most exciting adventure you've had. It can be about being lost and finding your way; it can be about a vision quest, a special time you had in nature, or a time when your fears got the best of you."

All except one student began writing. Clara sighed and walked back to a small, slender girl's desk. All she needed was for Deena, normally one of her most cooperative students, to start acting up. Deena was scrunched over a bundle on her lap.

"Deena, what's up? Why aren't you doing the assignment?" Clara asked kindly.

"Oh, Ms. Jordan, I wanted to surprise you at the end of class, but you ruined it. I brought you something." The bundle was moving. A small mew came from within its depths. "Here, he's yours."

Deena handed over the bundle, which by now was extremely active.

Clara peeled away the flaps of blanket. "Oh my gosh, it's a kitten, and it looks just like Oscar when he was a baby." She took the tiny smoky gray creature in both hands and kissed the top of its head. "Thank you, Deena. He's beautiful. I think I'll call him Oscar *Segundo*. She gave Deena a hug around the shoulders. "You're so thoughtful. Now I won't have to be alone anymore."

Clara visited Will and Louise over Christmas. Will, diminished by Alzheimer's Disease, barely recognized her. Following Clara's suggestion, Louise had hired a woman named Linda Jones to come in and care for him a few hours each day. "Even with help, it's getting too much for me," she sighed. "This is probably the last Christmas he'll be able to have at home."

They sat at the dinner table laden with an organic turkey Louise baked, yams, mashed potatoes, peas and onions, all the traditional foods Clara remembered from Christmases past. She took turns with Louise feeding Will, who could no longer manage utensils.

To Clara's astonishment, Louise was not upset when she learned about the reunion with Greta Suina, her biological mother.

"Oh dear, I was hoping you'd find a way to reconnect. It was Will who had problems about your finding your biological mother. And now that he's..." Tears streaming down her cheeks, she broke off mid-sentence.

Helpless, mindless, a shadow of his former self, Clara wanted to scream. The relief at being able to tell about her reunion was overshadowed by the grief she felt at her father's condition. He would have to become a resident of Whispering Pines, the local assisted living center. A cruel ending for a well-lived life. She held back tears as she reached over and hugged Louise.

"I'm here for you, Mom. Daddy has lived a good life. I've been researching the Internet on Alzheimer's. He will grow less and less aware of what's happening around him. It's harder on us than it is on him."

She hated talking about her father as if he weren't there, but when she stole a glance at him, his gray head had fallen over on his chest, and he seemed to be asleep. It was how he spent most of his days.

With Louise's help, Clara helped Will totter over to the couch, where they eased him into a sitting position. He woke up for a few minutes and was soon dozing.

"I just haven't had the energy to decorate very much this year," Louise apologized as she and Clara pulled up their chairs near the tabletop fake Christmas tree decorated with red chile lights Clara had sent a couple weeks before her trip.

After trying unsuccessfully to rouse Will from his slumber, they proceeded with their gift exchange. Louise gave Clara a soft black leather vest. "I thought it looked Southwestern, and it's something you can throw on with just about anything."

Clara gave Louise a decorated basket of ingredients from Santa Fe School of Cooking with directions for cooking an entire Mexican dinner. They took turns opening presents for Will, stacking them neatly on the table in front of him as though he would wake up and see them at any minute.

It was a poignant time for Clara, and after a week she was both sorry and relieved to catch the plane for Albuquerque. As Clara kissed Will goodbye, she held back tears at the realization that he didn't know her.

"Please come visit me, Mom. You can find someone to stay with Dad. You'd love seeing the school and meeting my students."

"We'll see, dear. You know how much your father and I love you. Sitters are expensive. With the illness, we have to really watch our expenses. Will always used to take off in the car when you were growing up, but I'm just not up to driving across the country, and I've never flown. It's too late to start now." She smiled weakly and gave her adopted daughter a hug.

Clara decided not to push matters. If she had to, she would drive out and get Louise and drive her to New Mexico. A taxi pulled up to the front door to deliver her to the airport. She waved back at her parents, stunned with how frail they both looked. They had always been her heroes and role models. Now they were diminished, vulnerable. She put on sunglasses to help conceal the bitter tears streaming down her cheeks.

The New Year brought a fresh semester to the American Indian Academy. Wren Taggert was going to finish the year as interim headmaster, but the school was advertising nationwide for a permanent headmaster, a Native American preferred. Clara's class published *Memories of Joseph Speckled Horse* and sold it for $5.00 a copy to nearly everyone at AIA, faculty, administration, and students alike. They were saving the profits for an end-of-the-year trip.

In early February, Red Mesa's afternoon temperatures skyrocketed to the mid-sixties. Fruit trees began to bud, and crocuses poked through the earth. Clara's new kitten, Oscar Segundo, was climbing trees and leaping from branch to branch.

"I know," Clara told her, "you'd rather be a bird. You're just like Oscar used to be, always up off the ground, going for the highest place you can reach."

As he had ever since the death of Henry DiMarco and the beginning of Larry Butt's trial, Jerome came to Clara's cabin at six a.m. to go for a run. He let himself in the unlocked door.

"We've got to stop meeting like this," Clara said, wearing one shoe and holding the other in her hand. "I just broke a shoelace and I can't find any spares. I don't know why I keep buying Nikes. They're always too wide for me. What's it like outside? Do I need more than my windbreaker?"

"More like spring than winter," said Jerome. "Here, let me have your shoe. I'm an expert at repairing laces." In a few minutes, Jerome had the lace back together and rethreaded through the eyelets. "Have a seat, madam. I'm Prince Charming and you're Cinderella. Let's see if the shoe fits."

Jerome pulled Clara's wooden kitchen chair out from the table. When Clara sat down, he knelt before her and took her left foot in both hands. Instead of putting the shoe on, he started gently massaging her foot.

"Oh, that feels wonderful," Clara said. "That's the foot that Estrellita's herbs cured. It's so much better now that I have to remind myself which one was injured."

Jerome's strong, muscular hands worked up from her toes to her ankle. He'd apparently forgotten about the shoe.

"Hey, what is this turning into?" Clara laughed. "A full body massage?"

"I wish," said Jerome as he slipped the well-worn Nike on Clara's long slender foot.

"Love me, love my feet, that's what I say. Come on, let's hit it. See if you can get me to do more speedwork. I'd really love to make a personal best in the Santa Fe Run-around. We only have until June to train, you know."

Clara stood up. Jerome was still kneeling. "How's your other foot," he asked. "Doesn't it need some intense massage?"

"Come on, Jer. You're supposed to be my coach. You said yesterday, you were going to help me smooth out my stride. I'm leading the stretches. Let's do some long slow toe touching."

After five minutes of stretching, they left the cabin and started running along the dirt road at the bottom of Clara's drive. For the first half mile, they ran slowly, about a ten-minute-per-mile pace.

"OK," said Jerome, "let's pick it up until we get to the school entrance." For the next half mile, they ran much faster. Jerome talked, but Clara had to save her breath for running. Her lungs ached and she had a stitch in her right side, but she concentrated on breathing deeply. Just when she thought she couldn't stand it any longer, the pain dissolved. By the time they reached the AIA sign, she'd forgotten everything else but the thrill of running.

Dawn transformed the land. As the sun bathed the adobe buildings of the school in light, the surrounding pinons turned from black to green. Clara and Jerome continued the dirt road all the way around the school and out to the highway, alternating between fast and slow running. Following Jerome's suggestions, Clara stretched her legs out, swung her arms more freely, and relaxed.

"I can't believe this," she said as they did a three-mile turn-around and headed back to Clara's cabin. "I feel like I'm running more gracefully. And once I get used to the breathing, it seems to be easier to run faster than plodding along. I guess I've been ready for a change for quite some time now and I just needed you to inspire me."

"Actually, it was the magical power of my foot treatment. How about another one tomorrow? I'll do both feet and then your speed will advance even faster and your style will become poetry in motion."

"You mean it's not, already?" Clara pretended disappointment.

"Well, yes, it is. I just mean it will be a sonnet instead of a ballad. Maybe even a haiku."

As they approached Clara's driveway, Jerome looked at his pedometer. "Stop at the mailbox, that's the ten-kilometer point."

Swinging her arms in broad arcs, Clara dashed the remaining 200 feet. At the mailbox, she raised both arms in victory.

"And the winner, in 48 minutes and 20 seconds," Jerome shouted into an imaginary microphone, "is the beautiful schoolteacher from Red Mesa, the unknown runner who is only just beginning to develop her potential, Ms. Clara Jordan. Stand back, you nasty reporters. Let the lady catch her breath."

Laughing at Jerome's imitation, Clara fell into Jerome's arms. "I'll have to collect the prize money later. Right now, this running star has students to teach."

Jerome's arms tightened around her and their lips met. It wasn't their first kiss, but it was electrifying.

197

After several minutes, Clara drew away. "Really, Jerome. After all the confusion of last semester, I need to be there on time. My class is only now beginning to calm down. And you know that Carnell. He's probably already been there for ten minutes."

"OK, but only if you'll let me take you out to dinner tonight. I thought we'd go to La Tertulia, the new Italian restaurant in Santa Fe. How about six o'clock?"

"Why, yes, I'd love to. Now I've really got to sprint." Grinning widely, she ran up the driveway and into her cabin. Jerome drove off in his Bronco, leaving a cloud of dust.

She took a quick shower, jumped into her favorite corduroy slacks, boots and a clean white blouse. She topped everything with the leather vest Louise had given her for Christmas. Almost ready to leave, she remembered Oscar Segundo.

"Here kitty, kitty, kitty. Here Oskie. Come here, kitty."

Clara looked for five minutes and was about to leave when she heard a faint meow from the bathroom. She suddenly remembered what the first Oscar did when he was a kitten. Opening her deep bathroom cabinet, she looked into the shelves. A furry gray head peeked out.

"You're just like your namesake," she laughed. "Wait till I tell the kids."

Epilogue

Jerome and Clara sat facing one another in a booth at Pranzo's Restaurant. They were celebrating the end of a tumultuous school year for Clara and a career change for Jerome. Hushed conversations and the rich aroma of pasta and tomatoes enveloped them.

Jerome had resigned from the police force and was going to work as a counselor at the Santa Fe Indian School. He ordered a bottle of Sauvignon Blanc and they toasted to the future.

In the interim after ordering, both Clara and Jerome stayed lost in thought. Clara realized that she dreaded going back to AIA for another year. She loved her students, she was good at teaching, but the new headmaster was supposedly an ogre. Jerome held her hands across the table.

"You won't believe this." She paused, then continued, "I'd like to move to Santa Fe with you. I have too many bad memories with the school. It's time for a change."

Jerome smiled broadly. "You must have read my mind. I know you'll still want to find out more about your birthmother, but San Ildefonso isn't that far from Santa Fe. I have a friend we can stay with until we find an apartment. I guessed that you'd probably given your notice to AIA about not returning."

Clara sighed. "I was embarrassed to tell you that, but yes, I did give my notice. Part of me feels like a failure. In my heart, I know the school and all that happened has to be left behind. I want to stay in New Mexico. I love the mountains, the incredible sky, the weather, the people. I'm done with the American Indian Academy. It feels...I don't know...cursed." Silently she added, *What I love most about being in New Mexico is you.*

Jerome ate his ravioli and listened as she continued talking. Clara scarcely touched her pasta alfredo. She named all the people she'd grown fond of, her favorite students, the parts of the American Indian Academy she'd miss.

Finally Jerome broke in. "What about your reason for moving out here in the first place? What about your birthmother?"

The waiter glided toward their table and recited a list of desserts. Clara was tempted, but she remembered that she hadn't found time to run for three days. She didn't want to gain weight. Jerome admitted that he was "bursting at the seams."

The plates cleared away, they continued talking. Both were grateful for this quiet time out. Jerome simply nodded and smiled as Clara continued, "I decided that my adoptive mom has too much on her plate right now. She's taking care of my dad, and he's sinking into dementia. Besides, Greta might not want to be found. She probably has other children and I have a strong feeling they don't know that I even exist. I am going to wait. My mind's made up. But, well... maybe I'm rushing things with *us*?"

Jerome held both Clara's hands to his lips and kissed them tenderly. "No, my love," he whispered, "You're right on time."